G000123591

OUT OF THE FRYING PAN

Judy Upton

HOBART BOOKS

HOBART BOOKS

OUT OF THE FRYING PAN

First Published in 2021
by
Hobart Books, Oxfordshire, England
hobartbooks.com

Printed and bound in Great Britain by Clays Ltd, Elcograf S.p.A.

Cover design by Rachel Hanks

Out Of The Frying Pan

By Judy Upton

PROLOGUE

The art is not to think. Do not under any circumstances hesitate. Use your fear, ride the adrenaline high and it will take you through. You don't need to think, just react. You'll *know* what to do.

The cashier is still and pale. Most go white, but some flush – adrenaline again. Her hands are steady and so are her eyes, focused on the gun, not the money. I shouldn't be looking at the money either, not even a small glance. Watch her, keep your attention on her eyes. If she's going to go for the button, her eyes will tell you. React, don't think. The door's taken care of. The alarm is just a sound, nothing more than that. In all probability you won't even hear it. The woman on the floor can't get up quickly from that position, and if she starts to move, you can put her straight back down there. She's under control. Everything is under control. The money's ready. Collect and go.

CHAPTER ONE

'It's not a big enough space.' Actually it is, but Gina's parking is crap. It's time for a quick escape while she's deciding whether to give the wheel a couple more turns for good measure. She glares as I slam the car door, indignant at being abandoned.

'There's plenty of room behind,' I shout over my shoulder and quickly cross the road to the building society, before she can ask me to guide her in.

'Have you considered changing to our Double Platinum Ninety Day Account?' I confess the idea hasn't been uppermost in my thoughts, but still let the over-tanned cashier hand me a glossy leaflet. I tell her the amount I need to withdraw this week, and her thin eyebrows dip as she peers at her screen. It doesn't bode well – if she can't even *see* my balance...

A man enters, wearing a black crash helmet. He waits behind me. I'm sure there's a sign telling customers that crash helmets mustn't be worn in the branch. I look but can't see it. I can however see Gina's blue Uno reflected in the security glass. It is now almost on the diagonal to the pavement. She pulls out to try again. The crash helmet guy turns to look. His motorbike is only one parked car away from my flatmate's perilous manoeuvres. He has my sympathy. The cashier offers me a pile of notes, while looking over my shoulder, probably watching Gina cack up the parking again. The woman's face immobilises and fades several shades beneath the bronzing powder. Then, as I involuntarily follow her gaze, I see the gun that Motorcycle Guy is directing between her over-plucked brows.

'On the floor.' Blood throbs in my ears. The carpet is unpleasantly acrylic beneath my long nails and smells of cancer-causing cleaning chemicals from a brand I avoid. Lying on my front isn't a good position for me; my stiff knee (a childhood car crash injury) has a tendency to lock and leave me stranded. I watch Motorcycle Guy's boots back slowly outside. The cashier gasps or sobs, still frozen to the spot. Perhaps he has the gun trained on her from outside the door. Then she moves, quickly, decisively. An alarm shrills at a sickening pitch. Rising on my good knee I risk a look. Motorcycle Guy – now reclassified as *the Bank Robber* – is astride his motorbike, but can't seem to get it to start. Behind the counter, a second cashier is saying 'Oh my God' over and over. Gina opens the car door, standing to get a look at the action. 'Stay in the fucking car you dim tart,' I silently will her. He's seen her. 'Please don't. Don't shoot her,' I quietly pray.

He shouts. Gina freezes. With the gun trained on her at chest height, he abandons the motorbike and runs across to the Uno, motions with the gun for Gina to get back in. I heave myself up – mercifully the leg hasn't locked – and run outside. He takes off his helmet to get in the car and I get a glimpse of his face. The car speeds away, ripping the bumper off its neighbour. Irrationally, I find myself wondering if

Gina's insurance company will hike up her premium again. Then my legs go. I sit down on the kerb.

* * * * *

My eyes are shut tight. Knuckles pound again and again, gradually breaking down resistance, making the plastilina softer, more malleable, pliable and responsive. I need to recreate that face in my mind, wipe out all else. I need to see that face in three dimensions before I can begin.

* * * * *

'Your pasta sauce is growing mushrooms.'

Bridie briskly bins it, and in minutes manages to whip up a fair imitation using a couple of tomatoes and a few of Gina's mysterious little bottles. Gina cooked, I cleaned – that was our agreement. I'm a good cleaner, so good in fact it's my certified profession.

Since Gina's abduction, three days ago, various friends have been looking in on me. Bridie in particular seems to relish the drama. Before this, I always got the impression she found my company a little tedious – someone to talk at, but too inclined to interrupt her flow and also, not being in showbiz, unable to fully grasp her problems. Since these problems invariably involve money: lack of it, work - lack of it, and hassles with the Department of Work and Pensions – I don't see as we're necessarily from different planets. To Bridie though, anyone who doesn't live, breathe and sleep acting might as well be a goldfish – company of sorts, but certainly not worth listening to.

5

Now for once she's letting me get a word in. I explain that young detective Nelson and her depressed-looking sidekick McGuire have, while asking exhaustive questions, given me no clues as to the state of their investigation. Surely as Gina's concerned flatmate, I deserve to be told something, to be given some kind of reassurance, some shred of hope? Bridie clasps my hand and widens her eyes in precisely expressed indignation.

'You *must* demand answers.' Her bosom rises beneath her plunge-cut black lycra top. 'Time is of the essence. She could be... lying helpless somewhere, poor little lamb.'

Describing Gina as a little lamb is not entirely accurate, but she certainly wears a lot of pale-coloured wool, which she likes to be as big and baggy as possible. It's also true there's something childlike about her. It's her way of seeing the world: shoplifting is a crime, drugs are evil, litter droppers should be made to clean the streets, parties should end at midnight or ten pm on weeknights. I hope I'm not making her sound insufferable because really she isn't – and she can cook remember? She's tidy, writes down phone messages accurately, and always volunteers to go to the shop when we're out of oat milk or bread – a model flatmate in fact. All of my friends, and most of my lovers, get on really well with her, although curiously they seem unable to remember her name. '...Yeah, she's a nice girl...err...wossname...' Wossname is twenty-three, though swathed in her puppy fat and cautious, pastel-shade cardigans, her age has been guessed as anything between eighteen and thirty.

Since Gina's been missing, I've started feeling guilty about my treatment of her. The 'Coronation Street' episodes I've recorded over before she could watch them. The nights I let my friends – and lovers – keep her awake. The times I've snapped at her for reminding me of the amount of her money I've borrowed that week. The petrol I've let her pay for – 'well it's your car.' Her Twixes I've eaten. Her *Best's* and *Bella's* I've left dog-eared and coffee stained. Her Nicky Clarke hairdryer I've broken. No wonder I found my voice rising aggressively whenever DS Nelson asked questions that impinged on my flatmate's olden-style morals and honour. 'No, of course he couldn't be someone she knew.' 'No, she doesn't know anyone like that.' 'Yes I'd know if she was seeing someone.' '…Because she'd tell me!' She'd tell me.

The phone rings twice and goes on to answerphone before I can reach the kitchen. Gina's father is treated to the sound of his daughter's self-conscious 'Vonnie and me must be out. Please leave us a message.' Cutting in, I apologise. I won't change the message because it seems like in some way wiping out Gina. I've never met her dad although he lives locally. She'd go round to his rather than inviting him here. I have been in regular phone contact with him since her abduction. He suggests we meet up to talk.

Bridie has a friend who's a spiritualist. 'She's only there on Thursdays and Fridays…' She probably sells insurance the rest of the week. '…*do* give her a ring. She helped poor Candice when her cat went missing. She saw the *actual* tree he was trapped in. The actual tree'. Candice had found this helpful, so perhaps mystic Luana also saw its location. Otherwise one tree looks very like another and there are around three trillion of them on Earth. Google it if you don't believe me. I tell Bridie I also have some other lines of enquiry to follow. She sits down gracefully on the arm of the sofa, her whole manner vividly expressing 'tell me all', but the truth is as yet I've no idea what these other lines will be. In fact I could do with some lines of something right now, but I've never dared try to score off Bridie (though surely she must use, she's an actor, for Christ's sake). The pasta is ready and mercifully distracts us both. Gina's abduction hasn't affected my appetite. I can't remember if I was born callous or whether it happened somewhere along the way.

Over dinner, Bridie talks of the Equity workshop she attended last weekend and how it released something she didn't know was inside her. She makes it sound a bit like flatulence and is so intense that in spite of myself I giggle. She feels my brow with a cool hand. The concern on her face would earn her a call back for 'Casualty'.

'I know it's awful. I know. But don't lose it, babe. You've got to be strong for …Gina…' Bridie remembered her name, that's a first. 'You've got to be strong. Promise?' I promise, and still dangerously on the edge of laughter, fetch my head.

I'm a sculptor. I know I just told you I'm a cleaner. I wasn't accentuating the positive. I could've said Bridie was a telesales marketer, but I didn't. I'm probably better at accentuating the positive when it's about someone else's life that's going down the crapper, rather than my own.

It's time to fill in the gap. Gina was abducted on Tuesday. On Wednesday and Thursday, the two whole days that have passed since Gina's carjacking by the building society raider, or the Bank Robber as I shall inaccurately but more economically dub him, I've had three chats with the boys and girls in blue, two at their place, one at mine. With my friend

8

Jake I've driven around the city looking for I don't know what. With Bridie's dogs I've searched for a scent of Gina, (having first let them sniff Gina's old Peacocks nightie), though unsurprisingly the trail went stone cold right after she and the Bank Robber drove off. The police made me help with a photo-fit of the robber. I said that as a sculptor I could create a better likeness. They smiled indulgently, but weren't impressed when I couldn't immediately come up with the goods. It takes a few days to create even a roughish piece from scratch even when as here I'm working from memory. I think they expected me to just grab a bit of Playdoh and whiz something up in a couple of minutes. Disinterested, they said I might like to show them when I'd finished it. Don't call us we'll call you – the old story.

'Such an expressive face, and classical. Definitely classical.' You're not supposed to be creaming your silk Frenchies over him, Bridie, this is the guy who's made off with my flatmate, remember? Bridie remembers almost in time. 'Yes, he's got a cruel mouth. You can see the desperation there.' It's an accurate portrayal in clay of how in my mind I see him at that moment, but whether it looks anything like him is another matter. 'I've seen him!' Bridie announces suddenly. 'I remember now. He was in the Tate Britain.' Eh? 'A portrait in an exhibition… Victorian paintings, pre-Raphaelite that kind of thing.' She takes my disappointed look as something else.

'Yes, I know they're not your scene, but that's where I've seen that melancholy face. I've a book or two at home he might be in, I'll bring them over.' Gina might be anywhere, alone and terrified, or suffering some terrible ordeal that at this point I don't feel able to verbalise to Bridie or anyone else. Or of course, she might be dead. Meanwhile Bridie is suggesting we leaf through art books. 'He has a solitary look,' she continues, oblivious to my sudden wish to be rid of her, 'and he's known suffering…' Well, that's really narrowing it down. 'You said he's pale so…'

'He doesn't get out in the sun much? Unless he's robbing building societies and abducting people on a nice day?' Bridie fortunately picks up on my churlish vibe, asks if I'm tired, and I manage to plead fatigue and send her home.

'Remember to ring Luana – the spiritualist, dear. I'll tell her to be expecting your call.' I'm tempted to say that if she's spiritual she'll know I'm going to contact her anyway, but I bite my lip.

CHAPTER TWO

After a rough night of wonderings and imaginings about Gina, I wake to the phone. Nobody dares call this early. Then I go cold and pick up. It's DS Nelson. They've found Gina's car up on the South Downs. They're doing tests on it now. Nelson reminds me I have her card.

'Don't hesitate to ring if you think of something, even the tiniest detail.'

'The investigation's not going well then?' I query. She hesitates, and then blusters, which in my opinion is never a good sign when it comes to cops, doctors or politicians.

I've recorded the regional news reports featuring Gina's abduction and watch them back as I eat my no-frills, budget range Cinnamon Crunch cereal, the Pre-Raphaelite Bank Robber's head watching me from the table. Janice from the agency calls and with patently fake sympathy asks if I might soon be returning to work. With two cleaners currently off sick and a third in Ayia Napa, they're currently a little overstretched.

'There's a Mr Williams, in his eighties and getting a wee bit wobbly. Lovely clean flat but does so worry about the dust mites. Emile usually does him, but he won't be back 'til next

11

Monday at the earliest.' I don't have to be there until two. That gives me time to do a little research into the subject of motorbikes. The old Yellow Pages that we use to block the draft beneath the kitchen sash window seems a good place to start. I rip out the section entitled 'Motorcycle and Scooter', imagining Gina looking horrified at this wanton act. Still, it should prove easier than squinting at my phone screen in the sunshine while walking along the street.

It seems a little tasteless to ask DS Nelson how soon before I can have the car back, but I ask anyway. She'll let me know. I walk down the hill into town, carrying the pages from the phone book and the head in a carrier bag. The head is heavy, and considering it's solely for identification purposes, making it life-size wasn't a particularly sensible idea.

I moved to Brighton four years ago to be near the sea. It's as simple as that. The happiest times I can remember were our annual seaside holidays at my Gran's bungalow in Portslade, or West Hove as she called it, to make it sound more upmarket. Back then it always seemed to rain throughout June. Aged ten or eleven I'd sit indoors making gluey little animals from the previous summer's shells, or venture out with my duck-handled umbrella, taking a bus to explore Brighton's North Laines. There I'd gaze in wide-eyed admiration at all the beautiful people – art students with Technicolor hair, miscellaneous piercings, Doc Martens and threadbare charity shop clothes. That's when I realised it. The seaside is the place where misfits, freaks and work-shirkers of all descriptions can find sanctuary and safety in numbers. Back home, I locked myself in the bathroom and bleached my hair with Mum's dye. That first time it turned out canary yellow, but it definitely felt like the start of something important. I was going to be different, daring, scary – and definitely very famous. I've only recently grown out of this delusion. I could have been a contender, but at thirty-five years of age, I'm a cleaner.

Sol is playing his fiddle outside M&S. I've not seen him for a month or two and it turns out he's been playing at some festival in Cornwall – busking, not on the official bill, of course. Inevitably I tell him the whole tale about Gina. He swiftly calculates he's earned enough small change for a cappuccino each and a slice of carrot cake between us. We go to the Inner Sanctum Café, where the coffee comes in giant shallow cups, which are pricey, because they know most of their clientele are artists who will make one cup last as long as possible. German industrial music is playing and a dusty mobile that appears to be made of bicycle parts hangs lopsidedly from the ceiling. Cassandra is serving at the counter, wearing a necklace that looks as though she's welded a dozen coat hanger hooks together. She peers uninvited at the Bank Robber's head to say it's good but derivative.

The thing about Sol is he's practical. In fact he's the most down-to-earth and thoroughly useful violinist I've ever met. It makes it possible to, for a while at least, ignore his little quirks. He suggests I widen my search to encompass petrol stations. 'Even if the bike was nicked he might've needed to fill the tank.' He asks Cassandra if the café has a phone book. She brings it over, her nail and washer earrings clanking against the scrap metal necklace. I'm surprised it doesn't create sparks. I wait until she's busy serving a dreadlocked student before tearing out the pages. Sol looks scandalised. Like Gina, he's so honest it's touching. Then he comes up with his second brainwave. If he takes a photo of the head he can mock up a type of wanted poster and display it in various pubs and cafes. Full of gratitude I rashly invite him round for dinner. He frowns. Maybe he's currently with another over-possessive girlfriend, he's always been prone to them.

'I'll drop by 'bout seven, yeah?' he says finally, 'but is it alright if I cook?' I nod, grateful really. I'm sure Sol's never been a casualty of my culinary endeavours, but someone's clearly been telling unfortunately true tales about my failings in the home economics department.

As I walk through Churchill Square, a young woman with spiked hair and cat's-eye, green-framed glasses tells me I look like the type of fun, 'up-for-it' type person they need for a new, reality TV show being filmed in our region called 'Sex On The Beach'.

'Does it pay?' Her bright smile drops slightly. Obviously I've asked a really stupid question.

'Um first I just have to like ask you this, okay?' she continues, still keen to hook me.

'Have you ever had sex on the beach?'

'Brighton beach?' She nods, still keen as mustard. I ask if she's seen it. Not yet, she's just down from London for the day. I tell her I'm not keen on pebbles up my arse.

'I'll take that as a 'no' then shall I?' She's already got her eye on another fun, up-for-it type coming out of WH Smith's, but still asks for my phone number, murmuring flatly, 'we might possibly be in touch.' On impulse I give her DS Nelson's card, as I've already transferred the number to my phone. 'Oh gosh, you're a police officer!' she squeals,

14

beaming, interest swiftly returning to her eyes. 'Oh, I'm definitely sure we'll be in touch.' She even gives me a friendly little wave as I depart.

* * * * *

In the second motorcycle shop I make the mistake of telling the tale of Gina's abduction.

'What make of bike was it?' asks the owner, before bombarding me with a barrage of technical questions about cylinders and so forth. His pitying contempt for my ignorant state follows me outside. In the third shop the proprietor asks me the question Sol, Bridie and the others have been too tactful to raise.

'Why don't you leave it to the police, love?' The guy is middle-aged and a bona fide biker, all grizzled chest hair, sagging greasy Black Sabbath vest and skull tattoos. I could tell him about my Portslade gran, the three break-ins the police could hardly be bothered to investigate and how after each one she became a little quieter, a little shakier, a little less able to go on. The fourth time she woke up with an intruder actually in her bedroom. She died a week later. But I don't tell him about my gran. Instead I say, 'I just feel I ought to do something.' He nods in approval and goes on to explain how he and a couple of no-doubt equally spawn-of-Satan-like colleagues dealt with the joy rider that totalled his favourite Kawasaki. It's not a tale for the squeamish, though it might make a good late night movie with Jean-Claude Van Damme.

There aren't many petrol stations in the centre of town. In the only one I can find, which is just off from the coast road, I have to wait while the cashier makes a meal out of serving the members of a very long queue. When it's my turn she clocks the sculpture as I take it from the bag and immediately points to a sign that says, *'We don't buy from trades-people.'*

'What? Do I look like the kind of person who'd expect a rip-off convenience store to buy an artwork?'

'You'd be surprised what people try to pay for their petrol with. One woman offered my boss a Vietnamese pot-bellied piglet when her card was declined.'

'He didn't take it?'

'He didn't.'

'Shame. Probably been a lot faster on that till than you.' Her mouth opens like an oxygen-deprived guppy, but I've temporarily run out of time. A geriatric with a dust mite fixation awaits me.

* * * * *

Gina's father introduces himself as 'Connell', his daughter's surname, and asks for a decaf. I only bought the jar by mistake. Gina usually shops. A small, neat man in an expensive-looking suit, Connell nurses his mug as his eyes scan the magazine, book, CD and DVD mountain in the alcove where we plan to one day have a cupboard. Does he think he'll find the answer among my charity shop bought Chili Peppers albums and Gina's vintage 'Friends' DVDs? It's not until he sits down I see the worry in his eyes. I tell him of my enquiries, feeling the need to reassure him that I'm doing my bit.

Connell last saw his daughter five days ago. He asks me much the same things as the police, but without tagging on bland reassurances. His hair is precisely cut, brown but greying. He has a very straight nose in a symmetrical face. He reminds me slightly of Cary Grant, but with a clipped Cockney accent. He knows how to flirt. He isn't flirting now, but I can see it in little things, the way he uses his eyes, or his hands to gesture. He follows me into the kitchen as I dump our mugs in the sink. He sees the Evening Argus's report of his daughter's abduction pinned to our corkboard. I don't think I'll show him the Bank Robber's head. To him it might seem a bit strange – his daughter's flatmate sculpting the man who made off with her. He remarks that they can't have got clear security camera pictures or they'd have published them. He asks if he can take the article, but I say I'll make a copy for him. 'He's probably a junkie' he says, 'It's usually smack-heads that do armed robbery. Need a lot of money and quickly. But why take my daughter? Why?'

Gina manages one of her father's chip shops, along St. James Street in Kemp Town. It strikes me that I've never seen him in there and I can't smell it on him, only 'Dune pour homme'. He must be much higher up the food chain than the fat fryer.

* * * * *

Sol talks passionately about Stravinsky while he deftly composes a risotto, and later over coffee laments how the only request he received while busking in Western Road earlier was 'Come On Eileen'. I'd hate to tell him but he does have that country-boy look of a Dexy's Midnight Runner about him. He should really stop wearing those plaid

17

waistcoats and neckerchiefs. His enquiries at petrol stations and motorcycle shops in the Hove and Portslade direction have met with no more success than mine on the eastern side of town. He has though, got his teeth into this investigation, even though he can't remember if he's actually met Gina. I'm sure he has, at several parties I've held here in the last year. Then again she does tend to just carry the dips around and not speak unless spoken to. In a packed room Gina would be the last person to stand out from the crowd.

Sol has borrowed Jake's van. When we've had a second coffee he suggests we head out of the city, across the Downs. Near the Seven Dials roundabout we see a fight outside a pub. Six huge bellies belonging to at least two men are rolling about on the pavement. Three police cars are in attendance. I feel like shouting out to the coppers to leave the human beer kegs to their brawl and get out there looking for Gina. I don't do it though.

I'm not someone who gets out in the country very often. I'm not much of a walker because of my knee, and I don't find the countryside as stimulating as perhaps I should. I find beauty in the colours of a club's lightshow, rather than a sunset, in rain on oily tarmac, rather than reflections on a pond. Then most of my work is nudes – and models tend not to like getting naked anywhere there are dog-walkers, nettles and gnats. It's also not that easy to sculpt outdoors. Too much or too little moisture affects the plastilina I like to work with.

The van's suspension is non-existent and the gear stick designed for a wrestler. We've no map or real plan – just cross the South Downs and drive around a bit. Teenagers who only work the evening shift are the cashiers of our first couple of petrol stations. Teen Boy One claims he doesn't really notice 'the punters', but he certainly notices the pert female bottom bending over the shop's ice-cream freezer, picking out her special edition Magnum while I'm trying to talk to him. Teen Boy Two, a beanpole with acne and a pierced brow, just shrugs and grunts.

In the shadow of the hills, we're heading west. In the One Stop Shop at Petrol Station Three, I realise Sol has a little notebook in his hand. Peering over his shoulder, I discover he's been listing the prices of various items – PG Tips tea bags, Sunny Delight, mint Aero, etc. in the different shops. I'd conveniently forgotten this obsessive side to his nature. Ask him why and he'll always say, 'Because I have to.' No wonder the Royal Philharmonic didn't want him. By Petrol Station Six, I could throttle the fiddle-playing obsessive. The stress of it makes me steal a Crunchie. At Petrol Station Nine, deep in West Sussex, Sol ponders whether the prices of chocolate bars alter in direct relation to the socio-economic make-up of the area. I'm sure it's an interesting topic for a discussion with Owen Jones or Jack Monroe on 'Question Time', but quite frankly my dear at this point in time I don't give a crap. The woman on the till, a dead ringer for Judith Chalmers, runs her cerise nails along the Bank Robber's clay cheekbones.

'Yes…' she cackles throatily, providing us with the nearest thing to a positive ID we've had, 'Looks a bit like a chap who comes in here sometimes.' She's not seen him on a motorbike, or in a car for that matter. 'Comes in for a few groceries. Got a dog with him. One of those skinny ones.'

'Greyhound?'

'That'd be it.'

Petrol Station Nine is outside Steyning, a largish village or smallish town, depending on how you look at it. This area clearly needs further, boots-on-the-ground investigation. On the way back, I let Sol drive while I draw up a roster for a stakeout. He agrees to take the early morning shift, as he won't sleep anyway. His mind will be racing through a statistical analysis of grocery prices across East and West Sussex, and in my unexpressed opinion it'll probably keep him hard for days. A quick ring around a few of my speed dial numbers yields Nuala willing to take the lunchtime shift as she'll be feeling relaxed after her aromatherapy, and Jake, available for the afternoon slot, as long as he can leave by two as the Aquatic Bees have a pub gig in Havant. Bridie can manage the afternoon if she can bring the dogs and leave in time for her movement class at six. I'd take a shift myself, but I still need the police to let me have Gina's car back. All but Sol can liaise with me via their mobiles, but he thinks, or rather knows, they're radioactive. All are under instructions to follow our quarry, at a discreet distance of course, should anyone fitting his description happen to show up.

Back in Brighton, we adjourn to the Prince Regent, where Sol joins a drum, flute and fiddle combo he vaguely knows, to play second fiddle, no pun intended. He never travels anywhere without his violin, ever ready to earn his next packet of crispy bacon and maple syrup Kettle Chips and count how many crisps it contains.

Muirinn, serving at the bar, recognises me and comes over. She needs Sol and me to come with her to Queen's Park at closing time. I agree, thinking it's a party invite, to someone's flat in the Queen's Park area of town. Instead, we find ourselves in the actual park, shivering in the middle of the vast expanse of grass, while Muirinn explains the principles of shape shifting. Apparently we're going to be put into a trance from which we will emerge as foxes. The cunning of the fox will give us a fresh insight into finding Gina. At least the Countryside Alliance doesn't have much of a following around here.

Muirinn starts her chanting; kicking out her feet, with strange yelping cries that echo as far as the lake and make a few distant dogs bark. Muirinn's eyes are wide as she shakes her gourd rattle, and I remember hearing she's endured painful tribal initiations all over Africa and learnt her craft from medicine men in Hawaii and Shamen in Cambodia. Not bad for a former head girl at Roedean. I start to feel light-headed. It must be the beer and the cold air. I look towards Sol. He stares back, but those are not his eyes. They are wild, feral, and it has to be said, animal. The chanting reaches a crescendo, echoing and reverberating down my spine. The stars in the night sky appear to be moving further away. I can hear the rustle of leaves and smell the soil. A worm is writhing in the grass in front of me, huge, serpent-like, coiling and uncoiling. Suddenly I'm running – running for the trees, then I'm running round the trees, round and round until I fall down on the grass panting. The forest. In the forest. Creatures all around me – moving, rustling, creeping.

Muirinn is breathing heavily too. She pushes a strand of hennaed hair back from her face. 'Well?' Sol says he thinks he's trod in dog shit. 'The forest. In the forest,' I mutter, without being entirely sure why. Muirinn nods, eyes shining. She assures me I've gained 'a deep spiritual insight by tuning into nature'. Then I notice all the livid scratches criss-crossing my ankles, complete with bramble thorns. I don't tend to buy cropped trousers but mine all tend to end up that way after one too many trips to the laundrette. Knowing my luck, every mosquito in the park has drawn blood from these little strips of exposed flesh too.

Next, Muirinn explains, we're going to become owls and see deep into the darkness. I hold up my hand to stop her before she can begin chanting again. Being a fox was knackering and hazardous enough; flying around among the branches at night doesn't sound like something I feel ready to handle. Muirinn nods, she understands that shape shifting can seem a little unnerving at first. Instead we adjourn to her Kemp Town attic flat for a glass of organic mead. Sol is interested in buying some leaves from the plants on her windowsill. 'They're scented geraniums, not weed,' I whisper when she's out of the room. Poor love, he's not very clued up for a musician. Sol shakes his head despairingly at my squareness.

'No, Vonnie, they are herbal Viagra.' Recovering myself, I ask him what he, since he's currently single, can possibly need it for. 'The Kent Karmic Festival approaches. Lots of hot, sweet hippy chicks.' Who presumably don't mind a man who needs to compare the prices on all the organic vegan burger stands. It's been a long evening. I make my excuses and head homeward.

As I turn into my street I see a fox standing stock still in the middle of the road. Our eyes meet and a chill passes through me. Then he's on his way, swinging nonchalantly off towards the wild garden of the crack den on the corner. At my door I turn and glance back, in time to see him taking a last look back at me – Sister Vixen. I shake my head to banish the thought. Brighton drives you bonkers, there's no two ways about it.

* * * * *

I get up late, having been twice woken in the night by heart-wrenching screams. Probably only another sister vixen getting hers, but each time I see Gina in my mind. I feel ragged and raw. Sol drops in on his way to his busking pitch to tell me he's seen zilch on his stakeout shift. Next up is Nuala, the performance poet. The Arts Council should be subsidising this stakeout. She calls near the end of her shift, her words punchy, rhythmic and telling me she's seen sweet FA. At least she's bringing me over some scented candles, a few Moroccan joss sticks she knows I'll love, and an ounce of hash.

Fortunately, I don't have time to listen to Nuala's latest piece. She does like a repeating rhyme and the last one she tried on me had every sentence ending 'break it, fake it, make it, shake it' and so on. I used to have one of those self-hypnosis CDs designed to help you sleep and it employed a similar use of repeated rhymes. On that occasion poor Nuala only got to the second verse and I was in the land of nod. She didn't know how to take it, or perhaps shake it. I send Nuala on her way, then roll a quick one and head off to work. I can smoke it waiting for the bus, unless any of the sisters from

23

the convent in the next street also happen to be waiting for a 5a.

Bridie rings on my mobile, while I'm hoovering Persian cat hairs in Hangleton. It's a private job I do on the side for an elderly couple, and Sundays are the best time to fit it in. She hasn't seen anything on her shift either but being out in the country is 'such a pure experience'. The way she describes it, you'd think it was 'Gorillas In The Mist' or something. She feels totally revitalised and it seems to be helping Salome the Peke's nasal congestion. I try to tell her about my shape shifting but today as usual she won't let me finish a sentence. While we're talking, or rather she's talking, she pauses for a beautifully timed little gasp mid-sentence. 'I can hear a motorbike! He's pulling up to the pumps. Oh my God. My God. Give me some instructions. What should I do? I think the bike's one of those... you know, those dinky little things from 'La Dolce Vita'. Come on, you know, dear, Fellini with the divine Marcello?' She's getting excited over a ruddy moped... and then the rider turns out to be female.

On the way home from work, I stop off for a small portion of chips at Gina's place of work, 'The New Atlantis'. I'm instantly able to identify the object of Gina's workplace crush. A young Valentino, Benito is Spanish and studying English for a few months in his gap year. He has to put some chips in the fryer. It'll give us a minute or so to get acquainted, over the sound of the sizzle.

'Benito, I'm Vonnie, Gina's flatmate...'

'Ah, Gina, but where is she?' His big brown eyes are gorgeous. There's no fool like a thirty-five year old fool.

Clearly no one has told him what has happened to his manager. I explain about Gina's abduction. He's really shocked, unconsciously raking his fingers through his curly hair.' I cannot believe. I cannot. Gina.' He shakes his head. 'This is so terrible. Isn't it?' He looks on the verge of tears. I want to hug him. The counter and spitting fryer are in the way, otherwise I would, though only to offer comfort naturally. 'Terrible. I wonder why she is not here from Thursday.'

'Tuesday,' I correct him. 'She worked Tuesday morning then...' He's shaking his head, confused.

'She not 'ere from... she does not come in Thursday, Friday, the weekend.'

'This weekend?'

'Two weekends – this weekend and the other.' An older woman with bags under her eyes, who has worked there a while, elbows in to remove the sizzling chips from the fat. She wraps them with a glare at Benito, presumably because a small queue has built up while we've been chatting. 'Eileen, when came Gina last time?'

'Must've been Thursday before last. Suppose being the boss's daughter she can have time off whenever she likes. Be nice if she'd arranged cover for herself though wouldn't it?' Her tone is world-weary and slightly bitter.

'Eileen, this is 'err friend. Something terrible 'as happened.' I fill Eileen in on the details and reassure her as convincingly as I can that the police are doing their best. Eileen is flabbergasted by the news, rubbing her hands together in a washing gesture and mutters 'dear' and 'oh dear' several times almost beneath her breath.

Gina enjoyed her job, well most of the time, and certainly since Benito joined the staff a little over two months ago. Several times I'd caught her reading his stars as well as her own in the free paper. He's a Taurean. Once she went shopping with him after work, and once they'd had a coffee, 'a proper black one' together, but that's as far it has gone. Customers are waiting and Eileen moves away. Benito can't think of a reason why Gina should stay away from work. There hadn't been any rows or other problems.

'So she seemed perfectly happy?' I find myself gesturing as I speak. He watches my magenta nails as if mesmerised.

'I don't know,' he says at last. 'Before she go, she seemed maybe a little sad? Like she is… I don't know the word – But she say she is okay. She does not want to talk of it.' I nod. 'Also,' he adds, 'I think she might try to call me after she was taken. I have a missed call on my phone.' He shows me. The date and time fits.

'She didn't leave a message?'

'No.' This looks as though it could've been the last call she tried to make. Benito had just left work, and his phone had been in the pocket of his rucksack. Walking home through the noisy centre of town he had missed the call.

* * * * *

Gina's room still smells of hamster, even though Ferdinand reached the end of his two-year life span three months back. DS Nelson and her sidekick have taken a few of her personal

26

things, including, it seems, Gina's diary. That's a shame. It would've been useful, although I don't think she wrote in it regularly. Sol calls. He fancies taking another turn on the stakeout. There's no accounting for taste. I give him the evening shift from eight-thirty.

Going out on the town might seem an odd thing to do in the circumstances, but I feel the need to be immersed in a world other than the one inside my head. The only top of mine that's not in the laundry bin is a purple-rib sleeveless one. I drag it down over my push-up bra, and force a comb through the scarlet curls that match my lipstick. My state-of-the-art concealer won't make me look twenty one again, but it takes a few years off and I'm grateful for that.

With my knee problem, I dance like a rheumatic carthorse and probably over-compensate for my inflexible leg by flailing my arms about. My club of choice is currently The Seahorse, which is beneath the prom. They leave the front doors open unless a gale is blowing, and that means I can see the sea while I'm dancing. It gives me something to focus on – the horizon. I don't meet the eyes of the men in clubs. It's too like shopping in the dark. Feeling a hesitant touch on my arm, I give the skinny young man with a gap-toothed grin a piss-off glare. I've come here and entered this throng to find solitude.

The stakeout continues on Monday with a few personnel changes, including Muirinn, apparently shape-shifted to a kestrel for better vision. I can hear the wind blowing in the background when she calls. Can a kestrel use a Samsung Galaxy while hovering in the sky? I think she did say something about her spirit soaring and leaving her mortal body behind on Earth, but then which part of her entity is holding the ruddy phone? On Tuesday my stakeout is a little short-handed as everyone seems to have a class or workshop in something or the available shifts clash with their Job Centre Plus signing-on times. By Wednesday, surveillance of Petrol Station Nine is very patchy indeed. With Bridie at a hot stones session, there's no one to cover the afternoon and I'm back with Mr Williams and his dust mites until four. Badgering Nelson about the car has finally paid off though. I can collect it this morning.

* * * * *

The Uno is cleaner both inside and out than I've ever known it. It's far cleaner than the time Gina paid to have it valeted. Even her Rollo wrappers and my Rizlas are gone from the ashtray. A cop or Bank Robber hasn't nicked any of her CDs. I don't blame him or her. They're all by ex-members of boy bands with identically auto-tuned voices. Even a forensic sound engineer, if there is such a thing, couldn't tell the warblers of these miserable musical offerings apart. The glove compartment is still full of rubbish, but I suspect each item, from plastic spoon to motorway services tartar sauce sachet, has been carefully logged and noted by the white-coated boffins. Sol has missed his calling in life. He'd have been ace at working in forensics. The tiny faded teddy in a raincoat is still sitting there on the dash, and almost has me in tears.

I put in a couple of hours on the stakeout, but I'm crabby as hell with PMT today and eventually cross the road to the garage shop for some chocolate to cure the craving. The Judith Chalmers clone is on the till again. She smiles as far as her Botox will allow and says she saw me parked in the lay-by opposite.

'I nearly came over and brought you a cuppa, love. I suppose there's no news on your friend? It's so sad. It's a wicked world all right.' It's soon apparent who told her the whole story.

'Such a nice lady, a really lovely person. She told me all about it the first time she came in. I'm sure I've seen her when she was in 'Coronation Street'. Her face is familiar.' Bridie only had a walk-on – in 1986. 'I'm glad it wasn't me here when he came in. I don't know what I'd have done. Screamed probably.' It's a moment before I realise what she's saying. The Bank Robber or someone fitting his description had walked into the shop during the morning while her husband was on the till.

'It's a family business.' Naturally she'd told her old man all about it – building society raid, girl abducted, friend of a friend of an almost-famous actress. The 'suspect' had brought bread, biscuits, tea bags, milk, and dog food. Shame it wasn't on Sol's shift. He'd have burst in and told the guy he could purchase both the tea bags and milk cheaper a few miles down the road.

'He wanted brown bread but we only had white.' A health-conscious raider doesn't really fit with Connell's junkie theory. Then I go cold. Gina only eats white bread. Maybe this means nothing. Maybe I'm leaping ahead of myself.

'My husband asked him for his number. Said we'd give him a ring when the brown came in. He's quick he is, my Stevie.' I'm not so sure. How often does a convenience store

29

offer to phone you when the product you need comes in? '…said he didn't have a phone. But he didn't take the white bread, so perhaps he'll pop back in.' Most tellingly the dog was off the leash and the guy wasn't with a car. He can't have had a greyhound on the back of a motorcycle. He must live round here. Time for a spot of house to house.

The road is lined on one side only by red-brick council semis, or mostly ex-council now, judging by the oak-look doors, stone-cladding and double-glazing styles ranging from ultra-bland to chichi mock Victorian. The first house yields a dog owner, a Pomeranian – the dog not the woman – but she doesn't know anyone with a greyhound. The next house belongs to someone who has only recently moved to the village and isn't able to help. Her neighbour won't open the door beyond the chain and is monosyllabic. I take his two short, muttered syllables to be telling me where to go, and depart. Then there's a tree-lined break between dwellings, before a roses-round-the door kind of cottage. A severely permed blonde sixty-something, smelling of pot pourri answers the elaborately chiming doorbell. She has cats not dogs, she informs me sniffily. Next up is a weighty Scot who suggests I try 'the farm', up a little track opposite, where someone has 'a wee doggie'.

A genuinely tweedy farmer, a blue-eyed border collie peering between his legs, answers the door of the farmhouse. Perhaps this is the wee doggie. 'You've got the wrong farm. It's the next 'un. Fella with a lurcher.' I tell him it's a greyhound I'm looking for. 'Nay, it's a lurcher. Brindle lurcher.'

The next farm is a fair way up the lane, hidden away behind a thick bank of trees. The gate is wrapped in barbed wire, which gives it a rather threatening vibe. I almost expect to have a rifle pointed at my head by a red-faced farmer bellowing, 'Get orf my land,' before I've even set foot on it, but the place seems to be deserted. The rough tree-lined track up to the house also leads to a small green clearing containing a rusting caravan, some broken wooden pallets and splitting plastic sacks of something vaguely agricultural next to it. Outside the caravan, a dog bowl nestles in the grass.

The caravan looks like it's only narrowly survived a nasty collision. A lurcher is asleep on the floor. It is certainly a breed a non-dog person could conceivably mistake for a greyhound. In my younger days I'd sculpt the occasional dog and cat, so I do know my breeds. Surprisingly it hasn't heard my approach. I tap on the window. The dog still doesn't stir. 'Gina?' I tap louder. It's unlikely she's in there, twice as unlikely that she can hear me, but I must keep trying and hoping. The sound of footsteps spins me around. I twist my knee as I stumble, boot skidding in the mud. My shoulder bag slides to the ground. A man is approaching. I stoop for and find the Swiss Army penknife I keep in my bag for all kinds of emergencies. Trying to think fast, I have another rummage for inspiration and find some salt twists and an ancient ketchup sachet nicked from ASDA's cafe in the bottom of it. The knife moves swiftly to my pocket and I split the sachet and squirt its contents down the inside of my sagging sock.

The man stands a little way off, clearly not expecting to encounter a stranger near his caravan. I don't know if it's the guy from the building society raid. The face I sculpted is the only pictorial memory of him now in my mind. I don't remember his cheekbones as this prominent, I thought his hair was dark brown and shorter. This guy has long, wet-looking black hair. 'Thank God... I fell in the woods. I've cut my ankle on something.' He comes closer, eyeing me quizzically. I show him my ketchup-smeared hand. 'I don't suppose you live around here...' His expression becomes wary. 'You don't happen to have a first aid kit or anything?'

'Wait there.' His accent suggests he's a fellow Londoner, whatever else he may or may not be. It shouldn't give me comfort but in an odd way it does. He pulls the dented door open and disappears inside the caravan, reappearing after a moment with a tube of Savlon and an unopened bandage. He must have a first aid box. I limp over to the door of the caravan. 'Could you get me some water – I think I need to wash it.' Actually I think I need him to allow me a closer look inside the caravan.

'No running water.' he says. I make a big show of painfully sitting down on his doorstep, twisting around so not to turn my back on him. It would be so easy for him to cosh me and put me wherever he's put... stop thinking like this. As I half-turn, I catch sight of a black crash helmet on a chair. Stomach lurching, my breath comes out in an audible gasp. 'It stings,' I say to cover my panic, not looking at him. 'No water or electricity?'

'Honest,' he says as if I'm accusing him of fibbing. 'I've just been up to the farm for a bath.' He's very pale and there's a calmness and stillness about him. He doesn't strike me as likely to be a junkie. All the serious druggies I've encountered have been a little twitchy at least. His caravan is clean and tidy, but impersonal, hardly a home. The dog staggers arthritically over and sniffs my back. I hope it doesn't have a taste for ketchup. Its eyes are glassy and muzzle grizzled. He gently pushes it away.

'What's his name?'

'Her,' he corrects me, ' Peggy.' While the dog distracts him I do my best to make it look like a painful wound I'm cleaning up. Then I get the bandage on as he scrutinises me.

'What were you doing in the woods?' The tone's light enough, but I feel vaguely threatened.

'Went for a walk.' If he's been living here any length of time he'll know I'm not from these parts. 'I'm staying with a friend in the town. Thought I'd have a little explore… being it's so sunny today.' He doesn't comment, but the gaze of his cold grey eyes unnerves me. The only advantages I have are the penknife in my pocket and the fact he probably believes I can hardly walk. I stand up.

'Thanks…' I pull myself up in the doorway. Steadying myself on the wall I feel some keys hanging on a peg, beneath my hand. Flipping the string off the peg, I let them slip silently up sleeve.

'You didn't walk all the way out here?' Again I can't tell if it's an accusation or whether my fear is making me read more into it than is meant.

'No, I'm parked in the lane.' I concentrate on my hobbling, expecting him to do no more than watch me from the doorway. Instead he's beside me.

'Lean on me,' he commands rather than offers. I slip my arm around his shoulders and let him take my weight. His hair brushes my face. He smells of shower gel, so was probably telling the truth about the bath at the farmhouse.

In the lane, the man stops dead, almost pitching me forward onto the road. He's spotted Gina's car, and there's fear in his eyes. Now I know for certain he's the one responsible for Gina's disappearance. Taking my arm from around his neck, I hobble towards the car. Will he knock me down? Or shoot me in the back? Then a thought strikes me. Maybe it is only the shock of seeing *a* blue Fiat Uno, any blue Uno. My mind races; is there anything about the car that immediately distinguishes it from other blue Unos, apart from the number plate? I remember Gina's little faded teddy on the dash. He must've noticed that when he took the car. If he comes any closer he'll see it. Can he remember the registration? Will he let me get in and drive away?

I scramble into the car, and force myself to belt up before locking the door, so as not to look like anything is wrong. As I look up, I see he's walking away towards the caravan. He doesn't look back.

* * * * *

Luana's bungalow is decorated in a minimalist, IKEA style. I suppose I was expecting black drapes with moons and stars on them. She doesn't have a headscarf either but she does have long, dangling shell earrings. It's a bad sign, as are the wind chimes in the window. Her taste is something straight out of a daytime TV home makeover show. She has wooden letters on the top of the bookshelf spelling out 'Love Your

Life'. If she leaves me alone I might be tempted to swap the places of the second and first words. She also collects air plants, which are stuck to pieces of cork or more shells. It's hard to tell if they're alive or have long breathed their last. The same could almost be said for the glassy-eyed Luana – no stranger to the Diazepam bottle, I suspect. Clasping my hands intensely, she speaks in a husky east European accent. 'You vill find her. I knows you vill.' She talks of omens and portents, but it all sounds too eye-of-toad-and tongue-of-newt for me to relate to. She's seen trees. Oh hell, it seems like we're back to my inner fox cub.

'A house with climbing plants.' That's different at least.

'Wisteria? Or ivy?' The glassy stare focuses but remains a few degrees colder than ice.

'What is this weesteriarrh?' Unfortunately she's not a gardener. 'Gina is there, but not alone,' she continues. If he's tall, dark and handsome, I'm crossing her palm with a recently expired debit card and going home before the bullshit deepens any further. This is far too general; it's taking up my time and threatens to muddle my thinking.

'A young man who has had problems, but now he is healed. He is new. He is showing Gina herself.' What does that mean? Is he screwing her? Gina once admitted to me she'd never had a sexual experience. She'd not met anyone she'd want to share one with, which is fair enough. I sometimes wish I'd been a bit more discerning.

I want to leave, but Luana wants to draw me a picture of the house from her vision. I fervently hope it's only a quick sketch. Fortunately it turns out to be little more than a few lines. She apologises for the deficiencies of her art. The house has four square windows. It's detached with trees around it. If the trees are going to have big round apples on them then it's somewhere I definitely recognise. It's the house I and most of my infant class used to draw, even those of us who, like me, lived in a grotty high rise in Thornton Heath.

* * * * *

I'm watching 'Angel Heart' on Sony Movies when Benito phones. I like it when private eye Mickey Rourke tells Lisa Bonet to call him if she hears anything, and to call him if she doesn't. I wish I were cool enough to say something like that to Benito. He does though want to meet up. He's remembered some things, 'maybe not important things, just some things' about Gina's last week at work. We'll meet during his lunch hour.

Writing to the Bank Robber takes some time. It has to be a letter because I've no other way of contacting him. I'm going to have to address it to 'The Caravan on Rowes Farm, just outside of Steyning'. No postcode of course. Still, the post office has managed to get letters to Santa in the past, haven't they? Hopefully after that feat this'll be a doddle. Here is what I wrote. *'I have your bike keys. I want to see you again. Be at Primrose's – Steyning High Street, 3pm on Friday. From the Woman With The Injured Leg.'* I'll have to send it first class though, I'm not forking out for all that recorded, signed-for extravagance they always try to hard sell you at the post office. The keys I filched from the hook in the caravan appear to be two identical sets. Hopefully he can't use the motorbike without them. It'll make him more likely to turn up. I can't imagine he'd want to see me again for any other reason, unless he's desperate for female company. Judging by the amount of money he made off with, that's hardly likely to be the case. If I'd that kind of cash, I'd be in Ibiza now, with an Armani aftershave model on each arm. Don't judge me too harshly for that, I'm sure you would do something similar.

* * * * *

Benito wants to leave his job. Now Gina's gone, there's no one to make it bearable. He says Eileen is kind but has no sense of humour, and the boss (Gina's dad) has twice failed to pay him for all his hours, taking advantage of the fact that it's hard for him to get to grips with his finances in his second language and a still slightly unfamiliar currency. We're meeting in a café a few doors along from the chippy. He's brought something to show me – the engagement calendar from the shop. Provided by a chip shop supplies firm, it has pictures from the industry, who are mostly jolly, smiling folk in pristine white coats, hair nets and hats. For January they are working on a saveloy production line and in February they are putting gherkins in jars. Each page has a dark border smeared with floury fingerprints. On the printed part, various names are scrawled showing the work rotas, among them Gina's, along with notes such as 'E's birthday', 'E's holiday'. Benito turns back to last month. Two weeks in, it says in Gina's handwriting, 'Finish early – Meet R!!!'

'She writed this,' his slim finger traces forward a week. Here it is again. 'R at 5.'

'A man?'

'Could be, yes? She talk-ed about a friend sometimes. A name I do not remember.' I try out a few names beginning

37

with 'R' of both sexes. He finds Roger funny. 'We have a customer – Mr Rogers,' he rolls the R. 'Always I laugh when I see him. I cannot 'elp it. Eileen says 'to roger' is to… you know.' I know. The only man I've heard Gina mention in recent weeks is Benito himself. She seemed smitten. Gina has an old friend from her school days, Jo-Ann. I try the name on Benito. 'I remember Jo-Ann. Tall, y'know? And she talked of you, Vonnie.' Nice things, I hope. I'm fast warming to him and not only because he smells deliciously of batter. I've brought him a posh black coffee and a blueberry muffin. He thanks me politely, eating the cake like it's the first food he's had in a fortnight. Either he isn't allowed to eat at the chip shop or he's sick of fried food.

'Something strange, Vonnie. Gina begin to… to listen to different music. Like classico?' He mimes conducting to make the point. 'No words, just music. Like shop music.' I nod. 'Maybe this new friend give 'err CDs or download.' I can look among the CDs when I get home. Gina doesn't currently have a working computer. She spilt Ovaltine into her laptop a couple of months back and hasn't yet got around to replacing it. She uses her phone for everything, so if there are downloads or messages from 'R' or anyone else, they'd be on there. I wish I knew where that phone is. Presuming she had it on her when she was carjacked, then it's not in the flat. It's almost time for us both to go back to work. As he gets up to leave, Benito adds as an afterthought, 'and sometimes she 'ad phone-calls. 'err mobile ring-ed and she go outside.' The police can check this out by accessing her phone records if they haven't already done so. I thank him for his help and time. 'No problem.'

'Call me if you hear anything and call me if you don't.'

* * * * *

DS Nelson seems glad I called. She says they're thinking about making a TV appeal with Gina's father taking part. They're also following up a number of new leads. She is, as a matter of course, checking Gina's mobile phone records. I ask if they're any closer to finding the man on the motorbike. She says she can't divulge this information at present. Being as this is the case, I don't divulge I'm meeting him tomorrow. Fair's fair.

* * * * *

Mr Williams collects antique foreign coins. I use a lot of Windolene and elbow grease on his glass display cabinets. The most important factor in determining a coin's value, he tells me with pride, is its condition. He never picks them up without protective gloves on. The earliest ones he has are Chinese, from several centuries before Christ. I ask him if I can leave something with him. It's a folder of information sealed in an envelope. If I fail to return for it by six pm he's to call the police station and ask them to collect it. He's to say it's from Yvonne Sharpe for DS Nelson. 'Six on the dot,' he mutters to himself. The room has four wind-up clocks, all of which keep the correct time. I think I can depend on him.

* * * * *

I find a number for Jo-Ann. She and Gina haven't got around to meeting up for several months. She's recently started a new job working nights at some warehouse delivery place, so they've not been free to go to the pictures regularly like they used to. She's very concerned about Gina when I explain the situation, but can't shed any light on the mysterious 'R'. 'We both knew a Rebecca at school, and I suppose they might still be in touch.' She says she'll call if she finds her number. I remember the three exclamation marks after 'R'. Somehow I don't think it is anyone called Rebecca.

CHAPTER THREE

I arrive at the Primrose Café over an hour early and order a veggie lasagne for lunch. It's generously proportioned with lots of aubergines escaping from the sides. I hope to conduct this meeting, if indeed it happens, inside rather than outside the café. A confrontation in the street is the last thing I want and I feel safer in an enclosed, public space. Most people have already had lunch and are starting to leave, which does at least mean I can choose a window table. There are two women serving and Radio Sussex plays softly behind the counter. Across the road, two trendy mums are comparing identically clad babies. I suppose the tots are too young to be embarrassed by their fashion faux pas. Drizzle speckles the slightly steamy window beside me. I've brought along a book to read while I'm waiting. The library didn't have anything on solving abductions or dealing effectively with the criminal fraternity, but this self-defence tome might prove interesting, though with my gammy knee, some of the high kicks aren't entirely viable. It's why I've never attempted to read the Kama Sutra.

Ten to three and I put the book away, and order another coffee. There's only an elderly couple left in the café, but unfortunately they're on the table next to mine. They're talking about whether to buy a tablet computer. She's keener

41

than him, mainly so she can Skype her daughter who is living in Greece. He thinks it might be a mixed blessing, as he'll then find it impossible to avoid the golf club's WhatsApp group. It's already been the cause of one marriage break up and a 'clubhouse rage' incident, as he puts it. One of the café staff comes over and gives my table a thorough wipe. I suspect that means 'order something else or hit the road.' Unfortunately for her, I haven't fully drained my cup and lift it protectively to stop it being whisked away. I'm a café veteran fully qualified in meaningful lingering. To get me out of here she'll have to try harder than that. Nothing short of pressing the fire alarm will do it.

It's raining steadily now. I swill the remaining couple of centimetres of tepid latte around in my cup, but finally there he is, across the road. I don't know how he got here without the motorbike. Walked presumably. It would only have taken about ten minutes from the farm, I calculate. Regardless as to his mode of travel, he is wearing a motorcycle jacket and jeans, and, unlike at the caravan, glasses. He's spotted me in my window seat, so I hold up the keys, unsmiling. He beckons me to come out. I shake my head. He waits. If it weren't for the rain, maybe he could stubbornly stand there for an hour until the place closes at four. He crosses the road, looks through the window, hands in his pockets. Perhaps he suspects police involvement. He may have the gun he used in the robbery inside a jacket pocket. He could be a psychopath who will just walk in, coolly shoot me in the head and take the keys. If he is, it's too late to do anything about it now.

The Bank Robber strolls in, walks over to the counter, all the time looking around, checking that no one but the two women working there are present. They both have their backs to him, washing up. He appears to be checking for blind corners and the single door to the toilets has not escaped his attention either. One of the women turns to face him, and he orders a coffee without so much as a look in my direction. He's very cool about it.

The Bank Robber's body language is still relaxed and confident as he pushes the coffee towards me, holding out his hand for his keys. I ask him to sit down. Quietly he says he hasn't time. I'm so tense I hastily lift the cup and scald my lip on the coffee. 'We need to talk.'

'I don't think so.' If he does assume, as I've hoped, that I've invited him here because I fancy him, then he isn't flattered or curious and it doesn't seem to be mutual. Maybe he doesn't like women who make the running. Control freaks often don't. There's definitely something about him that makes me think he likes to be the one in control, and for the moment he thinks he is.

'We need to talk about my friend Gina.' He doesn't react. Somehow he doesn't seem to get it. I struggle to keep my voice matter-of-fact, as I add softly, 'Who you carjacked and abducted ten days ago.' Fear flickers across his face. His mouth twitches slightly.

'I don't know who or what you're talking about, but I'd like my keys, if you don't mind.' His voice is still steady and his eyes have only given him away for a moment. The thing is, I tell him, I do actually mind. I'll scream for help if he does anything other than slowly sit down opposite me. For a moment I think he's going to forcibly search me for the keys

43

anyway, then he looks towards the window, and I think he's prepared to leave empty-handed.

Seemingly changing his mind, the Bank Robber sits. He pushes his chair back, studying me from a little distance, getting the measure of what he's up against. He looks very smart today – almost as if he was expecting this to be some kind of date. With a dark red shirt beneath his biker jacket setting off his tied-back hair, he doesn't look at all out of place in the village teashop. If things stay this civil, the pensioners on the next table will be thinking we're 'a nice young couple'. Speaking softly, I tell him I have compiled a dossier of information on him, which I've left at a friend's. If I'm not there to pick it up in person unharmed and alone, at six pm, my friend is to open it, read it, and call the police. The Bank Robber repeats that he doesn't know what I'm talking about, looking me in the eye the whole time. He's certainly a convincing liar. I tell him I don't care about anything but getting Gina back.

'I'd have gone to the police with what I've got. If I thought it would help her. But what if they lock you up and you don't talk? If she's still alive, she could be starving, she could be dying.' Unmoved, he repeats that he has no idea what I'm on about and asks for his keys, with more of a threat implied this time. I know if I hold out any longer he'll take them anyway, risking the café staff seeing what'll appear as no more than a domestic tussle before making his getaway. 'If you leave without telling me anything, I'll be straight on the phone to the police. I know you think I'll do that anyway, but I haven't so far have I? There's a small chance I might not shop you if you cooperate. A small chance is all you've got.' He lifts his head slightly in a gesture of contempt, and folds his gloved fingers under his chin. For a very long minute neither of us moves. Needing to resolve this, I take the keys from my pocket and lay them on the table. Before I can remove my hand, his pounces like lightning, his fingers painfully crushing my hand against the keys. His eyes are cold like those of a cat with a sparrow beneath its claws.

'I don't know what sort of game you think you're playing. But I'm not someone you can play with.' He increases the pressure. 'I don't play.' He releases me suddenly and takes his keys.

'So talk to me.' I try.

'Go into the bathroom.' he says.

In the ladies loo, I transfer the penknife from my shoulder bag to my jeans pocket again. I wait for maybe a two minutes. I've convinced myself he's left the café, when he walks in. Wordlessly, he indicates I enter a cubicle. I hesitate, but there's nowhere else to go, he's blocking the exit. He follows me in. There's so little room I'm backed up over the toilet. He still smells of shower gel. He takes my bag and rummages in it and checks my mobile is switched off. Then he asks me to unbutton my shirt. I look him in the eye, but don't see any emotion I recognise. I don't think there's anything sexual in his request, but then remember that rape is actually about power and control. My fingers fumble on the buttons. I favour fitted shirts, and this one is now a size too small, so unfortunately I'm slightly busting out. When I've finished, he reaches inside with one gloved hand, feeling along the edge of my bra, around to the back and then on the other side. He only uses his fingers and doesn't cup or grip my breasts. His touch is light and neither rough not particularly gentle. 'Just checking you're not recording our conversation.' He then moves down to my waistband, and pockets. He finds the penknife and shows me it, before putting it in his own pocket. Unbolting the door, he steps back from me. I button my shirt. 'Who are you?' he says.

'Where is she?' I answer. He shifts his weight, leaning against basins, with a quick glance towards the door. I can read him now – his look is troubled. 'Is she alive or dead. Just tell me that.'

'I don't…'

'Don't say you don't know what I'm talking about. You do, you bastard.' He almost seems to flinch at 'bastard', as if he's some thoroughly decent bloke facing an unjust accusation. I'm pretty sure he isn't going to hit or shoot me for the present, at any rate.

'I don't know where she is,' he says at last, sullen, as if I've somehow forced this admission out of him, if indeed it is an admission. I remember how he looked me in the eye as he calmly lied over not knowing what I was talking about. I wait for more information but it doesn't come.

'Do you read the news? Of course you do. You need to keep one step ahead.'

'I didn't…' he stops himself.

'Tell me what you did. I was there in the building society. I'm the woman you made lie on the floor, remember?' His face says he doesn't. He really only saw me from behind, I suppose. 'Your bike wouldn't start. You hijacked Gina. And then?' He puts a hand across his eyes for a moment, and then leaning heavily on the basin he is copiously sick.

My first reaction is it means he's killed her. My second is to wonder how I should take advantage of the situation, while he has his back to me, but I can't think what to do. Perhaps it was in a later chapter of the self-defence book. Meticulously, he washes the vomit down the sink, leaving no trace, and barely giving me a glance, he heads for the door.

The rain is bouncing off the pavement as I follow the Bank Robber from the café, almost running to keep up with his stride. He crosses the road and heads for the town car park, walking straight up to the passenger door of Gina's car, where he waits for me. He must have either recognised it on his way to our rendezvous, or he was already watching from somewhere nearby when I arrived. I get in and open the door for him. I assume he's decided we're taking a trip somewhere. This isn't ideal but I don't have a lot of choice if I want to keep up with my only live link to Gina's disappearance. 'Where to?'

'Just drive.'

A couple of times, when in my nervousness, I brake a little harshly, the Bank Robber gives me a sharp look. 'Still feeling queasy?' I ask. No answer. He tells me to pull over in a lay-by on the quiet country road. Perhaps he's going to kill me here, or more likely, order me out and take the car. He gets out and he's sick again, straight into the rain-shiny blackberry bushes. I ask if he wants to sit for a minute and he says 'okay'. A broken twig falls from the tree canopy above and hits the bonnet, making us both jump. Psychic Luana said something about trees in relation to Gina. I've still got her little tree drawing in my bag. I take it out and look at it. There is no detached house with apple trees nearby. The Bank Robber watches me without comment as I fold it up and put it back in my bag. The rhythm of the windscreen wipers seeps into my head. Maybe five minutes pass. A magpie flies down onto the road. Unfortunately it's a single one. 'Good afternoon Mr Magpie.' I'm not usually superstitious, but this is one of those occasions where I'd rather hedge my bets. I realise Mr Magpie has found a freshly flattened squirrel on the verge. He begins a spirited tug of war to remove its intestines. I give the Bank Robber a sidewise glance. He's noticed the grisly goings on. He'll probably need to throw up again, I think, but he doesn't seem affected.

'I can take you to where I left her. That's all I can do,' he says at last. I nod. It's a start.

'And then? You'll leave town, I suppose?'

'When you go back to the police…' He doesn't say 'if'. '…You better hope they find me before I find you.' He issues his threats pragmatically, almost wearily. It was the same when he said, 'I don't play' while crushing my fingers. It hurt enough to make the point but no more than that. My knowledge of criminals has mainly been gained from low-budget gangster movies, which is all they seem to show on the free channels some nights. In a film, I'd have had my fingers broken by now at the very least, and I'd have certainly seen something of the gun he must surely be carrying.

We ascend the flyover outside of Shoreham and head along the dual carriageway back into Brighton. The Bank

Robber doesn't give me any directions at this stage, so I drop into the centre of town.

'Keep going,' he says suddenly, as I try to slow up as we pass the building society. Asked what he said to Gina, he replies he only gave her directions, adding 'She was in the wrong lane at this point.' I'm outraged he has the nerve to be critical of her driving, and find myself hypocritically defending her.

'Jesus! In the circumstances are you bloody surprised!' Unrepentant, he adds that she nearly got them rear-ended at Preston Circus. It's called 'hesitation' and she failed her test six times due to it. I can't face up to the fact I might never see her again. I might never know what's happened to her. It makes me hate him, and hate myself for letting him into her car for a second time. As we leave the town, her faded little teddy, it's once-brown fur now a sun-bleached mauve, topples off the dash. He picks it up, and I snatch it away from him.

We're heading up the South Downs. The houses are becoming larger and spreading out and then its fields on either side of the road. At a long lay-by, so big it could almost be called a car park, the Bank Robber tells me to pull in. I think maybe he's going to puke again, but it isn't that. This is, he says where he left Gina. The rain is drumming on the roof. Beyond this point the road disappears over the hilltop and starts to descend. He says he'd left a second, borrowed motorbike there, just out of sight, over the hedge. It was in case anyone back in the city had taken the number or got a good description of the first one. I get out, taking the car keys, and step through a near gap in the hedge. He follows and

points out a faint tyre mark on the mud 'There.' We stand
and look back at the car, rain pouring down upon us. He had
Gina's original set of car keys. He'd taken them upon leaving
her in the car. He'd got on his second bike and then looked
back. 'She was on her mobile. I'd slipped up. In the rush to
get away, I hadn't checked her bag.' He went back. She'd
locked the car door from inside but of course he had the keys.
She screamed as he snatched the mobile phone from her
hand and threw it into the hedgerow. The hedge is thick,
matted hawthorn and bramble with a barbed wire fence
embedded in it.

'It was getting dark. You left her stranded here, with no
means of calling for help.'

'Look, I don't give a monkey's, okay.' The sharpness of
his tone suggests he's rattled by the situation.

'You will if anything's happened to her,' I flare up, looking
him in the eye. 'You'll be the one who gets the blame for it.
Even if it wasn't you.' He turns away, contemptuous again.

Suddenly I've had enough of this, enough of him. I run
back to the car and I'm driving away down the road before I
realise he hasn't even tried to come after me. As my heartbeat
slows I wonder what on earth I've been doing, and what I'm
still doing. I've now squandered my only lead to Gina's
whereabouts by leaving him at the roadside. As I look for a
place to do a U turn, I still don't know if I believe what he's
told me.

The road is deserted when I return. The rain is torrential.
I've only been a few minutes; I can't see where he can have
gone unless he was immediately able to hitch a lift. Gina

50

disappeared with no logical explanation, and now the Bank Robber has vanished. Maybe there's some kind of Bermuda Triangle a few kilometres outside Brighton. Sol would probably buy into a parallel universe theory, Bridie would call one of her mumbo jumbo merchants and Jake would put it down to my smoking habits. Then I see him, walking down the ploughed field beyond the hedge, head down against the driving rain. He starts and stumbles at my blast on the horn. Here there is no gap in the hedge and he starts to climb over. I almost lean out to warn him about the barbed wire but stop myself. Why should I care? He makes it unscathed anyway. He's drenched and his boots are covered in mud. He gets in the car before opening his gloved hand to show me a mud-caked metallic blue mobile phone.

Rain silvers the Bank Robber's hair and runs down his face. He examines the phone, still wearing gloves, and presses a button.

'Last number dialled.' I look but don't recognise it. He rings it, listens. No answer. I try to take the phone but he holds it out of my reach. 'You might call the police.'

I insist I want the police to look at Gina's phone. He shrugs and pockets it. The rain is easing a little. 'What now?' I ask. He wants a lift home. 'And then what? You'll scarper pretty sharpish, won't you?' He says I haven't left him much choice.

* * * * *

I tell the Bank Robber I need some petrol, intending to pull in to the Judith Chalmers petrol station. With a bit of eye contact, maybe I can get her to call the police. Getting him

51

arrested is the only way to find out what else he knows. Once he disappears, my one direct link with Gina's disappearance will have evaporated. I wish I was as much of a fan of detective fiction as my Gran. I'm sure she would've known the right questions to ask him. If I was as clued up as her, I might have found out something useful. She always knew who had done it before she reached the halfway point of an audio book. The Bank Robber checks the gauge and says there's enough petrol for now. I can fill up after dropping him off.

As we reach the tree tunnel, an improbable horror film fog starts to engulf the road ahead. The caravan is in the clearing beyond. Getting nearer, I realise the fog isn't fog but smoke, and it's coming from behind the trees. The Bank Robber sits up straight and looks at me. I realise what he of course knows – there's nothing beyond those trees but his caravan.

Snatching my keys from the ignition, the Bank Robber leaps from the car and sprints through the trees. There's lots of smoke, even inside the car it's making my eyes and nose sting, creeping, tickling and choking down my throat. While I'm rubbing my eyes, he's gone, disappeared inside the burning caravan. I can't see flames, only smoke clouds pouring from the caravan. It looks like one of the cheap special effects in a student film Bridie once appeared in. Except there the woods were full of undergraduates pretending to be zombies. It's still raining. I leave the car, not knowing what to do, just wanting to do something. Suddenly the Bank Robber comes staggering out of the caravan, a body in a blanket cradled in his arms. Gina.

It's not Gina. It's his dog. He drops her heavily on the ground. She sprawls limp. He crouches over her, checking for signs of life, then lifts her again and runs with her to the car.

Peggy has a heartbeat. There's a vet in the village. The Bank Robber strokes the lurcher's head and talks to her throughout the five-minute journey.

The vet is in the middle of early evening clinic, but is brisk and efficient in the emergency, admitting Peggy and immediately administering oxygen. We sit in the waiting room under the empathetic eyes of other pet owners. I look at the Bank Robber, and he's looking at me, with hatred in his eyes. 'If she dies…' I realise he thinks I'm part of this, whatever 'this' is.

* * * * *

The vet tells us it's touch and go. They'll keep Peggy in, in their intensive care section. Already she's on a drip. They want contact details. He tells me to give them mine and knowing they assume we're a couple, I give my address and mobile phone number. I hope I don't get the bill, I think uncharitably, but know there's safety in the vet having my address. However murderous the Bank Robber's intentions were just now, he surely wouldn't do anything to me at present. Not if he's rational.

Back in the car, the Bank Robber doesn't immediately hand me the keys. I need to talk to him. I can feel his anger, so I start talking. I say I know he's thinking the fire has something to do with me. He thinks I was luring him away with my café meeting, but why then have I brought him back here, if I knew of the danger that would put me in? I tell him

I've no way of proving my innocence, the same as he can't prove to me he hasn't killed Gina. Silence. Water runs down the windscreen. His face is taut with tension and smeared with ash. For the first time in his presence I am immobilised by fear.

The Bank Robber reminds me I must phone my friend before six and tell him I'm safe or the police will be alerted. I'd completely forgotten about Mr Williams. I make the call and let Mr Williams know I'll call in for the envelope the next day. Poor love, he hasn't a clue what I'm on about. He can't remember if I've left anything with him or not. Then he calls me 'Sophia', muddling me up with another cleaner who works for the same company. I know I'm too reckless for my own good sometimes. I just hope I'm not too reckless for Gina's. The Bank Robber gets out the car. He tells me to drive off. I ask him for Gina's mobile phone. He tells me not to push my luck.

* * * * *

I wake at three am. I think I can hear somebody in the flat. I fumble to find my mobile to call the police but realise I must've left it in the lounge. I wait for a while, huddled up in my duvet, still almost certain there's an intruder in the place. I can't hear very much. It's the occasional light thud, rustle, or other sound. It could be the neighbours, they've never been the quietest, but it sounds nearer. I'm starting to think it could be someone in the lounge or in Gina's bedroom. For a moment I almost wonder if it is Gina. It's possible she's come back, and because it's the middle of the night she's creeping about quietly so as not to wake me. She's thoughtful like that. If it is Gina though, she'd know that by now I'd be worried sick about her, surely? She'd tap on my door or put her head around to say she was home and that she was sorry. I'm sure she would. Almost sure anyway. I tiptoe over to my bedroom door, slowly lowering the handle to open it a crack. It doesn't move. I try again. Then I realise that the key that should be on the inside isn't there. Crouching to peer through the keyhole I see it is blocked. I've been locked in.

CHAPTER FOUR

A key turning in the bedroom door lock wakes me. I scream, but it's Bridie, in her pink tracksuit. At least she looks more of a bombsite than I do, after going to bed in my clothes with my make-up on. She offers me her little bottle of rescue remedy, suggesting I place a drop on my tongue. What I need is a stiff gin. Or three. It's seven am. After I'd discovered the bedroom had been locked, I'd yelled, screamed, hammered on it and the wall, but our neighbours are drunks who tend to be in a stupor by closing time and there's no one living on the top floor at present. I did try banging on the floor, where the people with the hordes of kids live, but clearly no one there heard me either. Either that, or if they did they couldn't be arsed to investigate. It doesn't exactly give me a warm feeling about being a resident of this block. 'Friends' it ain't, and right now I'd even settle for a few neighbours from 'Neighbours', even the murderous ones.

Bridie had got up for her morning jog along the prom with the dogs, and found a key ring on her doormat. Recognising it as my ancient Garfield fob, a present from Gina, she'd come straight round to find out what was happening. 'Him?' I wonder, pointing at the sculpted head.

'How did whoever it was know where...?' Bridie trails off, as she sees my address book from my shoulder bag lying open on the sofa. Her surname is Addison, and as it is arranged in alphabetical order she's the first entry. My cash and bank card are still in my bag and untouched.

'And how did whoever it was know where I lived in the first place?' I ask.

'You didn't give that Bank Robber your address?'

'Of course not. ...But after the robbery he had Gina's car... with her driving licence no doubt still in the glove compartment.' Now I'm not feeling too clever.

'Well, if it was him, at least he didn't leave you to rot eh?' she says, giving the head an approving nod. She adds in an equally irritating tone that the fact I'm neither raped nor murdered bodes well in respect of Gina. I hadn't really thought about this, but it's a valid point. The Bank Robber isn't psychotic, not on a power trip, and there's nothing creepy about him. He doesn't seem to have a bad temper; he's not been violent to me, or even made much in the way of threats. Bridie shakes her head knowingly. 'But don't you go getting any ideas into your head – if that's a fair likeness,' she indicates the head, 'he's definitely a dish, but you've been out with enough deadbeats and no-hopers. It's time to find a respectable, responsible man with prospects.' I grin in spite of myself.

'Alright, Jane Austen.'

'Don't mock me, Yvonne, you're in your late thirties now.'

'No! I'm thirty five, Bridie!'

57

'Don't leave it until you're my age when there's simply nothing left out there worth having.' Bridie is around ten years my senior, at an estimate. She wears it so well it's hard to tell. It's just in the things she says sometimes like TV programmes she grew up with, or music she liked when she was a teenager. Stuff I've not heard of.

'I'm sure that's an exaggeration. There's bound to still be a decent catch or two out there.'

'No, mark my words Vonn. You need to snap up a nice doctor, solicitor or architect pretty sharpish. Someone who'll pay the mortgage on a nice semi in Hove while you sculpt to your heart's content.'

'Urgh. That would be so... so conventional. It would affect my work. Not needing to struggle. It would become bland and safe. It wouldn't *live*.'

'Nonsense! That's just a romantic notion. If I'd married a millionaire it wouldn't stop me becoming Brighton's answer to Dame Judi or Helen... It would help because I'd have money to hang out at all the fashionable places where the casting people and directors go. I'd be eating at The Ivy at least twice a week. And you know you can buy your way to a premiere? I'd be a fixture on the red carpet in front of the paps.'

We decide that whether it was the Bank Robber or a person unknown who has paid me a nocturnal visit, we should look around and check carefully if anything has been moved or is missing. I can't see anything amiss in the living room or kitchen. Reluctantly, I lead the way into Gina's bedroom. Here, some things have definitely been moved, albeit carefully. A book has been left on top of her duvet cover. It wasn't there yesterday. I know that for a fact. It's a travel guide to South America. 'Perhaps your Bank Robber's thinking of fleeing to Brazil. Like Phil Collins and the other Great Train Robbers.'

'It wasn't Phil Collins! Only in the film… You're thinking of Ronnie Biggs.' I stop. 'Wait a minute, I don't think this can be Gina's book.'

'Why not?'

'I've never seen it on a shelf and it's not the sort of thing she'd read. 'I mean she's hardly a globe trotter.'

'People can dream, Vonnie. I'm always reading books on being in the movies. And I don't mean yet another ten minute film by bloody students.'

'If Gina had wanted to go anywhere, I'm sure her dad could've stumped up the cash. But she didn't… doesn't. She once told me she'd only ever been abroad once. To France on a school trip. She hated it. Was sick on the ferry.'

'Should've gone by Eurostar.'

'It wasn't like that was an option. It was a cheapo school trip to Dieppe from Newhaven. It was the same when I was at school. No swanky train through the Chunnel for us.' Bridie went to a grammar school in Kent. Clearly they do things differently there. 'But the point is, Gina hated the ferry and is terrified of flying. She told me that once, when I said I fancied a weekend in Marbella and asked her along. So I can't imagine her owning a book on South America.'

'So let's recap,' Bridie says, 'Someone lets themselves into your place? How? Using Gina's door keys, possibly? Or a hair grip like in the movies.'

'I don't think that works, even if anyone still wears hair grips.'

'Never mind hair grips. Why does our person or persons unknown leave a book on her bed?'

'It doesn't make sense.' I agree. 'Unless they had to leave in a hurry and forgot it, or possibly it didn't contain the information they were looking for.' I can't think of anything missing from her room, but there might well be. It is cluttered to say the least, so not that easy to tell. There's a whole shelf of little plastic trolls for starters. Even if ten of these monstrosities are missing, I doubt I'd notice.

* * * * *

I know Karim who works in Waterstones fairly well. We both started to attend this open mic night, where poets get up and read their work. I think we were both at a loose end at the time. On the third occasion, one very middle-class rapper aged about eighteen seemed to be ranting on for far longer than his designated five minutes. Then he said a line that went something like 'In this nation, I burn with consternation' but instead I heard 'constipation'. In situations like that, where everyone's serious, intense, listening, well I can't help myself. The giggles come fatally easily. I'm like it at funerals too. Anyway, I looked across at Karim and saw by the way he was hunched over trying to stare at his hands that he was on the verge of corpsing too. He must've misheard the same word. Perhaps like me he's no stranger to prescriptions for what is known in the IBS community as sluggish transit. I managed to hold my laughter back for a moment longer, but Karim was less fortunate and he has a laugh that fully lives up to the term guffaw. Neither of us dared go to the open mic night again. I think like me he'd only been there in the first place because it had been advertised on flyers in nearly every café in town. They do say with advertising that the more times you see the promotion, the more likely you are to eventually act on it.

Like me, Karim spends an inordinate amount of time in cafés, though in his case, so he says, it's to gain characters and plots for his short stories. He wants to be the new F. Scott Fitzgerald or Ernest Hemingway, and in his view, present day Brighton is the new Jazz Age Paris. I've read a few of Karim's tales and they're fine if you like stories about eavesdropping on arty people sitting in Brighton cafés. There's one where I'm sure a character is based on me. She's a painter rather than a sculptor, but the way she keeps whining about having no money, and throwing herself at random guys as they walk in, begging them to buy her a latte, does ring a bell or six. Come to think of it though, it could probably be based upon just about everyone I know. The moral of Karim's tale is, I suppose, if you enter a café and judge by the conversation that you're in the presence of actors, writers or artists, and you don't look thrift-shop Bohemian enough to be one yourself, it's probably best to leave right away. If you don't, it won't be long before someone catches your eye, pretends an interest in you or suggests that maybe you've met them before. You'll end up joining their table and then you'll notice all the empty cups. 'Are you getting a coffee yourself?' you'll be asked. Not 'would you like a coffee?' Of course you'll be buying yourself a drink, as you wouldn't have entered the café otherwise, but the arty crowd know that. They're also banking on the fact that you'll feel guilty about only treating yourself to a beverage. Once you've been suckered into maxing out your card or emptying your wallet, conversation will start up again, and you'll feel part of the in-crowd. You'll soon however start to notice a subtle but important change now you've fulfilled your role as provider. No longer will anyone pretend to have an interest in you, what you do, or any opinion you might happen to hold. Everyone will have returned to their favourite topic of conversation, which is themselves. Don't say I didn't warn you.

The travel books are, as I recall, conveniently located on Karim's floor in the bookshop, so I think it might be worth a visit. Bridie waits, idly browsing the 'Italy' section, as she does love to nip off to Tuscany whenever finances allow. Karim isn't particularly busy so I show him the travel book and explain about Gina being missing for eleven days. It turns out he'd seen me in the shop's café with Gina on several occasions, but if she had bought that book, he didn't believe he'd been the one to sell it to her. 'If I had, I'd have asked after you, Vonnie, and I'd remember doing that. But I don't remember ever seeing your friend here without you.' At least he actually noticed Gina and recalled what she looks like. That's more than most people I've spoken to so far have done. He asks to examine the book and comments that it doesn't bear a sticky price label. 'Not every book here does, but many do. Though if it was bought as a present of course someone might have removed the label.' I try to think of someone who might've bought Gina a book but draw a blank unless it was her father.

Karim takes the book on South America over to the appropriate shelf in the travel section, but it seems to be a volume they don't currently have in stock.

'Maybe she bought the last copy,' muses Bridie. Karim opens it to check the inside pages.

'It's not that up to date,' he says, showing us the publication date. It is 1996, so it's positively ancient. 'If you want a travel guide you tend to purchase a recent one, as things may have changed.' Returning to his till, he runs the scanner over the barcode. 'Ah! Looks like we don't currently stock it. Maybe she brought it online or in a second-hand place.' I groan inwardly at the second suggestion. Although the number of exclusively second-hand book emporiums in the city has decreased dramatically in recent years, as people have moved to internet purchases, the amount of charity shops and flea-markets, all offering at least a bookcase full of 'pre-loved' books, has grown. I've never been keen on the needle in a haystack phrase, as when does anyone apart from scarecrow costumiers sit in a field and sew, but I'm sure you get the idea. Checking out every vendor of second-hand books in Brighton and Hove would take forever. There's also the possibility she ordered it online, though Gina wasn't big on internet shopping, possibly because I used to grumble about getting up in the morning to receive or sign for parcels. I'd usually still be in bed after she'd gone to work, so she'd have to rely on my goodwill, always in short supply in the morning. Often I ignore the doorbell anyway whatever time of day the damn thing rings.

As Karim hands the book back to me, something falls out. It's a piece of paper, folded in half to create a makeshift bookmark. I snatch it up, open it and find it's a list of classes and courses taking place at The Old Stores Arts Centre in Hove.

'Our next stop then?' suggests Bridie.

'Why not?'

* * * * *

As Bridie and I enter The Old Stores, we can hear Sister Sledge's 'Frankie' playing in the main hall and see people of a certain age bouncing around to it with pom-poms in their hands. A notice on the door says: 'Veteran All Stars Cheerleading Team.' I ask the woman on reception if she could tell me what class my flatmate has been attending here. It turn out she can't enlighten me for reasons of data protection. We wander around the building, discovering a group of nature-lovers holding a meeting in a smaller room about protecting harvest mouse habitats, and a life-drawing session in the bar. These though are daytime groups, and I don't remember Gina having a regular daytime class or group. The list from the book is of evening classes, though I suppose she could conceivably have picked it up and used it as a bookmark while waiting for a daytime class to start. Benito did say something about her not being in work for a few days prior to her abduction. I'd been mainly in my studio or on my cleaning round at the end of that week, so I can't say whether she was at home or elsewhere. If Gina went out, and had left before I got up, I would have assumed she was at work.

Gina used to stay in and watch the TV most evenings if she wasn't working, and perhaps do a bit of knitting. I on the other hand, would be out most nights, including almost every

Friday and Saturday. If Gina attended a regular evening event here, I probably wouldn't have noticed. I tend to meet up with Bridie, Jake, Sol and the rest and we have bite to eat somewhere cheap, before moving on to one of a number of pubs, bars and clubs, depending on how the mood takes us. This means I'd probably have left the flat to pre-load and scoff something before the time Gina would've needed to leave to attend a class. Me and my friends are regulars anywhere and everywhere. If a gallery has a private view with free plonk, if there's a film we all fancy seeing, or a new stage play where we know at least some of the cast, then those events will be incorporated into our evening's revels. We tend to finish off the night, post club, at the all-night café. Then I crawl home, and if I've forgotten my keys or can't find the lock, Gina will have to get up and come to the door in her pyjamas. Like I've said, I took her for granted. I've never known her be out after midnight herself though. It's almost as if she feared the night bus would, at the witching hour, turn back into a pumpkin pulled by mice. By the way it smells on occasion she might not be entirely mistaken on that score.

The Old Stores bar is where the life-drawing is happening, and since I'm on nodding acquaintance with several of the participants and the model, we nip in quietly and order a couple of coffees. Bridie seems slightly distracted by the fact the group are sketching a naked middle-aged man, but as I spend half my life working on nudes, to me being in a familiar environment actually helps me focus.

I've taught art classes of various kinds myself over the last few years, which is why I know a few names and faces in the group. If the tutor for this session, who I haven't met, does decide to ask why we're not drawing, I'm sure I can grab a sheet of paper and a pencil and pull something passable together. In fact I'm rather tempted to get stuck in. Drawing is a compulsion with me and has been ever since I was small. After my parents split up, my mum worked as a travelling hairdresser and beautician. With no choice other than to take a small daughter along to appointments with her, crayons, a sketch pad and the command 'sit there and draw something' were my out-of-school routine. Different houses, different clients and their family members and pets gave me plenty of subjects. Mum was very encouraging, telling anyone who listened her daughter would be a famous artist one day. She'd display my pictures on the fridge and walls of our one-bedroom flat, where they served a useful function in covering up both the damp patches and cracks in the plaster.

Aged eight I won a local drawing competition, for a picture of mum perming an elderly woman's hair. I was offered as a prize a children's art course in either drawing or sculpture. Thinking a change might be in order, I opted to try sculpting. Up to this point I'd only had the chance to make one small pen-holding pot out of clay at school. The class bully had stomped on it before it got anywhere near the kiln, so I never even saw it in its finished state. Most of the kids had only cared about throwing the clay at the ceiling and seeing how much of it stuck there. By contrast, in the sculpture class I won I was shown how to make wire frames for more inspiring and elaborate models such as horses, dogs and people. An amazing new world of three-dimensional self-expression opened up before me. I made a woman about to throw a stick, her dog poised in readiness to fetch it. The tutor loved it. I now knew what I wanted to do in life. Mum though wasn't too keen that I'd switched from paintings to creating something she occasionally referred to as 'dust magnets'. In her view, famous artists who made money painted pictures rather than made useless ornaments. When the competition organisers had rung to tell her I'd won the prize, she'd also been disappointed to learn it was a course, not money. She'd encouraged me to enter as it had said 'various prizes' and she'd hoped it included cash to pay for my next winter coat and pair of school shoes. Also, as we soon discovered, sculpting materials, unless you stick to plasticine and plaster, are expensive. I started to favour air drying clay, as we didn't have access to a kiln, and Mum drew the line where any of the colourful sculpting materials you slow cook in the oven were concerned. Air drying clay was less messy than plaster or plasticine, which inevitably became trodden into the rugs and broke the hoover, but it was pricey and I couldn't afford it in sufficient quantities to make anything more than the smallest figures. Still it taught me about detail, and again, using a wire frame to create figures in action poses. I did start sketching again too, but now it was mainly to serve my sculptures. When my school days ended and I applied for art college, while the other students sat waiting for their interviews clutching portfolios, I sat with a cardboard box on my lap, wanting to show only my 3D work. I got accepted, took a shop job in the evenings to fund my studies and my life journey to becoming a penniless sculptor began.

'Could Gina have been attending an art class?' queries Bridie. 'More fool her,' I feel like saying. Perhaps if I'd never lifted a pencil, I'd be plying a lucrative trade of some kind today. I've never known Gina draw. She doesn't even doodle on the phone pad, which to me is extraordinary. I find it hard to resist any sheet of paper, in whatever form it takes. There's an advertising board opposite our flat, and late last year it had an advert on it, which had the one printed word 'imagine' in its centre. I think it was a logo or catch phrase for some fancy drink that's passed me by. Anyway, I couldn't look out of my bedroom window and see that great expanse of unadorned white paper without feeling troubled and restless. For once I understood Sol's compulsive need to complete a specific task. One night, or to be more accurate, one early morning, when I'd come in from a night on the town, I could resist it no more. Somehow, I found myself out there with my marker pens, doodling. As Brighton started to wake up I sheepishly slunk back indoors, leaving behind a wall of hurriedly sketched people, dogs, cats, cars and lampposts. That empty expanse of paper had after all asked me to 'imagine'. Now it bore witness to the fact. The next night I added to it, and the next and the next. Recently Jake has pointed me in the direction of an Instagram site, where there's footage, shot by streetlight, presumably from another flat in the street, of me at work on my impromptu and spontaneous mural. Thank God I'd had the sense to put my hood up before starting. It's not that the execution of the piece is patchy and piecemeal, and that as a composition it lacks a certain cohesion. It's simply I don't want some irate billboard site owner coming after me with a baseball bat, or having me arrested for damage to property.

Gina, as I say, has as far as I know, zero interest in becoming an artist. She prefers homely crafts like knitting cat blankets for charity, and felting. I find myself explaining the concept of felting to Bridie. She takes her phone out and finds there is indeed a felting group, who have recently been busy making fluffy seagulls to exhibit on the pier. It's held on a Tuesday afternoon, and Gina's shifts mean she wouldn't have been able to attend regularly. There's an email address for the tutor though. Her name is Rachel. 'Could be 'R?' I send her a quick message to check if Gina is in her group. Friday and Saturday evening activities at the Old Stores tend to be of a more physical nature. I'm not sure I can imagine Gina at Zumba Fitness, something called U Can Dance, or Boxercise. Then there's a choir. 'Does she sing?' asks Bridie.

'In the bath. Justin Bieber songs. Badly.'

'Look at the choir master's name though. 'Ron Richmond – RR!' Bridie jabs at the flyer for emphasis. They say that having a surname with the same initial as your first name makes you more likely to be famous. Most of the examples they always give though didn't start off with the double initial, like Marilyn Monroe or Adam Ant. Ron Richmond doesn't have an email listed, only a phone number. There's an email for Boxercise, but no tutor's name. I'm guessing it's kind of boxing to keep fit. I send an email, just addressing the coach 'hi there'. I'll ring Ron and the others when I get home. Over a second coffee, Bridie and I agree the Bank Robber is still our only definite link to Gina's disappearance. We decide to drive up to Steyning again and see what information we can get from the vet who was treating his dog.

CHAPTER FIVE

As Bridie and I drive into the tree tunnel just outside of Steyning, we hear the alarming crack of a gunshot, followed quickly by a second one. I stop the car and we sit motionless, looking at each other open-mouthed, unsure for a moment what to do. A couple of minutes pass without us hearing any further sounds of a worrying nature, so we decide it's as safe as it's going to get to leave the car. Keeping low, we clamber over a fence into the muddy woodland beyond, stopping on the edge of the clearing containing the charred remains of the caravan. A man is lying on the ground clutching his leg, a shotgun beside him.

There's a lot of blood on the man's jeans just below the knee. It's thick and black. I kick the gun further away from him before telling him we're calling for help. He nods, gritting his teeth, as Bridie dials 999. The man is thickset, forties, with a shaven head and a ring in each ear. Judging by a livid scar across his scalp and another below his eye he's no stranger to the rougher side of life. Apart from saying, 'Shit' and 'Arghhhh!' he isn't a great talker. Bridie tries to ask him what happened. 'Bastard…' he growls, 'Bastard!' I leave Bridie optimistically trying to give the man a drop or two of her rescue remedy. I've spotted a pile of freshly dug earth near the remains of the Bank Robber's mobile home. A makeshift

70

cross, made of two scraps of charred wood tied together with string, has the word 'Peggy' written on it in marker pen. The poor old dog – there's no need for that return trip to the vet's now. I rejoin Bridie who is trying to get the man to take part in a visualisation exercise she learnt in Goa on a Shakespeare tour to conquer the pain. 'Imagine you're on a beautiful tropical beach'. If he was, I imagine he'd have a flock of salivating vultures circling above him by now.

The man becomes a little more animated when the paramedics arrive. He seems keener to talk to them than us, and if he's written Bridie and me off as a couple of cranks, I can't say as I blame him. I hear him mentioning 'accident' and 'shooting crows' as they stretcher him into the ambulance.

* * * * *

'It's the book that still bothers me,' I confess to Bridie over a comforting hot chocolate in The Inner Sanctum Café, back in the urban normality of Hove.

'Not somebody getting shot?' She regards me slightly quizzically. The thing is, I can hazard a guess what the shooting was about. My hypothesis would involve the Bank Robber, Connell, aggravated arson and a now-deceased dog called Peggy. All of this may or may not have some connection to Gina's current whereabouts. I tend towards the belief it has more to do with Connell wanting to blame and punish someone over the carjacking rather than anything directly connected to his daughter's current plight.

'I mean why would Gina have a book on South America?' Frustratingly, Bridie says it's the kind of thing the police are paid to investigate. Her conclusion from two appearances in

'The Bill' is that the police always make sense of these things. Usually within forty-five minutes plus advert breaks. It's not quite the way things seem to be panning out here. The ends are not being neatly tied up before the credits roll. Regarding the man in the woods, Bridie is sure that the Bank Robber must've shot him. I think she's right, though keep it to myself. 'Trust you to get involved with someone dangerous.'

'I'm not 'involved…' She waves her hand airily to stop further protest on this point.

'We're dealing with ruthless people, Vonnie,' she continues, 'And from now on we ought to tread more carefully.' She sips her fair trade chai latte pensively, 'Though we must still absolutely see this thing through and do our utmost to find your flatmate.' She stops, and then adds as an afterthought, 'And if they happen to turn this whole thing into a primetime TV drama, I'm playing myself okay? Olivia Colman is so not getting this one.'

Jake arrives with a thick pile of flyers for his band's latest gig, and a complicated looking form as a PDF downloaded on his phone. He wants to apply for an arts scheme where entertainers – or in his case, a rock band – play to workers in factories or shops and get paid for it.

'The Aquatic Bees could play inside Waitrose instead of busking outside like Sol does.' I sense the usual rivalry at work here. 'It would be so much better on a rainy day. We could cover songs like Pulp's 'Common People' – that mentions a supermarket.' I scroll wearily through the massive form he's barely made a start on.

'I don't imagine many common people shop at Waitrose.'

'Well, The Clash's 'Lost In The Supermarket' then,' he counters, defensively. Bridie leans over and notices Jake's only filled in his name, address, and as is customary with these things, reduced his age by five years. There are lots of questions along the lines of identifying your key skills, your vision and value. You have to tell them where you hope this generous career break will take you. No doubt you're supposed to talk up the likelihood of global domination being the direct result of strumming a chord or so in the corner of a shop. Then there's a budget, in which they hope you'll have some matching funding from other sources. It seems to me if there was any other money sloshing about for musicians no one would be sweating over this form. 'If I ask for too little I'll be left out of pocket on the band's travel and food and if I ask for too much they'll bin my form.' Bridie says she'll ask around and see if she knows anyone who's previously made a successful application. The idea is Jake can hopefully pretty much copy his or her answers for the price of a beer. I wonder if the funding bodies will ever cotton on that this is the reason everyone's application for any pot of money always looks exactly the same.

My mobile rings, conveniently saving me from the hell that is applying for arts funding. It's the police in the form of Nelson's depressed sidekick McGuire – only today he's sounding a little smug. They've something they want me to see.

* * * * *

McGuire registers my disappointment as he shows me the mud-splashed mobile phone and tells me it was dropped in at front desk this morning. 'A man found it while walking his

73

dog.' A dog that has since expired due to a caravan fire that was probably arson and is somehow connected to a man getting accidentally shot nearby, I muse to myself. The phone has my number on it, which was how the police made the connection. Gina did occasionally call when she was going to be late home from work – most often because the shop takings wouldn't balance for one reason or another.

McGuire tells me that they are currently in the process of getting complete call breakdowns from the phone company. He shows me the other numbers on the phone and asks if I recognise any of them. I don't apart from my own, Connell's and Benito's, and he won't let me write any of them down. I ask if he'll be able to identify them all. He tells me he is remaining positive and that DS Nelson is currently out following up other lines of enquiry. Like me then, she is probably spending large amounts of time sitting with her cronies in a coffee shop or pub somewhere trying to work out what to do next.

I tell McGuire about the book about South America. He says that ports and airport departures have already been checked as a matter of course. 'There's no way Gina will have flown down to Rio without us knowing about it.'

'Rio?' He tells me he was just quoting an old song and he didn't mean to sound flippant. I think he's more worried about me putting in a complaint than finding Gina.

* * * * *

Despite not having a name for the shooting victim, I'm able to get directions to his ward. I arrive to discover Connell already at the man's bedside. He doesn't appear to have brought chocolates or flowers, but then I'm not sure you're allowed blooms in hospital now. Perhaps the crow shooter isn't that keen on confectionery either. I'm on the point of turning and leaving when the man sees me. He beckons. Connell turns his head and sees me. His eyes narrow with suspicion. The man explains to Connell that I'm one of the women who found him.

'Really?' Connell says flatly before telling him we're already acquainted. 'That's something of a coincidence isn't it?' There's something weird and slightly menacing about Connell today, and his eyes bore into mine as he asks whether I saw anything or anyone before finding his friend 'Phil' lying on the ground. I say that Bridie and I were simply driving past and heard a couple of shots.

'Aiming at those bloody crows,' the man says, unconvincingly. 'Must've tripped on a tree root.' Connell nods, backing up this cock and bull story. I'm definitely not buying it, but look away so they don't see the scepticism in my eyes. Phil doesn't look like a farmer or gamekeeper to me, or probably anyone else for that matter. I am of course not wishing to stereotype people in any way, but in the woods he was wearing slip-on shoes, not wellies, plus a townie's leather jacket. Okay, I'm totally stereotyping him, I admit it.

'So what were you and your friend doing out that way, Yvonne?' Connell's tone is more conversational now, but I'm not fooled. I tell him I'd been offered a cleaning job at a biggish house in Ashurst, and thought I'd drop in and see exactly what it involved before saying yes or no to it. My fingers are crossed in my lap. 'Oh yes, Gina once told me that's your line of work.' He says this in that dismissive and slightly snobbish tone people often adopt when I mention my bread-and-butter job. Yes, I'm a domestic, a skivvy, feel free to look down on me or suggest I should be in the ruddy workhouse. 'If you ever fancy a job in one of my shops…' he offers. I bristle.

'Well now, if you happen to own a vegan chippy then give us a call, yeah. Because I find the concept of cooking sentient beings who are a vital part of our ecosystem morally indefensible.' I smile sweetly. 'And the same goes for shooting crows, Philip. For your information they do a great job cleaning up road kill and other carrion.' I think Connell probably knows I'm aware the crow-shooting alibi is utter bollocks, but he's not going to say so. Phil jokes weakly that it's probably the last time he'll be shooting at anything with feathers, and gives Connell a look that he doesn't acknowledge. I wouldn't go expecting sick pay Phil. Your P45, or however else Connell makes cuts to his staff, will I suspect shortly be on its way.

Phil tells us he will only be kept in overnight for observation.

'So what job do you do for Mr Connell?' I ask, as if making conversation.

'Van driver.' Connell hastily interjects.

'Oh right. Delivering fish and chips?'

'Corporate clients only. And supplies to the shops.' Again it is Connell answering.

'Oh right.' It sounds perfectly plausible, but then so does the rest of the hospital bedside bullshit I've just had to listen to.

Out of the corner of my eye I see DS Nelson approaching the ward. Things are looking up. I give her a smile and nudge Connell to let her know Phil is about to exceed the 'only two visitors at any one time' notice. Nelson, like Connell, looks surprised and more than a little irked to see me. Come to think of it, Phil hadn't looked especially chuffed to see his angel of mercy materialize at his side either. Connell stands, explaining rather unnecessarily to the officer that Phil works for him and is also a family friend. 'So I came as soon as I heard he'd been involved in an accident.'

'A shooting incident,' she corrects him, slightly ominously for Phil. Connell though tries to switch her focus onto me.

'Yvonne Sharpe here is the person who discovered Phil.' Thanks for that, Connell, I think darkly. I wasn't aware he knew my surname either. He's clearly done some delving where I'm concerned. I decide to offer no further information to him or the police.

'Yvonne was on her way to a cleaning job.' I grimace. When the DS had previously asked what I do for a living, I'd said I was a sculptor. Now she knows I'm also a cleaner, she's going to start being more patronising towards me, I can pretty much guarantee it. DS Nelson is, however, for the present, more interested in speaking to Phil alone. She'd like us to leave her to it. I get up even quicker than I do in the theatre when someone's ordered interval drinks. Connell's still on his feet and out of the door ahead of me.

Connell suggests, when we're both safely out of Nelson's earshot in the corridor, that I might like to go for a quick a drink with him. I try to decline, telling him I've a deadline on a commission.

'Commission?'

'As a sculptor. Two figures running.'

'Ah.' Is he saying that because he's remembered this is my main occupation, I wonder, or had his daughter only told him about my cleaning role? I don't want to think any ill of you, Gina in the current circumstances, but you could have accentuated my career positives. I mean I've shown you my Instagram and LinkedIn for God's sake, and you've visited my studio, even though when you did you found my work either shocking or slightly comic, judging by your giggles, coy sideways glances and remarks about 'men's dangly bits'.

'Why are the people running? In this... model you're making?' Model – how dare he! It's not Airfix or Lego!

'They're athletes.'

'Oh.' I'd would have liked to have said instead 'it's because they're being chased by a gunman while out shooting crows,' but it doesn't do to get too cute with folk you have severe misgivings about.

I continue trying to wriggle out of having a drink with Connell, as we cross the hospital car park. I don't want him grilling me any further about why I happened to be so close to the location where someone happened to take a shot at one of his employees. I don't expect he believes the 'just driving by' story. I know I wouldn't if our roles were reversed.

Connell stops before even reaching his car to tell me he has some news. It's something he wanted to tell me earlier, but couldn't in front of a police officer, he explains. He doesn't really want to mention it out here either. Looking around as if he expects us to be overheard, or followed, he automatically make me do the same, as an odd kind of reflex. I think he knows that, as soon as he said he has something important to tell me, my curiosity will ensure I go with him. They say curiosity killed the cat, but unless someone spells out to me exactly how the death occurred, I'm going to remain eternally inquisitive. I don't just mean about the apocryphal moggy's demise either.

* * * * *

I've never been in this pub before. It's tucked away behind the seafront and is squeezed between two shop fronts that look in danger of squeezing the last of the life out of it. Inside, its air conditioning seems non-existent and there's smoke wafting in from a group of ancient gaspers having a fag or six in front of the door. The bar is heavily populated by brawny older guys in faded dad jeans and football shirts. If I was a man I wouldn't feel particularly relaxed about walking into this bar. As a woman I feel perfectly safe. It's one of those places where if you're a fella and you accidentally queue jump at the bar, slop your drink on someone's scuffled brogue, or brush against them, they're immediately wanting to 'take it outside'. It's an unwritten rule which even in the twenty first century has been unaffected by the Equality Act. If you're a woman and you queue jump or accidentally jostle, you'll simply get an 'alright, love?' or some such. I might call myself a feminist who demands to be treated the same as any man, so it does feel a tad hypocritical, but there are times when this kind of discrimination is a positive relief.

'You know why she came up the hospital, don't you?' I say of DS Nelson. Connell sips his pint, ruminatively. 'I don't imagine it's a stray shotgun pellet lodged in your friend's leg. I think it was a bullet that clipped him and the hospital reported their suspicions.' Connell puts down his glass.

'Vonnie, if you've had anything to do with my daughter's disappearance…' I'm startled. That came from nowhere. I shake my head vigorously and tell him I know less about it than he does. 'Then please stop speculating about things you and I have no knowledge of. My van driver was out shooting. It's a hobby of his. Someone else was no doubt after rabbits or pheasants, saw a movement and didn't expect it to be a person in the line of fire.'

'Ah right.'

'What do you mean by that, Yvonne?'

'I was agreeing with you, Mr Connell. Maybe a gamekeeper or farmer thought he was trespassing. It is private land.'

'How do you know that?'

'There's a big enough sign you can't miss it.'

'I see. Though I'm not sure Phil knew that.'

'He does now.' Connell sighs audibly.

'Look,' I insist, 'I'm merely trying to find out everything I can about Gina vanishing, and assume that's what you're doing too. If I sometimes ask too many questions, or say the wrong thing, it's because I'm not getting answers from anyone that make any sense to me.'

I know Gina idolised her dad. I think he's a thoroughly dodgy geezer, but I still think theirs was a fairly healthy relationship. It's simply intuition again I know, but she was my flatmate and I saw her face light up with affection when he called, and heard her relaxed, laughing manner with him as they bantered. I envied her that.

Connell knows about the mobile phone being handed in. He says they asked him if he'd seen it and told him it's blue and shiny. I nod and confirm this.

'Did you overhear her making any calls on it recently?'

'Eavesdrop on my flatmate? No, I've only ever seen and heard her on the landline at home.'

'Calling anyone in particular?'

'Her friends. You. Work.'

'No one different recently?'

'No.'

'Had her manner on the phone changed recently?'

'Not as far as I'm aware. That's just it, Mr Connell, there's been nothing different about Gina really in recent weeks.'

'She didn't seem suddenly more... I don't know... troubled? Worried?' I shake my head. It should be me asking the questions. I try to switch it around, the way the shrinks

81

do on a TV drama. Not that I'm going to utter 'tell me about your childhood' or try some Freudian analysis.

'Have *you* noticed anything like that?' This is about you, Connell, not me, time to open up to Doctor Vonnie.

'Maybe dads don't notice things changing with their daughters,' he says sadly, as if we've finally touched a nerve. 'Maybe they're the last to notice. But I'd always imagined she didn't have any secrets from me. Do you think that's being naïve?' Of course it is. Everyone keeps secrets from everyone else. Show me a person with no secrets, and I'll show you a person with no human interactions. Connell, of course knows this as well as I do. He's a weary old dog that's been dragged round the block a few times on a cold winter's night, if you know what I'm saying. Perhaps though it's the old 'King Lear' thing. A daughter can do no wrong even if it's Bridie playing one of the two ugly sisters, you know the one with the name that sounds like an STD.

I'm not talking from my own experience of fathers here. My dad was a van driver, mum was high maintenance and wanted the best of everything, so he had to work endless shifts, forgoing his own interests and rarely seeing his friends. They separated when I was six. My art, when he occasionally saw an example of it, didn't make him proud. My lack of interest in football, on the occasional Sundays when I saw him, made me hardly worth a conversation. We do keep in touch. He calls once a year at Christmas, before going out for a drink with the mates he now has plenty of time to see since a back injury ended the van driving.

I think I would rather have had a dad like Connell. I mean because he is close to Gina, not because he runs a dubious-sounding small-time fish and chips empire.

'So you don't think Gina kept secrets from you, and as far as I know, she wasn't keeping any major ones from me. But...' I hesitate, 'Were there things you didn't tell her? Secrets of your own that could have a bearing on what has happened here?' His eyes burn, but he doesn't reply. I sense I've gone too far and decide to row back a little. 'I'm not asking you to tell me anything. I don't need to know stuff about you or your life. I'm just saying it might be an area you haven't fully explored yourself. Could the kidnapping in any way be more about you than Gina?'

'Maybe.' I wait but he offers nothing further. It may be a way to end the subject that he orders the same again for us both with just a nod to the barman. I'm drinking halves. I'm not usually a beer person, but I'm trying to be matey in the hope of discovering anything he knows. Clearly he's not prepared to end our little chat just yet. I presume there is still something he'd like to get off his chest.

'I've been doing some research,' he says at last, lowering his tone. Not in the library, I think I'm fairly safe to assume. 'The guy the cops are looking for... the armed robber... I've found out a few things...' I wait. 'He's not from around here.' This sounds so like a line from an old Western that I have to cover my mouth to stop the corners twitching. 'Down from London it seems.' I grunt. So am I, and I don't like the 'we don't want you city folk coming down here' implication I imagine goes along with that remark. It's ridiculous anyway, if London and Brighton didn't like each other, why build the road and the railway? Besides Brighton and Hove is a city now too, albeit a weirdly two-centred one. I thought Connell's accent was cockney, but perhaps it's actually Brightonian. There are only subtle differences. 'I made a few discreet enquiries up there,' he continues.

'In the Smoke?' I ask, deadpan. Do Brightonians even call London 'the Smoke'? I mean Sussex has its own issues with pollution despite the coast.

'Yes, I talked to one or two… well, old acquaintances shall we say?' I don't comment. 'It seems he's not well liked, err, in the fraternity as it were. Works alone, muscles in on other people's turf. No known associates. Bit of a lone wolf.'

'Has he ever hurt anyone?' Connell nods. 'In the course of a robbery, yeah. And some guys who tried to have a word with him like… they didn't come out of it too well, or so I heard. Up in Manchester that was. He seems to have been all over.'

'Has he ever… well carjacked anyone before?'

'Not to my knowledge.'

'Has he been in touch with you at all?'

'*He* hasn't. But I've had a letter.' I start. Something has happened and Connell's only telling me now, as we approach the dregs of our second beers.

'A letter? Not a ransom note?'

'A ransom note. Or pretty much… but I've got serious doubts about it being genuine.' He adds he thinks someone has seen the story in the papers or online and is trying to make a little easy money by making a mug of him. The letter is now with his solicitor and they're working out how to proceed from here.

'You've not taken it to the police?' He hasn't. He wants to be ultra-careful and handle things his own way.

'I can reach people the police can't. People will talk to me who wouldn't talk to a cop in a million years.' This could be because the police don't have folk like Phil the Crow Shooter asking the questions. However, now Connell has almost levelled with me about the deep dubiousness of a number of the people in his social circle, the more I worry for Gina's safety. If one of his acquaintances in the 'fraternity' as he put it has abducted Gina over something Connell has done, then she could be in very serious trouble indeed. She has now been missing for eleven days after all. If truth be told, I'm more than beginning to think she'll never be found alive.

As if reading my thoughts, Connell says, 'If you were kidnapping someone for a ransom, you'd get in touch almost straight away. You wouldn't leave it this long. And I'm not sure in this day and age you'd use the post. I mean there are plenty of encrypted apps. You can even use an email server where your identity can't be traced or routed.'

'Perhaps the kidnappers are crap with technology.'

'Like I said, I don't believe the letter is from the person who's abducted her. It's from some crank, fantasist or chancer. Someone out to cash in, or simply to stir trouble.'

'Like an online troll, if they were using the internet?'

'Or a poison pen letter.'

I ask what the ransom note said. He has clearly memorised it, though it's so short that's no great feat. '*We have your daughter. You will pay £500,000. Let us know you have the money, by putting a plant in your window.*'

'What?' I can't believe what I think I heard. 'A plant? Have you?'

'Yes. I don't have houseplants, so I dug up a fuchsia… at least that's what I think it's called… out the garden and put it on display. Since then I've kept a watch on the window twenty-four seven.'

'Apart from now while you're down the pub?'

'I've rigged up a surveillance camera. I can check it from my phone. Not everyone over fifty is a Luddite, Yvonne.'

'What else did the note say?'

'That was it.'

* * * * *

Back home, I roll a quick spliff to smoke while embarking on my phone calls. It'll hopefully make me a little more relaxed and chatty as I work my way through the evening class contacts. I don't smoke a lot of dope these days. I find it blunts rather than sharpens my creative edge, in a way it didn't seem to do when I was younger.

I call Ron 'call me Ronnie' Richmond. He says the membership of the choir is very 'fluid'. I don't really know what he means, and ask him to explain.

It seems he has his regulars but you can 'just rock up on the night if you want' as he puts it. Ideally people book and pay their tenner in advance but if not he accepts cash on the door. I describe Gina but he says the choir is very popular and attracts all ages and abilities.

'She's not really a singer.'

'Nonsense!' barks Ronnie from the landline speaker, making me jump with this sudden emphasis, 'Everyone can sing, Veronica. We are all born to sing.' I had told him my name was Vonnie. Perhaps he's slightly deaf. I can imagine this could be an asset for a guy fronting a community choir that accepts anybody and everybody. He's terribly public school and slightly tigger-ish on the phone. By his voice I'd say he's probably in his sixties or seventies. A favourer of navy blue blazers and old school ties at a guess. Ronnie goes on to tell me the group is a joyous celebration of togetherness to encourage confidence and well-being. The idea of a community choir is all very well, but I've still no idea if Gina has ever been part of it. It looks like I might have to go along and join in the next session. I'd rather stick pins in my eyes, but if it leads me step closer to finding Gina it'll be worth it. You can download the songs in advance apparently. They might be anything from 'Yellow Submarine' to 'Smells Like Teen Spirit', according to Ronnie. I hope he can't hear my shudder over the phone.

I try giving the *U Can Dance* tutor a bell but only get an answer phone message, which has annoyingly been recorded with Madonna's 'Into The Groove' playing in the background. Due to the name of the class I take it this is deliberate. Unfortunately the teacher's name is René, so he's another possible 'R' from the chip shop calendar I need to persevere and make contact with. Boxercise is led by a woman called Lila. I almost cheer out loud when she says her name. It's unlikely to be her class Gina was attending, but I decide to ask anyway.

'Gina… hmmm, maybe.' I describe my flatmate. 'Yes, I think so. Came along once or twice. Not sure it was for her. I've seen her since though, waiting in the foyer for the evening events to begin, so I think she might still be coming here, but attending a different activity.'

I sink into a bath full of bubbles and reflect that it's not the only thing I'm now up to my neck in. Gina and Boxercise, it just doesn't fit. I asked Lila what it involves and as I'd suspected it's a boxing-based fitness regime. The issue is I can't imagine Gina taking part in something like that. She's never shown any interest in boxing whatsoever. The only thing that could make sense of it was if Gina was newly afraid of being attacked or possibly abducted, and was learning self-defence skills to protect herself. What a pity that she hadn't treated the Bank Robber to a swift uppercut, if she'd been training like Nicola Adams. When I said to Lila I imagined Boxercise was in part to teach participants some fighting moves, she stressed this was in fact definitely not the case. She couldn't speak for other teachers of boxing-related skills, but her class was purely about fun, fitness and weight loss. There were no combat techniques involved and Lila herself is a pacifist who doesn't believe in 'the ethics of teaching people to hurt each other'.

I don't know if Gina took this class for a short while in an attempt to improve her physique or simply to have fun and meet new people. Judging by the shapeless baggy cardies and long skirts she favoured, perhaps she did have a body confidence issue. When our clothes were hanging side by side on the radiator to dry, mine were at least two sizes smaller, yet physically we're around the same size. Alternatively, agony aunts are very fond of telling singletons looking for a relationship to join an evening class, especially one that takes him or her out of his or her comfort zone. I've read this many times. Perhaps that was what Gina was looking for, and a possible Mr Right simply didn't attend this class so she moved on. The other possibility is she was actually looking for self-defence lessons and had booked these sessions by accident thinking this was what it involved. In spite of the expense, I pour some more hot water into the tub, scalding my toes in the process. There is another reason Gina could've left the class of course. Perhaps she did meet someone there, someone she didn't want to see again, like a stalker, sex pest or equally sinister person. I might have to come back to Boxercise, even going so far as to join it myself, if no more urgent clues to Gina's current plight emerge in the next day or so.

Through the open door I can see the Bank Robber's sculpted head on our scuffed old coffee table. 'Are you holding Gina for ransom?' I mentally ask, staring into that solemn face. 'Surely you can't have known she was a fish and chip shop heiress when you hijacked her. One with a dad who's reasonably loaded but is in all probability a bit of a gangster.' The phone rings. I pick up. No one is there. Dripping water onto the carpet, which can only be a good thing considering I've not shampooed it for a while, I dial

1471. The caller withheld their number. I'm just back in the bath and it starts to ring again. This time I can't be arsed.

I had intended upon an early night, but find myself drifting down to the Glass Heart Gallery for a private view, to prop up the bar and take a cursory look at the work of a rival sculptor. Collections of small papier-mâché blobs in salmon pink and spring green have got this sculptor a forthcoming London exhibition. They remind me of the kind of vomit you see on the average pavement on a Sunday morning, though possibly without the chunks of sweet corn. *'Eerily evocative of a lunar landscape, where the spaces are as vital as the shapes themselves'* reads a critic's blurb that the sculptor has modestly displayed alongside her lack of talent. I'm on my third glass of free fizz and angrily haranguing some hapless sap about the current state of the art scene in this country when I spot Cassandra waving from across the room. I excuse myself from the guy I'm boring rigid and join her and her latest girlfriend Kaylin. Kaylin, like Cassandra, has the scrap metal jewellery thing going on. They probably met at a necklace welding workshop. Kaylin, it turns out, has recently designed a website to promote local sculptors' work. She wants to know if I'd like to exhibit in her virtual gallery. She takes her small and very nifty laptop from her shoulder bag and proceeds to give me a tour. It looks good, and its Instagram followers are already over six thousand despite the site only being up for a couple of months. She will, as an art dealer, take a small percentage if anyone buys my work. This is the future, not physical exhibitions, she says. I'm not so sure. It might work well for paintings but sculpture is a tactile medium. You need to touch it and experience it from all angles to fully connect with a piece. Nevertheless her knowledgeable enthusiasm for my figurines starts to make me feel more positive about being a sculptor again. This feeling grows as over another glass of plonk Cass and Kaylin start disparaging the 'puke' sculptor's efforts.

Kaylin asks if I'm going to be taking part in the Artist's Open Houses again during the forthcoming Brighton Festival. I nod, but then start to wonder. Gina never minds me turning the flat into a gallery for a few weekends in May, and enjoys serving tea and biscuits to the visitors who turn up. Last year, Cassandra had a jewellery display in our flat, Esther exhibited her acrylic seascapes, Bridie her embroidered cushions and hand-made greetings cards and Ferdy, his muscular phalluses. I slept in my sleeping bag in Gina's room with our collective junk piled around us, as the rest of the flat, including the loo, was our gallery. We must've had nearly five hundred visitors and I sold four of my smaller pieces. If Gina doesn't turn up though, I won't still be here in May. I'll need to move out as I can't afford to pay the rent of the flat on my own. I'm starting to feel too old for flat sharing anyway, but I don't see how I'll ever afford a place of my own. Cassandra says if the worst comes to the worst she'll help me find someone else's where I can exhibit for Open Houses. I'd only really counted her as an acquaintance before tonight, but now she's mentally upgraded to friend status.

With Cass and Kaylin, I go out for a veggie burger when the last of the punters have gone. After we've stuffed our faces, we decide to burn the calories off again, strutting our stuff at Audio until almost 2:00 am. I find myself throwing up in my regular drain, one block from the flat. It feels almost like old times, only with no Gina to disturb when I stagger in. Once home, I fall into bed without putting on the light. Not just because it would hurt my bleary eyes, but there are times when the faded photos of my heroes and heroines looking down from the wall, remind me what a big nothing my life has amounted to. Tonight Marlon, Monty, Nico, Patti and the rest of you, I need to sleep without your judgement. Maybe it's not all my fault, maybe it isn't possible to be anyone substantial any more – unless through reality TV, a talent show or your own YouTube channel. Even the puke sculptor will be over by next year, overtaken by the next emergent hopeful. These days, unless you're exceptionally lucky, an artist's career is like a sandcastle on the beach.

Something else I've been wondering about is whether there is any connection between the fact that famous artists through history have tended to be both male and self-centred. When I first read about their lives full of abandoned lovers, cast-off friends and ruined creditors, I felt it must be all part and parcel of having an artistic temperament and so answerable only to your muse. Perhaps to be a true artist you needed a selfish, ruthless streak. It seemed almost romantic to be like that, despite the tales of lovers and models driven to suicide, having breakdowns or ending their days in poverty. I don't believe that any more. I don't think being an artist excuses thoughtlessness and cruelty. A genius doesn't need to be a person who treats others badly. If I've been behaving like a spoilt teenager for fifteen years longer than I've any right to, under the mistaken notion it made me 'arty', then it all stops now. Tonight I've made a decision. I'm finally going to grow up. Mind you, I have made this pledge to myself before, and in fairness I'm doing so whilst sitting in bed finishing off a Pot Noodle.

CHAPTER SIX

I don't really feel like working and it is a Sunday, but I've a client, an ex-athlete, who has commissioned a small piece of two figures running. Although I've completed all the preliminary sketches with live models, and uploaded them to a computer program that converts them to three-dimensional diagrams, I'm yet to work them in clay. Eventually these competing women lunging for the finishing line will be cast in bronze, but first I need to recreate all those stretching muscles and sinews in detail. Although I have the computer screen showing the 3D renditions of my sketches in front of me for reference, I work mostly by feel. These days it would be easy to photograph the models from various angles, convert the 2D pictures to 3D and create the sculpture with a 3D printer. It would be highly accurate and lifelike of course, but in its perfection it would, in my opinion, lose a great deal. The best photos tend not to be as powerful as the greatest paintings, and it's the same with computer rendered sculptures. I can breathe life into the piece by accentuating the yearning, the striving, the pain and the desire. I'm not likely to be made completely obsolete by new technology yet.

To work however I have to be in the right frame of mind. I have to be in a kind of reverie where my hands lead my mind, rather than the other way around. My thoughts drift while my fingers 'see'. I can't really describe the process with much more clarity than that. It is however a fragile state to achieve, almost a kind of meditation. My worries about Gina are hampering me today. When René the dance tutor rings back and says he could manage a quick chat, I discover he's recently finished teaching a class at a building containing dance and fitness studios, only a few doors along from this one. I suggest he pops in to my studio and stick the kettle on in readiness.

I think René is French by his accent, but his says he's Belgian, and implores me not to mention Hercule Poirot. 'Why would I?'

'The moustache. It is nothing like his. Nothing.' Considering he is talking about a fictional character depicted onscreen by numerous actors with everything from a dapper Chaplin to a full pair of handlebars perhaps he's being a little over sensitive.

He's walking round the studio looking at my sculptures, or rather caressing them. This is a good thing. They are meant to provoke a sensual, tactile reaction, and it does tend to only be us uptight British folk who ask permission first. I can tell René is a dancer. Every step and movement has spring, style and grace. 'You like the masculine form, eh?'

'I do. And it earns me a living. Seventy percent of my commissions for naked figures are of men, against thirty percent for women.'

'And who buys them eh? Straight women? Gay men?'

'There's no one client type, though I've noticed people often commission or buy a ready-made sculpture similar to their own body type.'

'Ah! But I like this – larger, older men.' He indicates a piece on a shelf of statues often overlooked for the works depicting young, beautiful bodies. 'This body has a story, it has lived.' I estimate that René is, like me, in his thirties, or perhaps a well-preserved forties. He has blond, possibly bleached, slicked-back hair and something of the bullfighter in his strut and strong jutting jaw.

On arrival, he spent ages perusing my box of herbal teas until he found an infusion containing ginseng. He then inhaled the resulting brew so deeply I thought he'd end up with it running down his nose. Not a great look, even for a dancing Adonis. René interests me, I admit it. I don't mean sexually, well I don't think I do. Perhaps having a ginseng blend myself out of politeness isn't such a great idea. It is after all supposed to turbo charge the libido, or so Bridie insists.

'So René…' I can't say his name without thinking of both ''Allo 'Allo!' and that 'Just Walk Away Renée' song by the Four Tops. Come to think of it there was René and Renata too wasn't there? Be gone ear-worm from hell! 'René, you said on the phone that Gina was attending your dance class?'

'One of my classes yes. Ballroom For Beginners.'

'U Can Dance?'

'Of course I can, darling.'

'The name of the class. On a Friday night.'

'Yes, that is the one.'

'And could she dance?' Here I'm expecting a similar reply to the one I received from the choir's leader about how 'everyone can dance' and how it comes from inside etc.

'No.'

'No? She couldn't dance?'

'But who cares eh? She have fun.'

'Did she come to class with anyone?'

'By herself. Many people do. When they need a partner, I pair them up.'

'Was there any special partner? Anyone Gina particularly clicked with?' He smiles.

'I think she mostly came to dance with me.'

'Ah.'

'You see she found me on Tik Tok.'

'Tik Tok?'

'You don't know what…' I tell him I'm aware it involves online sixty second videos of dogs looking self-conscious and cats playing the piano.

'I post my dances. Fun stuff.' He comes and sits beside me and takes out his phone. There he is in a long raincoat, carrying an umbrella and dancing on the prom. The music is Boney M's *'Hooray, Hooray, It's A Holi Holiday'* and as he dances he discards umbrella and coat. By some kind of editing wizardry the sky above turns blue, it's suddenly a lovely day, and he's cavorting and strutting to the music in nothing but a pair of purple budgie smugglers. Only they are more parrot smugglers if you get my meaning. 'Would you like to see another?'

'Err why not?' There are worse ways to spend a minute of my life. This time he's kind of a stripping headmaster to a song with the refrain 'Love's Unkind'. It's also from the 1970s and by Donna Summer, he tells me. He does more contemporary stuff including street dancing but the retro stuff gets the most hits. He also has another site where people subscribe and he'll do an originally themed dance especially for them for a fee.

'Nude?'

'No. Well not always.' It brings good serious money, he explains, allowing him to rent a luxury seafront apartment. This is a whole new world to me.

'Was Gina...'

'A subscriber? No. Just a big fan. Those are her words. I think she has a bit of a crush on me.'

'So that's why she came to your class?'

'I think so. And sometimes she'd stop behind to chat. She was interested in the cruise ships. I also work on cruises as a dance instructor. I have one booked for later this month in fact. I have a friend who takes the classes here while I'm away. I fly out to Brazil in a fortnight's time to teach tango classes on board.'

'Brazil… South America!'

'Yes, is there another one?' I roll my eyes at his sarcasm. I wasn't trying to impress him with my geography GCSE. I am of course remembering the travel book from Gina's room, the one containing the leaflet about his course. 'Gina likes the Latin dances. We have a Flamenco guitarist come in and play for us sometimes. She sat and talked to him.'

'What's his name?'

'Ah, yes all the women like to meet him. He's like catnip.'

'I'm not wanting to hit on him, René, I'm only asking his name.'

'Martin.' It doesn't start with an 'R' and doesn't sound particularly South American but I get his phone number off René regardless.

René heads on his way, to see a woman who is altering some shiny shirts for him, the ones that he wears when teaching Salsa. He has worked too hard on his abs at the gym, he says and now needs them taken out to accommodate the extra muscles. They're by some French designer I've not heard of. I'm not sure if he is flirting with me or simply trying to impress. He's hard to read, a bit like a cat.

In the back of my current sketchbook I've optimistically started a little list of suspects. There's the Bank Robber, though I almost believe he's not involved, there's Gina's dad, Connell, though why would he be asking himself for a ransom, and there's 'persons unknown, connected to Connell'. 'René Beauce', I write in. Is that even his real name? A quick check on the internet offers me loads more Tik Toks of him prancing about, though I think I'll save them for another time. I think René is definitely 'R!!!', but I find him a tad too self-obsessed to be a kidnapper. He didn't seem to have much interest in talking about Gina, but he certainly loved chatting about himself.

Benito answers the phone immediately and asks if there is any news. I don't mention the ransom note. I don't want to worry him about it. 'Did Gina ever mention a René Beauce?'

'Oh Vonnie, yes! She show me his videos. Dancing in his little pants, so funny!' He stops laughing abruptly. 'Oh you don't think he could be involved in her disappearance? I see the one of Brighton seafront.'

'I don't know, Benito.'

'She used to direct message him sometime.'

'Do you think she fancied him.'

'Mmm, I don't know. She never said that.'

'Okay, I'll keep you posted.' I will tell him about the ransom note later. I notice he didn't mention that Gina went to René's dance classes. In fact I got the impression he thinks she only knows him online. René seems to be Gina's little secret for one reason or another.

I pop round Bridie's on my way home. She's in her conservatory listening to a drama on Radio 4 online. Apparently the producer had rung her to ask if she was available to play a part, but had then not firmed up the gig. Bridie is now wondering which character she had been passed over for. I let her listen to the end, and luckily decide she hasn't missed out on anything too major. Then we have a glass of wine and I ask her about dancing and cruise ships. 'So it's a paid job, right? You don't have to pay to go onboard and hold dance classes.'

'I'd imagine it's reasonably well paid. Why didn't you invite me along when you met René? I could've got the measure of his reliability.' I tell her it was all rather short notice. 'What I'm getting at Bridie, is he's leaving the country in a couple of weeks.'

'Which is rather convenient.'

'Isn't it? But will he need a substantial sum of money to take with him, or will most of his expenses be paid?' She suggests phoning the company who are arranging the cruise. We try to look it up but there are several covering Brazil in the timeframe mentioned, and it seems that René, despite the size of his ego and Tik Tok following, is not a big enough name to be personally mentioned in his capacity as a dance instructor in any of their advertisements. This, I deduce is because cruises are aimed at an older demographic than Tik Tok. 'Tutored dance classes' are though mentioned among the activities offered by two cruise lines. Bridie rings both, pretending to be a dance tutor looking for work. She name drops people she's seen on 'Strictly Come Dancing' pretending they're dear friends and colleagues. It's truly a BAFTA worthy performance. Both times the answer is the same. Onboard entertainers are provided via talent agencies, and they are the ones handling the contractual details. 'Does it pay well?' Bridie purrs to the first woman. 'Only I'd be having to temporarily abandon my regular weekly classes here you understand?' The woman says she believes that freelance dance tutors are adequately recompensed and Bridie can get no more out of her.

The second cruise company's representative is slightly more forthcoming, furnishing us with the name of the talent agency they use to find dancers. Bridie duly calls Amanda at the agency, which also represents singers, comedians, magicians and TV presenters. Amanda says Bridie would need to send her show reel to be assessed and that takes time as 'we're only a small agency'. A one woman band in other words. If she likes what she sees (and she doesn't even bother with the pretence of using 'we') then she might possibly be able to put Bridie forward for cruise ship work, providing she was DBS checked etc. It does, according to Amanda, pay adequately, plus you've bed and board and the chance to see the world. It's not for everyone, she adds, but if you've no ties or commitments, such as a young family etc. then she'd thoroughly recommend it.

'A DBS check,' I say when Bridie has hung up. 'That's to see if you've a criminal record isn't it?' Bridie nods.

'Pretty standard. There may be travel restrictions if you've committed certain offences, and for all we know the dance classes might involve children. Actors need to have a check if they're going to be working with kids or vulnerable adults too.'

'So René is unlikely to have a criminal record?'

'Yes, or he wouldn't get teaching work. Did he strike you as in any way sinister?'

'Only the moustache.' I'm joking of course. I'm not someone who judges people by their facial furniture, or at least I hope I'm not. I rely on getting vibes about whether I can trust someone or not. In the past these have been fairly accurate, even when I've been stupid enough to ignore them. Since Gina's abduction though, my vibes have been in rather short supply. There's no one I've encountered so far who could really be classed as 'sinister', or 'suspicious'. Bridie says that the most successful criminals, especially con-artists, tend to present themselves very well. A cousin's neighbour gave twenty thousand pounds to an entrepreneur boyfriend who she thought was investing it for both their futures. He not only did a runner with her cash, he'd done the same thing to at least three others, and was a bigamist, working as a shelf stacker in Poundland. In court, his mother insisted he was the most honest, trustworthy son a woman could have.

Bridie thinks that if René turns out to have nothing to do with Gina's kidnap, I should make contact with him again upon his return. 'Bridie, he is not my...' She waves a hand to shush me.

'He's got a huge... ahem, online fan-base. Can you imagine how many of them might like a little sculpture of him prancing about in his underpants? While we've been chatting, she's checked out his Twitter account. There are links to a website selling mugs, key-rings and even cushions with his photo on. I stare, open-mouthed. 'The man is a brand. He shifts products. You could get in there, get a cheeky slice of that action.' I sigh. I just don't see myself as that kind of person. Making identical statues of an internet influencer because they'd sell well feels to me like selling out. As if reading my thoughts, Bridie puts her hand on my arm. 'The definition of not selling out is,' she tells me, 'Starving.'

When I get home there's a message from Connell to ring him. I do and he says he wants to keep me updated. I say I appreciate that. It's the truth, I do. We both want Gina back and I think it's the best – albeit slim – chance of it happening. His solicitor has noticed that the ransom note was in fact posted second class, eight days ago, according to the postmark. There's a street near Connell's with a very similar name. He lives in a close, it is a crescent. Connell's mail fairly often goes astray to the house with the same number in the close, especially if the postal worker isn't used to this round. Connell went round to that address and asked if they'd had any misdirected mail lately. The family living there had apparently recently received one letter that was meant for Connell. It had sat on their shelf beside the front door until the woman had, a few days later, decided to walk her border terrier via the crescent and pop Connell's by now very late letter through his door. If the ransom letter is bona-fide, then it seems to have arrived at the house in the close at least eight days ago. The kidnappers have left Connell no way of contacting them apart from putting the plant in the window. He's done that now of course, but very belatedly and they haven't been back in touch. It does sound now, even to me, like the note is probably a hoax, and the person behind it has since had second thoughts and decided not to see their attempt at extortion through.

I call Martin the flamenco guitarist. He has a strong Irish accent and sounds open and friendly. I remind him of playing for René's class, but when I mention Gina chatting to him, he can't immediately remember that much about the conversation. 'Oh,' he says suddenly, 'She bought my CD.'

'You were selling your music at the class?'

'Ah now we all have our little side hustle going on now don't we?' Could this be the 'classico' music Benito was talking about? I'd thought by his badly mimed conducting he meant something orchestral. It would certainly be a departure from her usual boy band stuff. 'She said she was buying it for a girl she knew. Said she'd love it.' Perhaps the 'girl' was Jo-Anne or Rebecca. Could it even possibly be me? My taste is pretty eclectic. I don't dislike flamenco music. I can't recall ever telling Gina it was a favourite of mine either. I check through our shared CD pile but the disc isn't there. Perhaps if Gina was going to give it to someone as a present, it's still in her room. I have a quick look but can't find it. Martin's music is also available as a download from his website. I treat myself to the short, free sample, as I'm not feeling particularly generous. He can certainly strum up a storm. It makes me want to stamp my feat, click-clack a pair of maracas and make the requisite whoops of delight. What it doesn't do is get me any nearer to solving the mystery of Gina's abduction.

* * * * *

Jake and Sol suggest a quiet evening in the pub, and I join them willingly enough. There's a new band playing a set at The Grapes Of Wrath who are supposed to be edgy and achingly cool. To me they're anything but. They're boringly posh, preppy and their lyrics are superficial and sung by a woman with a lopsided haircut, in a hoarse voice. There's nothing you can even sing along to. 'This one's 'A Pre-lude To A Dream',' she lisps.

'Prelude not preeeelude – what is she, American?'

'Actually she is, Vonnie,' whispers Jake. 'From Louisville.' This clearly makes it alright then, or at least gives her a thin excuse. Usually Sol and Jake spend the whole evening arguing during these kinds of gigs. If one likes the band the other is sure not to. This time it's different. Neither of them are terribly keen, but both seem to feel they ought to be. The band is apparently on everyone who is anyone's 'one to watch' list. They've already won a few 'most promising newcomers' things, locally at least. My thinking is that they're smug and pretentious, which no doubt mean I'm getting old and the generation gap is opening up like a vast chasm between my feet. I suggest another round of shots before it swallows me entirely. We're only drinking them because there's some promotion making them the cheapest way to get drunk tonight.

The band finish their set and I bring Sol and Jake both up to speed with the situation with Gina. Sol reveals he knows Martin the Irish flamenco guy, 'though his repertoire used to be more classical.'

'Classico?'

'Sorry?' Clearly I'll have to pay up and download Martin's entire album, unless Sol handily happens to have a copy of course. He doesn't. 'I like the guy, but...' he makes a face, 'his interpretations lack a little finesse.' This is the least scathing I've known Sol be about another musician's work.

Martin must be good. He's also about to join René on the suspects list, even if I'm not entirely sure why.

Jake asks me if Bridie has told me about The Old Pumping Station Escape Room. She hasn't. He ran into her earlier buying fluoride free toothpaste at Infinity Foods. She'd had a call back about a job there last week, but wasn't sure whether to go for the second audition.

'So what is it then? A play?' Jake shakes his head pityingly. Tonight, I'm clearly the least hip or clued-up person in the room. Apparently the escape room, which is going to be opening next month, involves groups of people, like those on a hen do or a work mates' outing, being locked up in a spooky room. In the room are various clues, along with a few red herrings, which they have to put together in order to escape. It's kind of 'Scooby Doo' for grown-ups, or people who refuse to grow up. Bridie has auditioned for the role of some kind of wise old hag who speaks in riddles. You can only speak to her through a metal grill, a bit like a priest in a confessional. Bridie has been 'almost offered the part' and the money is okay, but she's concerned it's not bona fide acting work. Jake says he'd jump at the chance of dressing up as an old crone and do it if he was her. 'I mean you never know who might come in and see you there. Some big name director…'

'Martin Scorsese?'

'Not quite that big, Vonnie.'

'Before they created this panic room…'

'*Escape* room, Vonn! Where have you been the last ten years?' Avoiding this kind of team bonding crap, clearly.

'Before they turned it into an Escape Room thing, it was a pumping station, you said, Jake?'

'That was many years ago. It's been abandoned for years. The point is, I was thinking of places locally where you could keep someone prisoner. First I thought of the Underground Studios but Benzedrine Hounds are recording a limited edition green vinyl promotional EP there this week.'

'But the pumping station is currently unoccupied?'

'Yeah. And funnily enough, I know a woman involved with the escape room venture who has a key.'

* * * * *

With the drink and the cold night air combining, we all feel pretty stoked and heroic as we storm into The Old Pumping Station. Just up on the South Downs, where Hove meets Hangleton, it has taken us two buses to get here. Unfortunately, Jake has thrown up on the top deck of the second one. He blames it on a rogue samosa earlier in the evening.

At the Old Pumping Station the oak front door has recently had some kind of screaming devil's face doorknocker affixed to it. The screw holes where the previous, less dramatic, door handle was once situated are still visible on either side of this kitsch monstrosity. The door opens with a long creak, straight out of 'The Munsters' and we can't immediately find a light switch. 'Gina! Gina!' We all yell and then listen in silence for a few moments. Somewhere a pipe

107

is dripping into what sounds like a metal basin. Shining my phone screen along the wall by the door, I realised a cylindrical device had been attached to the door where the hinges are and it is this that now makes it give that long horror movie creak. No doubt the dripping is some kind of elaborately constructed effect too, though if slow, loud drips were required the new owners could've saved themselves some dosh and purchased my flat's boiler second-hand.

Jake is walking ahead and treads on something. There is the sound of breaking glass. He recoils, fearing he is about to fall through a glass skylight, but again it seems to be an effect triggered by crossing a light beam, rather than something that is actually underfoot. It's convincing enough to make him hop about on one leg moaning about having severed an artery in his toe though. I could absolutely predict Sol telling him that technically toes don't have arteries in them. If this were 'Scooby Doo', sadly they'd both be contenders to play Shaggy rather than Fred. I'd like to be Daphne, but suspect I could be seen as a slightly archer version of Velma, without the specs naturally. When we do locate the light switches, none of them appear to be working, whether by accident, design or not paying the bills. We continue using our phones as rather ineffective flashlights to search the room.

I'm not scared by any amount of ghostly effects or the fake cobwebs that have been liberally sprayed around the room. My school friend Shannon's Halloween parties were tons better than this, plus she used to tip her mum's cherry brandy in the non-alcoholic punch when nobody was looking. I am a little unnerved though to be standing in a place that could be a serial killer's lair in one of those Scandi Noir dramas they put on BBC 4 after the watershed. There, anyone who's been kidnapped always comes to a very grisly end indeed. It's probably why the cops all wear those comforting Fair Isle jumpers, even while having sex. It's kind of, 'well, as we've just had to scrape up the melted skin of another victim, let's have a quick comfort shag, Bjorn.' Sol picks up something from the floor. It's a woman's earring. I scream, as he hands it to me. In a Scandi Noir drama it would have part of someone's ear attached, suitably bloodied of course. Also, if it were one of those shows, I'd instantly recognise it as belonging to my missing friend. Cue the titles and there's a second episode on the way to give us all insomnia. Fortunately there is nothing attached to the earring and I've remembered Gina doesn't have pierced ears. I once showed her where my belly bar used to be, and she'd looked nauseated at the thought.

We lock the escape room and escape, to retrace our steps to the nearest bus stop. I fervently hope the bus, when it comes, isn't the one Jake threw up in. The driver probably saw it on his CCTV anyway, I tell myself, and now won't stop for any of us ever again. I need to pee urgently and end up crouching in the kerb while the guys gallantly, or disgustedly, look the other way. Sol says that we might not have found the location where Gina is being held, but he might check out some other currently empty properties and abandoned squats. Jake thinks it's a good idea. They decide to do it together tomorrow night while I keep on with my own detective work. They use the phrase 'my detective work' not me, I hasten to add. I fear nothing I've done so far gives me much right to use it.

Fortunately, a different driver means a bus with no vomit upstairs. As we reach the top deck, Jake recognises Dembe, who he was in a band with some years ago. Dembe has since gone solo as a vocalist and, like Jake's Aquatic Bees, believes he is finally on the verge of making it. He's on his way to a house party over a shop in Sackville Road and invites us to join him.

Like Dembe, it seems everyone else who was asked to come to this bash has invited at least another three people. The windows have streamed up and there's not enough oxygen, let alone room to dance. I manage to battle my way to a window and open it, then have to stay put, stopping others from closing it again. Someone thrusts a glass of red wine into my hand and uses it as a pretext to start a conversation. Shouting above the drum and bass, my new acquaintance, like most of my old ones, has one topic of conversation – himself. Grabbing a huge handful of Twiglets from a bowl on the windowsill, I propel myself into the throng and let it swallow me up. On the other side of the room, if only I can get there, is a woman who once bought a small figurine from me. If I can reconnect, even to give her a crumpled business card, I might be able to persuade myself that I have at least been networking. Before I can reach my former customer however, another guy keen to find a woman to talk at looms up like a battleship and blocks my trajectory. He works for some kind of institute and is doing research into micro-surveillance. For a second or two I think a surveillance boffin might be useful where Gina's kidnap is concerned, but he starts rambling about nanobots implanted in feline microchips, and I realise I need to move on. Jake and Sol seem to have hooked up and I'm the only person standing alone, due to my fickleness or perhaps good sense. No one notices as I squeeze my way down the snog-fest of the stairs, knocking over a few abandoned glasses as I leave. Outside, it is starting to rain, and again there's an hour to wait until the next night bus.

* * * * *

By the time I get home, my head is pounding and my throat parched. I'm glad that for once I'd gone out in a waterproof coat. Not that it's much less damp in the flat. I can hear rain rattling against the leaky sash window and dribbling through the cracks onto the sill. As the elderly fluorescent tube in the kitchenette flickers to life, I spot a huddled shape on the living room sofa. I freeze, staring. 'Dirty little stop out,' sneers the Bank Robber. I switch on the main room's light, blinking against the glare. The first thing I notice is his face is bruised from left cheek to forehead. If someone had tried to give him a black eye they'd clearly just missed. He's also soaking wet from the rain again.

'You look awful,' I say, unthinkingly.

'Likewise.' I am instantly aware of my heat-smeared make-up and wine flushed cheeks. The clock on the wall says it approaching 5am, and I seem to be out of paracetamol.

'What do you want?'

'Same thing as you.' His tone is slightly unnerving and I break eye contact. I tell him what I want is him out of my flat. I'm a heavy sleeper when I'm drunk. I realise I don't know if he has recently broken in, or was already here when I got home.

'How did you get in? Do you have Gina's key?'

'No.' He takes a little metal key-like gadget from his pocket.

'You buy them online,' he explains, smugly. 'They open most front door latches. You need to lock your deadlock too if you want to keep intruders out.'

'I've lost the key.'

'Get the lock changed.'

'Did you let yourself in on Friday night too?'

'Eh? No. Why?' He seems surprised at this accusation. I take from that he may be telling the truth, though I've already learnt there are few certainties where the Bank Robber is concerned.

'Someone came in. There was no sign of a break in.'

'Your flatmate?'

'I don't believe Gina would've locked me in my bedroom and crept out again.'

'Is that what happened?' He finds this amusing.

'And Gina has no interest in South America.'

'Doesn't she?' I stop and gawp at him.

'What do you mean by that?' He stretches his hands above his head and arches his back. I notice he's not wearing gloves tonight.

'I don't think it's possible to know everything about someone.'

112

Angered by this remark and the presumption he can let himself in any time he feels like it, I insist he leaves, or I'll call the police. He ignores my threat. I grab a cup and throw it at him. It misses and seconds later comes whizzing back past my head. I get the feeling it was meant to miss. Unlike me, he appears annoyingly sober. Again I tell him I'm calling the police. My mobile is back in my bedroom but the landline phone is on the table in front of him. He goads me to come and get it. Judgement impaired by the hangover, I snatch at it and we wrestle. He smells of petrol and his hands are cold as ice. I find I have the phone and lift the receiver. It's dead, unplugged. He's smiling, I try to hit him over the head with a chair cushion, the only thing to hand, then catching a glimpse of my reflection in the mirror, realise how ridiculous all this is. World still swimming around me, I go and put the kettle on.

I draw up a hard chair, my dressing gown now wrapped round me while the flat's rather pathetic radiators warm up. The Bank Robber had expected me to sit on the sofa beside him, but I'm not feeling that cosy. 'You had a drink with her old man yesterday. Owns some chippies, don't he?'

'Which you know how?'

'Chippies or the fact you met him?'

'Both.'

'Asking around.'

'And spying on me clearly.'

'Spying on him, not you. He sent someone looking for me.'

113

'And he or she found you.'

'You think?'

'Your face. Or are you going to pretend you walked into a door?'

'Yeah, let's just say I did.' I put a mug of coffee on the table for him. He sniffs it, wrinkles his aquiline nose. The nerve of the guy.

'You dropped Gina's phone into the police station.'

'They need to have a few suspects.'

'I could give them your name.'

'Dead end.'

'Possibly.'

'Connell, the chip shop guy, does he have any suspicions?'

'He's had a ransom note.'

'How much?'

'Five hundred thousand.' The Bank Robber doesn't react. Unlike me, he's clearly not shocked by the sum. 'Is that peanuts to you then?'

'Hardly a life changing amount.'

'To you maybe. How much did you manage to 'withdraw' from the building society?'

'What you and Connell need to be thinking about is why that much. Do you know anyone who needs that kind of cash urgently?'

'Clearly you don't. Well unless you've already spent your building society withdrawal. On drugs? Gambling?'

'Women or motorbikes?' He grins. 'Wouldn't that sort of conspicuous spending over a few days have been noticed?'

'Are you a junkie?' It's come out a little more direct than I meant it to. He says the majority of people in his profession are. I can't help rolling my eyes at the word profession. If he notices, he chooses to ignore it. A few like him get a high from committing the actual robbery, not from shooting up afterwards, he explains. It's an adrenaline thing.

'Like bungee jumping?'

'Nothing like it. But it is addictive.' Wouldn't then he also enjoy the power game of kidnapping someone? Having everyone else waiting for him to make his next move? He says I make it sound interesting, but it's not something he'd consider. 'If you have to take a hostage, you want to get rid of them quick.' He sees the horror on my face. 'I mean release them as quick as possible, keep it calm, clean and get clear. I left your flatmate safe in her car, in a reasonably calm state of mind. I'd explained while we were driving that nothing would happen to her if she cooperated and once she knew that she was reasonably okay with it.'

'Really?' I say, blackly.

'Yes, I got her talking, you know, telling me stuff about herself to calm her nerves.'

The Bank Robber had found out from talking to Gina while she drove that she worked in a chip shop, had passed her driving test just over a year ago, and liked living in Brighton. 'And she said she liked Scotland too. She'd been on holiday there as a kid. So of course she was scared, but she wasn't terrified or she wouldn't have been up for chatting.'

'And you were totally in control?'

'I usually am.'

'Even when someone smacks you in the face?' His hand moves automatically to the bruise. 'Or you shoot Phil.'

'Is Phil a big bald bloke with earrings? Yeah, I dropped him. Caught me at a bad moment. Death of my dog.' I find myself nodding as if shooting a man is a reasonable reaction to finding out your canine companion is no more. That's the thing about the Bank Robber, he sucks you into his world and you start to think it's normal and natural, when it's anything but. He continues to explain he had finished burying Peggy, and was crouched beside her grave. 'She was twelve. She might've made thirteen if I hadn't done that raid.' He thinks the burning of the caravan was in retaliation. 'I looked up – and this bloke was aiming a shotgun at my head. He'd crept up from nowhere. A heavy type – someone's bully boy.' He adds that he could see that Phil wasn't going to shoot him and that he was to be taken somewhere or given a going over, so he'd 'clipped his wing a little'.

Later, the Bank Robber was heading out of town, planning to leave the area, when a car swerved into his motorbike and threw him onto the verge. Someone got out of the car and put his boot on his face, then the driver got out and kicked him in the stomach. Another car drew up, and a couple of young guys tried to get involved, thinking it was a road rage incident. The Bank Robber's bike was too badly damaged, but he got away on foot as a brawl developed between the good Samaritans and his attackers. He'd walked back here, some two miles.

'I already knew from the news that your flatmate is called Gina Connell. And I'd found out all I could about him. So all roads do seem to point at chip shop guy being behind this...' he indicates the bruise, 'and the guy with the shotgun.' He stands up, very stiffly, wincing, and leans on a chair.

'This is my theory – and don't blow a fuse, it's only my theory. The guy's a villain. He's got some little empire going on, which he runs with his rent-a-thugs.'

'And you're not a villain?'

'My point is, could he have done something to his own daughter?' I start to shake my head emphatically, even though I've not entirely discounted this theory yet myself. 'And be trying to frame me for it.' I tell him I don't think this is likely.

'Why would he do that?'

'She seems like an honest kid. A bit naïve maybe.'

'So?'

'So, suppose she idolises her old man, and then she finds out he's involved in something dodgy. And he thinks she might go to police.'

'She wouldn't though. They were close. She'd beg him to stop, but she wouldn't grass on her dad. I'm pretty sure of that.'

'And he'd know that, would he? If he's someone who's always having to look over his shoulder? If he's always been careful, and managed to silence anyone who crossed him, up to this point.'

'You talk about Connell silencing people, but we've no evidence of it. I can't imagine him having people thrown off the pier with their feet encased in concrete. I mean he runs a few chip shops. He's not The Godfather... more like The Codfather.' The Bank Robber doesn't find my feeble joke amusing.

'I didn't say I thought he was big time. In fact I'm pretty certain he isn't. But put yourself in your flatmate's shoes for a minute, if you were her and you'd be forced to be an unwilling getaway driver in a robbery, what would you do? Who'd you call?'

'The police. 999.'

'Or?'

'Dad.'

'As far as we know she didn't call either though, did she? Why?'

'But he would never hurt her. She was a real daddy's girl and from what I've heard from Connell she was the apple of his eye too.'

The Bank Robber isn't convinced, sneering that appearances can be deceptive. He hints that for all I know there might have been something incestuous going on. Indignantly I tell him that I know my flatmate better than some low-life who only met her when he bungled a robbery. He gets up, comes up close and lifts my head to make me look him in the eye.

'So you still think it's me, I'm the guilty one, do you?' I don't say anything. He releases me and steps back. 'If I'd taken her, then why'd I come back here?' I don't know. I don't have any answers. I've been crap at helping Gina, and if anything's happened to her, it's going to be on my conscience the rest of my life. I need space to think, I need time to get rid of this hangover. I slump down on the sofa. Uninvited the Bank Robber sits beside me. I glare at him, but see a weariness matching my own.

'How did you know where I live?'

'Like I said, you had a drink with Chip Shop yesterday.'

'You were there?' At a guess, when fishing around for information concerning Connell, the Bank Robber had discovered his regular boozer. Connell could have taken me to the nearest pub to the hospital, but he hadn't done so. It seems that had been a mistake for both of us. 'And you followed me home? Terrific.'

'You turned up on my doorstep unannounced. Seemed only fair to come to yours this time around.' I glower. I don't mind being the cat. I hate being the mouse.

'I'm going to have to tie you up now.' the Bank Robber states, matter-of-factly. I jump up from the sofa and hastily back away. 'Just while I have a shower.' he adds, I tell him there's no need for this measure and that I won't try to escape or phone anyone, but he's having none of it. He pulls down the cord tie that in daytime holds back the living room curtains and advances on me.

'No way are you tying me up!' He ignores me, stalking me around the sofa, then lithely leaps across it grabbing my wrist. 'I'll scream the place down.' I threaten.

'Not if you've any sense.'

'What'll you do about it? Shoot me? Someone will hear.'

'Oh there're quieter ways to silence someone.' Then we're wrestling again as he tries to get hold of both my wrists. I scream loudly and repeatedly.

'Okay. Okay. Look my guts are too sore for this,' he says suddenly releasing me. I tell him he needs to trust me, but he shakes his head. 'No I don't,' I say. I don't think alerting the police will achieve anything in terms of getting Gina back.

'Well thanks,' he replies, insincerely.

'And you're my only clue to Gina's disappearance.' I promise I'll sit and watch TV while he is in the bathroom. He shakes his head. I remember he smelt like he'd just had a bath when we first met. He certainly seems to have an obsession with cleanliness, but in fairness he is soaked through and muddy.

'Alright, if you can't let me out of your sight, take me in the bathroom with you.'

'So you can watch me shower?' he laughed, dryly.

I point out the various nude male sculptures and sketches around the flat.

'Won't be anything I've not seen before. Let me grab my sketchbook.' He looks at me slightly mockingly, then ushers me in front of him into the bathroom.

'I'd offer to face the wall but that won't really make much difference,' I say, as grinning, he takes in the mirrored tiled walls. The bathroom hasn't been decorated since the seventies. I like to think that this house has known wife swapping parties and orgies surrounded by bad wallpaper, fondue sets and dipping ducks before being broken up into flats.

The Bank Robber looks at his bruised, rain-sodden face in the mirror and unties the ragged bit of cloth holding his hair back. His sodden black rat's tails fall to his shoulders. He notices the bathroom door locks with a key and locks it. He unfastens the thin silver chain that is around his neck, slips the key on it and puts it back on. He takes his gun from his pocket, breaks it, removes the bullets and puts them and the gun safely in the dry sink dropping a hand towel over them. He unlaces and takes off his muddy boots and socks, then his jacket. He turns the water on before unbuttoning his shirt, stopping to look at me quizzically before discarding it on the floor. Below he has an army green vest, like the shirt, rain-sodden, which he pulls off over his head. He wasn't lying about getting kicked in the stomach. He's heavily bruised, in purples and yellows around the ribs – from the motorbike incident presumably.

'That looks painful.'

'Nothing broken or ruptured as far as I can tell.' He says, feeling his side gingerly, and wincing. 'They only got one good kick in before my rescuers showed up.' His chest is pale, with a silver vertical scar that disappears beneath a line of hair preventing me from guessing its cause. He unbuttons his jeans then stops, looks at me.

'Shit. This is a bit weird… are you really gonna draw me?'

'Yeah, you shy?' He shakes his head, turns away, shrugs and drops his jeans and pants in one and steps into the bath and under the showerhead, ignoring me. I move my pencil in long, soft strokes to capture the contours of his decidedly comely bum and strong straight back. There're no scratches from, say, someone's nails – as in someone trying to escape – and although I wouldn't say he works out religiously, this doesn't appear to be the body of a junkie. He looks over his shoulder, catches me working and laughs. He's relaxing a little in the warmth and steam. 'Enjoying this aren't you,' he says.

'Don't flatter yourself,' I retort, 'I've drawn fitter models.' Smirking, he studies the shampoo bottle, unscrews the cap and sniffs the contents.

'Got anything less girly?' I indicate another bottle. It's organic, unperfumed from Infinity Foods. I bought it after some scare story or other about sulphates and have not got round to opening it. The smell of this one meets his approval and he tosses his coarse rat-tails back from his face and lathers them up.

The quick drawing is coming along reasonably well. I love Degas' pastels of bathing women and wonder whether to make a larger version of this in similar colours. I smudge the lines to give the feel of the steam condensing on the mirrors. He finishes rinsing his hair, grabs a towel and deftly wraps it around his waist, before coming over to look at my sketch.

'Am I really that skinny?' he says, noticing that in the arched back view of his torso, the ribs are prominent. I nod. 'Perhaps you're right, I do need to work out more.' He shakes his hair back, spraying me with water droplets.

'And eat occasionally,' I say. He helps himself to another towel to dry his face and hair.

'That sounds like an offer. What've you got?'

'Can you make do with beans on toast?'

'With an egg maybe?'

'I'm vegan.'

'A vegan egg then. Or veggie bacon?' Talk about taking liberties.

'Fine. But you can fry it.'

I could dearly do with some shut-eye, but it's not going to happen while the Bank Robber's in my flat. He arranges his clothes neatly over the radiators throughout the flat, before making our brunch, frying it whilst wearing only a towel wrapped around his waist, despite the obvious health and safety issues this poses.

'Eat up,' he tells me, 'Soon as my things are dry, we've someone to visit.'

* * * * *

A solitary seagull is making a racket on the roof opposite the flat 'We're off to pay a social call,' the Bank Robber says as he dumps our plates and mugs in the sink, on top of the pile of washing up already left there. I clean and do other folk's housework when I'm working, but never seem to get around to tackling the washing up at home.

'So who are we going to see?'

'Chip Shop.' I don't think he means the New Atlantis. I think he's referring to its owner. Personally I don't think going round to Connell's is a good idea, and feel even less enthused when I realise the Bank Robber intends visiting while Connell is out of the house. He is though, insistent and says it's the best chance of finding out what is really going on with Gina. I'm not sure I agree, and I don't like the sound of what seems to me a lot like committing a burglary. The Bank Robber says he requires someone to call Connell and the rest of his cronies out of his house while we let ourselves in to look around. I say that if by someone he is meaning me, then I don't even know where Connell lives. 'Nice try.' He says it's on my phone pad and he's already noted it down. I tell the Bank Robber I don't trust either him or Connell. He laughs and says he'd think I was mad if I did. I do however know someone else who can call Connell to get him out of his house. I know Gina had keys to her dad's place. I imagine

124

Connell won't be reliant on a flimsy latch that can be beaten by some gadget bought on eBay. I'll try to find the keys and then we can let ourselves in. That way it won't be breaking and entering, or at least that's what I'm trying to tell myself. I still know this really isn't a good idea.

* * * * *

At the shop, Benito tries to dissuade me from my plan. As I tell it, it's just me wanting to have a look chez Connell. I don't mention the Bank Robber at all, despite the fact he's waiting outside in the car. Benito doesn't like Connell, and believes he's a dangerous man. I ask what would make him come down the shop. 'If we maybe have a problem. Maybe the freezer, it stop working.' He agrees reluctantly to a little sabotage. 'For you, for Gina.' Anxiously he tells me to be careful, big eyes filled with concern. My heart fluttering like a teenager, I find myself giving him a peck on the cheek.

'Sure I'll be careful, sweetheart.'

CHAPTER SEVEN

Connell's house is huge, a 1930s flat roofed Art Deco beauty resembling an ocean liner from the golden days of crossing the Atlantic. He has neat, miniature, round trees in large tubs flanking the door, and what appears from the ground to be a tennis court up on the roof. It looks like a great place for sipping cocktails in fine weather too. With my nosy nature, I should've become an estate agent. I wonder if it's too late to swap polishing posh properties for flogging them. The Bank Robber tells me to stop the car a little further up the crescent. We'll need to head on foot into the next street, where there's a narrow access alley leading to the back gardens of this section of the street. We have both back and front door keys on Gina's fob, but I know Connell's camera is watching the front window, waiting for the kidnappers to check if he is displaying the requested foliage.

The back garden is large and well maintained. There are chairs and a table on a paved patio area surrounded by a trellis trailing vines. This would be another tranquil spot to enjoy a chilled glass of something, possibly grown from the grapes that may in summer hang above. I wonder if Connell does the gardening himself, but doubt it, being as he said he had no plants indoors. In my experience as a cleaner, amateur gardeners can never have enough houseplants surrounding them. I've never seen a horticulture enthusiast's abode without leafy things sprouting everywhere. The Bank Robber is not admiring the garden, but looking up at the burglar alarm. We have the keys, I remind him. We don't have the alarm code, he reminds me back. It will probably go off but we can afford to ignore it for up to three minutes, he believes. I wonder if he's spent time outside the police station with a stopwatch, timing their responses to call-outs. On reflection, it's more like something Sol would do, though in his case merely to furnish himself with some fascinating statistics to analyse at his leisure. Three minutes seems like a very short time to me, but as I've left Gina's car only a street away, I suppose even with my iffy leg it wouldn't take long to get clear. Being seen or filmed by the neighbours might be an issue though. 'Won't happen if we don't run,' according to the Bank Robber. I don't completely share his confidence.

I turn the key in the lock. The alarm appears not to have been set. There are no beeps counting down to cacophony. I let out a slow, relieved breath. Then a dog starts barking and suddenly it's there at the end of the marble-floored hallway. It's a huge German shepherd, its ears pinned back, baring teeth and spitting saliva. The Bank Robber immediately crouches and talks to the dog. It continues to bark but less emphatically. First its teeth disappear, and then its ears prick up. The Bank Robber takes his time with the Alsatian, until his 'dog whisperer' technique finally shuts off the barking, and the animal trots amiably after us down the long hall.

Connell is not a man who needs a cleaner – his house is spotless, though I suspect it's because he does have it cleaned, rather than polishing all that brass and parquetry himself. The furniture is mainly Art Deco and the paintings on the walls fit the period. They appear to be originals – not by any major names I recognise, but good work if you happen to like Cubism. It makes me wonder why there isn't a current Mrs Connell. Surely some former model and all round gold digger should have got her shellac nails into this guy. I realise I don't know a lot about Gina's mother apart from that she's dead. Had Gina talked about her and I hadn't listened? I feel another pang of guilt. What kind of friend am I?

The Bank Robber doesn't seem to be a reader of 'House Beautiful'. I point out the beauty of the worn but polished leather sofa, its depth of colour and the wear and tear making it even more desirable. He just grunts and moves through into the majestic drawing room, calling the dog to follow. I gaze up at the candelabra, and in awe at the spacious conservatory of spotless glass beyond. The Bank Robber has moved on into the kitchen. He's pulled a photo from the wall near to the range that takes up the space of three normal cookers. It shows Connell in sunglasses on board a lavish yacht. 'Think this might be his?' I know Gina occasionally used to go sailing with her dad at weekends. I'd imagined something small with an actual sail. 'We could always pop down the marina and check it out later,' he says.

'Is this how you see yourself in a few years' time?'

'Old crook with a big house?' he grins. 'Nah, nah, not me.'

'Odd that he lives here alone... well apart from the maintenance staff that must visit.'

'It's not that odd. I mean he must think 'who can I trust?' He probably can't let people get that close.' I wonder if it's only Connell he's talking about here. 'Did you see the mini-bar though? I expect he has the ladies down at weekends. And his mates from the nineties, talking about old times. The rackets they ran at the dog track, the cops who were in their pockets.' I'm not sure how serious he is being.

It's Connell's study that the Bank Robber is looking for. It turns out to be sandwiched between the drawing room and front room and lined with fitted bookshelves, some containing books, some file boxes. Connell seems to prefer spy fiction and non-fiction, and also has tomes on various periods in history.

The Bank Robber pulls the desk drawers out on the desk and starts to go through them. He has already persuaded the dog to lie down in the doorway of the room. 'Keep an eye on her. She'll hear before we do if anyone comes in.' I start to check the files. There are reams of paperwork – shop figures, account details – but nothing that means much to me. My own accounts as a skint self-employed person are much, much simpler than this, but there's nothing here to suggest anything that would be out of the ordinary for someone who owned a chain of fish and chip shops that were doing reasonably well. I do find a name of an accountant and a law firm and make a note of those on my phone. I go back and look at a few of the non-fiction books about MI5, the CIA and KGB. What I'm looking for is any kind of dedication. Lots of people have a general interest in espionage, but a dedication might mean Connell has or had links to that world.

* * * * *

The dog pricks its ears. The Bank Robber is instantly on his guard. He signals me to stay back in the room, and positions himself behind the doorway, moving so his shadow is obscured. I've yet to find any dedications in the books the intelligence services, but I'd have liked longer to look. As Connell's key turns in the lock of the front door, my stomach turns over. I'm up to my neck in this. At the moment it's burglary or trespass at the least. If the Bank Robber shoots him, I'm an accessory. If I shout out to warn Connell, maybe I'll be shot, or maybe Connell will shoot the Bank Robber. Does he carry a gun? Is he alone? Gina, I just want to find you safe and sound. I didn't sign up to any of this.

The dog runs to Connell, who scratches her ears. 'Yes, yes, girl, I'm home.' Then he looks up and sees the 45 pointed at his chest. 'Okay, alright... take it easy,' says Connell, immediately standing still. 'I know exactly who you are. You don't want to get yourself in any worse trouble than you're already in.'

'Hands on your head, slowly,' says the Bank Robber, also maintaining his composure. Connell complies. 'Patronising prick,' he adds. Connell sees me and looks questioningly. The Bank Robber pushes him against the wall, checks in his pockets, and pats him down, before indicating that Connell joins us in the study. He pats the back of the swivel chair at the desk. Connell sits.

'What have you done to her? You bastard, tell me that!' Connell finally flares up. Receiving no answer, he turns his attention to me. 'She trusted you, Yvonne, thought you were her friend. I might've guessed you'd be involved in some way.'

'Look, Mr Connell, I have nothing to do with Gina's disappearance, as I keep telling you,' I explain, trying to keep my voice steady. 'I'm trying to find her. As I see it, we can all insult and distrust each other until the cows come home, or we can try to work together and pool information.' I'm not convincing him, I can see it. The Bank Robber leans against the wall, gun trained on Connell's back, Connell's traitor of a dog dozing at his feet. I continue, 'I didn't think the police search was moving fast enough so I did some detective work of my own. As you know, I was there at the building society. I tracked down her abductor here myself and I've heard his side of the story. He says he left Gina in the car on the road to Devil's Dyke at around four pm,'

'She made a phone call on her mobile as soon as I'd walked away,' adds the Bank Robber. 'I made the mistake of leaving it with her.' Connell swings round in the chair to face him. 'I was figuring it was you she called, as it wasn't the police.' Connell just continues to glare murderously at the man with the gun.

'So,' says the Bank Robber, 'you send a few of your heavies after me, and they're not quite as quick or smart as they think they are. And you know what? I think you're trying to set me up because you've done something to your own daughter that you want to cover up.' Connell looks at the Bank Robber, trying to get the measure of him. 'And you had my caravan burnt out, killing my dog, so you see if anyone currently present has hurt that girl, my money would be on you.'

Connell looks away. There's now a sadness about him. I can hear a clock chiming in the lounge. Connell stands.

'Hey,' says the Bank Robber, 'No fast movements and keep away from the desk.' Connell leads us slowly out into the hall.

'When I saw you here, I was hoping this was it, you'd come here to negotiate – to name your price.' He turns back to face the Bank Robber. 'You're right, I've done my homework on you, Finn.' I start. The Bank Robber has a name of sorts. I should start using it. 'I've followed your little spree around the country. Learned all the details. And I thought, he's somehow realised what he's got in my daughter – someone whose father has a certain amount of money, and he's trying it on, trying his luck. Someone who doesn't care whose territory he works on, whose toes he treads on. Someone who'll take a risk, a reckless risk for the money. And I comforted myself with the fact that is all Gina would mean to you – just the ransom. I could find no evidence that you'd ever hurt an innocent party, and I was holding on to that. Desperately.'

'So now I think you know I haven't got her.' Finn says.

'I'm beginning to think it's unlikely,' Connell concedes 'But no, I don't know that.'

'But what do you know about the people who've got her?' asks Finn. 'Facts I mean. Cold hard facts.'

'Nothing,' Connell says curtly.

'Nothing at all?' Finn queries. 'You've not been so thorough in researching them then?'

'I've tried, but I'm still drawing blanks. Nobody knows anything. Then I suspect you've found the same thing, if you've been asking around yourself?'

'Yep,' agrees Finn. 'No one knows, or if they do, they ain't saying.'

'Though presumably Yvonne has told you about the ransom note?'

'It doesn't make any sense. The letter. The plant in the window. I mean, what century are we in?'

'Exactly.'

'I've never even heard of anything like it.'

'I know.' At least they're in agreement about something.

'And your security camera trained on the road? What you got?'

'You told him about that too?' Connell is not pleased with me, I can tell.

'Mr Connell, he doesn't have Gina.'

'So why are you both here? And how did you get in my house?'

'Gina's keys. We…' I look at the Bank Robber but sense he isn't going to back me up. 'I mean, we thought we might find something here that help us understand where she might be being held.'

'You mean you thought that I, her father, was in some way involved. Jesus, Yvonne…'

'I'm sorry…'

'Don't be,' Connell replies, 'You're trying to help Gina. You don't know me very well, and so you don't know that of course the last thing I'd do is anything to hurt her. Look, I'm not angry with you for coming here, alright? Not even for bringing him with you…'

'She didn't bring me. I'd found your address and I was coming anyway,' says Finn. 'Anyone who gets one of his henchies to stomp on my face is gonna get a little social call sooner or later.' He shrugs, unapologetically. 'It's just how I am.'

'So what do you plan to do, eh?'

'I don't. That's just it. It's not about me, Connell. You're the one who's got the note. You're the one with the missing daughter. I'd say the kidnappers have let you know the next move is yours, like it or not.'

* * * * *

Connell and I sit at a table in the conservatory, a fountain trickling away in front of us. Watching the water sparkling across the rocks, might I suppose, be relaxing under different circumstances. Finn is prowling around the garden, Connell's dog following him.

'He's a nasty piece of work.' Connell indicates Finn.

'Your dog seems to like him.'

'Rita never was the discerning type. So, is what you were saying in there the truth? You managed to track him down after the robbery?' I tell it to Connell like it was. Being in the building society, my investigations, up until meeting Finn in the café. When I get to the meeting in the café, Connell laughs dryly. 'You were taking one hell of a stupid risk.' I say maybe, but as the Bank Robber had behaved with logic during the raid, and didn't seem to be psychologically unstable when I met him at the caravan in the woods, I felt he was probably not some irrational killer. Connell nods. 'See when Gina was taken I suspected the worst... a young woman abducted – we know how that usually ends.' He meets my eyes.

'From a psychological point of view, it's usually someone whose turn-on is rape or murder. Or sometimes one leads to the other – where the rapist kills the victim so he isn't identified.' I tell him I've been trying not to think like this.

Connell says he finds it better to face things head on.

'Yes, but what are we facing?' I ask. When he received the ransom demand, he admits he felt more hopeful. 'That's if the ransom note is genuine. If someone has got her and money is their motive.'

'You're more sure it is genuine now?'

'What else do we have to go on? I'm not one hundred percent convinced, but if anything else had happened to her... well I think we'd have some idea by now.'

'Will you pay the ransom?' He gives me a look, and again I feel I'm still at least partly under suspicion.

'Whatever it takes... though let us say I doubt if they'll ever be able to do something like this again.' Connell leans forward, lowering his voice, although Finn isn't near enough to overhear. 'So you think there's no chance Finn there has sold her on to the kidnapper – whoever they may be?' I tell him I'm trying to keep an open mind, but that Finn seemed genuinely shocked by Gina vanishing, and more than a little rattled by it. Connell nods. 'It's brought him bigger headlines and more attention than he'd bargained for. Plus, being connected to a girl going missing probably isn't part of the reputation he wants. He wants to be respected as some kind of Robin Hood figure. I've seen it all before. Hired a few young fellas like that in the past,' Connell says, adding, 'For security roles. Strictly legit.' I think though he knows I don't buy this last part. 'But ultimately they don't stick around… don't want to work for anyone else see? Too big for their boots.' Finn is oblivious, still checking out the grounds. I don't know what he's looking for – footprints, possibly.

Connell takes out his phone and switches to the camera footage. 'I haven't checked this for a couple of hours. Let's see if there's been any movement outside the front window.' He puts the phone down on the table and we both watch the captured footage. 'It's motion sensitive, designed for filming wildlife really, but unfortunately it's a reasonably busy street. There are cars, cycles and pedestrians passing all the time.'

'Are we looking for a head turning this way, whether driving or walking by?'

'I don't know what we're looking for, Yvonne. Anything out of the ordinary? I only hope we're in time… that I replied to the message before they'd given up on me. If they think there's no chance of them getting the ransom…' On impulse I squeeze his hand.

'The ball's in their court, Mr Connell. They could've sent you another letter almost straight away when they didn't immediately see your signal, making threats to put the pressure on you. They haven't and that makes me think they're still waiting. You'll hear from them again soon. I'm pretty sure of that.' Actually I'm not pretty sure of anything, but we need to stay positive and be ready, come what may.

The doorbell rings. It's loud enough to be heard from anywhere in the garden. Finn disappears inside the house before Connell can rise to his feet. We both follow. As we reach the back door I hear a thud. Rushing into the hall I find Finn with his boot on the neck of man around our own age, gun aimed at his head. Behind me, Connell is looking on and the man is looking appealingly at him.

'He was only following instructions, Finn. And I'll pay for repairs to your bike.' Connell tries to placate the Bank Robber.

'Is he the fuck that burned my dog?' Finn's voice sounds calmer than his physical tautness suggests.

'No.' Finn doesn't move. 'Look – Bella, my dog, she's pregnant,' Connell continues. 'I'll give you one of the pups, a pedigree...' Finn takes his boot off the man.

'I don't want a pup. You take good care of them, eh? Better care than you did of your daughter.'

Without warning, Connell lunges at Finn but Finn's too quick, leaping lithely back and covering both Connell and the man on the floor with the gun.

137

'Wanna die, Connell?' I'm clammy with fear, nails digging into my palms.

'Guys,' I plead, my voice shaking, 'Can we just calm it right down?'

'Yeah, oh yeah,' says Finn, running high on adrenaline now, 'these bastards killed my dog, nearly killed me.' He indicates the guy on the ground, 'That scumbag knocked me off my bike, put his boot on my face. Not feeling so clever now are you?' He kicks at the man's head. The man flinches back but Finn's boot doesn't make contact.

I swallow hard and walk over to Finn.

'Are you gonna hurt somebody?' I ask. He ignores me, gun still trained on Connell, tension in every line of his body. 'Come on Finn, this thing ends when we find Gina. That's what we've all got to do. That's how it ends.' He lowers the gun a little. There's a pause in which no one moves. It probably only lasts a few seconds but feels like a lifetime. Then, slowly, Connell backs up and the man on the floor starts to stand and also backs away. Connell still looks Finn steadily in the eye.

'I want to find my daughter, okay? Nothing else matters to me. I just want her back.' Finn stares back for a moment, then walks out, still facing Connell and his muscle-bound friend. He swears to himself under his breath. I move to follow him.

'Yvonne,' Connell calls after me. 'Watch yourself with him.' I nod. I will.

* * * * *

I drive in silence back towards the centre of town. Finn, beside me, is still angry and pumped. I don't have anything to say to him. Going to Connell's hasn't achieved anything and has nearly ended in bloodshed. I wish I hadn't gone along with the idea in the first place. After the ugly scenes at Connell's I can't help thinking if 'our side' are behaving like this under pressure, how brutal and ruthless might the people holding Gina be? From the burning of the caravan, I realised Connell was capable of orchestrating violent acts, and Finn clearly is cut from the same cloth. I've mixed with a few dodgy people in my time, but dating a serial shoplifter and partying with a few pill pushers has nothing on this. I think I can now say that I've descended a good few steps lower on the ladder to the criminal underworld. I'm not too proud of it either.

I also believe Finn when he says there may be little any of us can do until the people holding Gina make their next move, however frustrating that might be for each of us. I intend spending the afternoon working in my studio as I'd planned before Finn invaded my flat, but first I'm meeting Bridie and her friend Annelise for a coffee and pastry in Kensington Gardens. I tell Finn he's welcome to join us, if only to keep things civil between us. In truth, I'd feel far more relaxed meeting my friends without a brooding, trigger-happy gunman in tow. Mercifully it seems he doesn't fancy a natter over hot beverages in the North Laines. 'I'll tell you where I want to be dropped off,' he growls. This turns out to be along the coast road, just east of the remains of the West Pier. 'Wait,' I say as he gets out of the car, 'How do I get in touch if I need to speak to you?'

'You don't, Yvonne.' I shiver as he says my name.

139

'Call me Vonnie.' He hesitates.

'Give me your phone…' I unlock and hand it over, slightly reluctantly, hoping he's not going to make off with it. He types in his number. 'In emergency only, right?' I don't know why he thinks I might call him for any other reason. He's certainly not making the invite list for my next party or private view. As he disappears up a side street I park up and wander up onto the prom, still early for my lunchtime meet-up. Gulls perilously bob up and down on the angry grey waves, somehow avoiding being dashed into the buckled legs of the fire-blackened pier. Do the others even notice, I wonder, if one of them is dashed against the wreckage, and drowned? For all I know they do, and there's more loyalty among seabirds than humans. I check my phone. The number Finn has left appears to be a London landline. Perhaps that's where he lives or is now heading.

Annelise has bought a new handbag in deep blue with long, sequin-tipped streamers hanging down from it. She works full-time in a small boutique in the Laines and can't resist blowing most of her wages on the latest stock. To Annelise, a must-have means a 'must-have today'. Now and again she holds a little soirée where she lets the rest of us buy those of her purchases she's tired of. The idea is to hold off until she's had at least five glasses of wine, then she'll let her wonderfully sloganed t-shirts and hand-crafted silver bangles go for a song, literally on some occasions.

I bring Bridie up to speed on developments, though she's very disapproving about my continuing to have anything to do with the Bank Robber. Annelise is more interested in hearing about Connell's furnishings. 'Do you think he had an interior designer do his place?' I shrug, my knowledge of such things limited to daytime TV home makeovers, which I often end up watching during my cleaning jobs to relieve the tedium. Not that they do that, they tend to make it ten times worse. 'How would you sum up the over-all effect? Does he go for genuine Deco, shabby chic, that French country house thing, or post-modernist minimalism?' She wants to know about Connell's curtains, rugs and lighting, but to tell the truth, I wasn't there collecting swatches and taking photos for Instagram. I was more concerned about preventing the guys from killing each other.

Finally Annelise redeems herself. 'With our shop, when you're employed to style a house, half the job is liaising with the small firms and individual designers who provide the stock.' She goes on to explain that if there's a problem or misunderstanding, it's as often with one of these other small businesses than with a customer. 'When you ask if James Connell has enemies, I'd look among his suppliers for starters. I mean if you had grotty fish and chips in one of his shops, you'd just avoid going back there and post him a stinky review on every travel and restaurant site you could find, right? So it's not likely to be a customer he's narked off, who's now trying to extort money from him. It's someone he's done business with.'

Bridie adds that she supposes farmers provide the potatoes and fishermen the fish.

This sounds so obvious that I'm about to say, 'no shit, Sherlock,' but Annalise butts in instead. 'The potatoes will be via a wholesalers.' Some of the fish might well come from a fish market, though she knows a jewellery designer who has

141

his own fishing boat as a hobby, and does sell to a few shops locally. 'Jonty likes to catch his own dinner and that's so primal don't you think?' She says she'll ask him where the fishermen and possibly fisherwomen hang out in case I want to talk to any of them, to see if they have or have had dealings with Connell.

I head into a newsagents for a packet of chewy mints, as I like to munch them while I'm sculpting. There's a paragraph mentioning something more about the building society raid on the front page. It leads to a longer article on one of the inside pages. The woman behind the till gives me a fierce glare for reading the merchandise rather than buying it, which is a little unfair, considering her shop must've made a mint (albeit fairly small) out of my confectionery purchases over time. On the inside page is a photo of Gina. It's not one I recognise, perhaps supplied by her dad. She looks younger than she actually is. I'm irked he couldn't provide a more up-to-date one. It's not helpful if someone spots her and thinks to themselves, 'oh, but the missing girl is younger'. There's also a description of the Bank Robber and although he was wearing a crash helmet until he left the building society with his scarf up over his mouth, someone else has obviously glimpsed him getting into the car. The write up is a little general, though it gets his eye colour right and mentions he has long dark hair. The police never published my attempt at a photo-fit, as far as I'm aware. I don't know why as it wasn't really that bad. The most interesting thing in the article is that the building society are now offering an unspecified award for information that leads to the robber being arrested. That will put Finn under a fair bit of pressure I should think, if indeed he finds out about it.

I buy the paper. It might be of use, if I continue with the idea of using my cork board in the kitchen as a low-rent version of those incident walls they have in TV crime dramas. My original intention was to pin my ideas and thoughts to it and make a few diagonal lines between them with some of Gina's red knitting wool. That's a bit like the cops do on the telly. Whether they do it in real life though and whether if they do it's any help to them, I couldn't begin to guess. I've also thought of starting a new board on Pinterest dedicated to Gina's abduction, which my friends could also add images and jotted ideas to. Unfortunately I haven't got round to even making a proper start on the cork board. Something else inevitably eats up all my time. That's the problem with trying to juggle two jobs and an amateur investigation. It's pretty full on, all things considered. 'Another coffee?' suggests Annelise. If she's buying for once, I don't mind if I do.

CHAPTER EIGHT

In my studio, I'm still working on the sprinters. A few more days and they'll be ready to go off to the foundry where moulds will be taken and they'll be cast in bronze. Jake modelled for them both, and I have a number of photos of him naked in various running positions in front of me. He's lithe and athletic as he once pole-vaulted nationally and narrowly missed making the Olympic team. He's also received some eye-watering injuries from his time in the sport. He still laments the fact that his pole vaulting didn't win him a medal, thinking it might've been another route to the fame and recognition that he, like me and most of our other mates, still foolishly craves.

I still think he's got more chance of making it with his music, whether with the Aquatic Bees or as a solo artist. After all I can't name any British pole-vaulters who've gone on to achieve riches and acclaim. Once Jake and I had a bit of a thing going on, so I felt easy about asking him to pose for the running figures. Most of my sculptures are based on old friends or ex-lovers, and could be recognised by anyone who knew them intimately. For me it's satisfying to get details like Jake's long middle fingers and Sol's slightly snubbed nose exactly right. I don't know why my former lovers always end up being my friends. I suppose it's no bad thing. I wouldn't want to be someone with a legacy of bitter ex-boyfriends. I've never fully understood love, romance or whatever you call it. I don't know why it suddenly sparks aflame, burns brightly for a while and then fizzles out. It still feels that even now I haven't fully got the hang of it. There's something I'm lacking or not grasping. I often think about it and of lovers from the distant and less distant past when I'm working. It sometimes feels that by my capturing the human form frozen in a pose, I am, for my customers, capturing that highest, strongest, purist moment of love, and preserving it for all time.

As my hands model, my mind returns to my list of suspects. I still think there are some major stones I've left unturned. I've recently discovered Gina had areas in her life she didn't share with me, involving YouTubers and evening classes, but they're hardly the kind of dark revelations that might lead to a kidnapping. I've looked on the social media sites connected to all the evening class tutors, and then cross-referenced them with those of any named participants. All I've found so far are hundreds of photos of smiling people, parties, holidays and pets, plus some of two people who have to Instagram their every cup of hot chocolate, complete with marshmallows on the top. If I'd found a suspicious person of interest among the class participants and upon cross-referencing, found a website linked to something like conspiracy theories, the occult or anything downright peculiar even by Brighton standards, then onto my list that individual would've gone. Instead I've had to add 'the evening class weirdo theory' to my list of suspects with as yet no names attached. Surely every evening class has someone who is a little odd? Mind you, if there is an evening class connection, it could as well be someone who presents as perfectly normal. There's a woman called Petra who attends Rene's class. She goes skiing, has three kids and a Labrador and loves buying scented candles. When I last looked, some of those things can be quite pricey. Not £500,000 kind of pricey, however. I can't stick Petra on the list because I've got a bad case of lifestyle envy by scrolling her socials. I need to keep looking elsewhere.

I've also still not discounted the notion that this isn't about my flatmate at all, but her father. I think Annelise is right and the next line of unofficial enquiries should be a delve into his business practices and interests. I'm not sure potato wholesalers and fish suppliers are the way to go, nor the saveloy bottlers from the chip shop calendar for that matter. I've checked out Connell's lawyer, a Mr David Sullars, whose name I found on a contract back at his house. This solicitor is on LinkedIn and is part of a chambers just off of Grand Parade. I'll drop by on my way home.

* * * * *

Connell's solicitor is based in a large building with shops on the ground floor and offices both below and above. These offices, according to a row of doorbells, belong to either the legal firm, an employment agency or a language school. The lawyer offers sessions to briefly discuss your legal problems for £25 a time. I have that much on me in cash, but up until now it was destined to buy my week's groceries. I'm buzzed in by a man with such a soft voice I have to put my ear against the entry-phone to hear his instructions. I head up steep stairs with a well-worn, moss-green carpet that badly needs hovering. Perhaps I can save myself the cash and persuade the lawyer I'm here to pitch my services as a cleaner for his premises. I push open a door with the firm's name on and suddenly everything is spotless and positively reeking of furniture polish. It seems I will have to risk my Lidl shop after all. The young man with the soft voice turns out to be the lawyer's personal assistant. 'Hmmm,' he says, typing away on a keyboard to find me the soonest appointment he can. 'Mr Sullars, something, something, something.' His voice reminds me of the first cheap flat screen TV Gina bought for our flat. The picture quality was a vast improvement on our boxy, old TV, but we went from being able to hear every word in our favourite dramas and documentaries to not having a clue what people were saying. At first I thought I'd got some kind of early onset deafness caused by too many club nights dancing to party bangers, until I realised Gina was in the same predicament. Here I feel like shouting, 'Speak up young man! Don't mumble!' like a pensioner at a Theatre Royal matinee. Instead I merely say, 'Sorry?'

'I said Mr Sullars has some leave booked for next week, and we're completely booked up for the rest of this one.' He's off to Klosters skiing, no doubt, or an island resort in Phuket. I tell the whispering PA I'll check in with my own diary secretary and come back to him with regard to scheduling. Then money still in my purse, I go to buy my groceries.

It might sound as though I've reached another dead end because I can't immediately see Connell's solicitor, but that's not strictly true. It wasn't him I'd been hoping to see. It was the inside of his office. I've only made it to the reception so far, but I'll call that a partial triumph. It's good for my motivation to think this way, or so the self-help books Bridie keeps passing on to me insist. You know the type of thing. Every door slammed in your face brings you one step closer to the one that stays open. It's probably bollocks, but a little bit of fragile optimism doesn't do anyone any harm.

* * * * *

Benito seems delighted by my offer of a home-cooked evening meal and promises to be there as soon as he finishes his shift. As luck would have it, Lidl is having a Spanish week, so it'll be tortilla wraps containing Manchego cheese, chilies and sun-dried tomatoes, with a nice bottle of Rioja. I know Manchego isn't vegan, but shallow creature that I am, I do lapse occasionally, especially when I want to impress. Don't judge me too harshly for that.

Benito apologises for still smelling of work, but the whiff of the fryer is no problem to me. He's polite about my slightly burnt offering, and enthusiastic about the wine. I tell him my plan. When we've eaten, we'll both head down to Grand Parade. The solicitor keeps office hours so his chambers will be closed, but the language school has evening classes for those wanting to study English.

Benito listens in silence to my plan and examines with interest the nifty little gadget I have purchased online for opening locks. He wants to know what it's called. 'A Bank Robber special,' I say. He nods when I mention Mr Sullars and reveals he has actually seen him.

'Yes, Connell's lawman. One time he is in the chip shop when I arrive. Lots of papers all over a table.' Not chip papers either by the sound of it. 'He and Connell they do some kind of urgent business that day. If you get sack-ed, I think this is the man who write you.'

'Has Connell sacked anyone recently?' Benito shrugs.

'Maybe. I don't know. Not in our shop.'

'So how do you know he sacks people?' I persist.

'Ah, Eileen say it. I think it has happened there. When I not work there.'

'Before you worked there?'

'Yes. Maybe a friend of Eileen was sack-ed, I don't know. I think I remember her saying this. When she tell me off for giving away too many sheets.'

'Sheets?'

'Shits?'

'No, err... probably not. Sheets of newspaper... no... err, serviettes, napkins?' I mime spreading one on my lap.

'Yes sheets! Err, napkins.'

'So you gave out too many napkins and she mentioned Connell sacking someone because of this?'

'Not because of that. To tell me to be careful I think. Not to do more things wrong.' I pour us both another glass of red. Working in a chip shop sounds like a worse minimum wage gig than cleaning. Benito sips his wine pensively and says that when he had called Connell into the shop earlier, he had first warmed up one of the fish freezer's thermometers, to make the boss think there might be a problem. Connell had swapped the thermometer for one from where they keep frozen pies, and waited to check whether the problem was with the freezer itself or the temperature recording. He stressed this was the procedure to follow if it happened again, and certainly not to move or throw away any possibly thawing stock without consulting him first. Connell had gone outside several times while at The New Atlantis, to make hushed phone calls, and Eileen had heard him address the person he was talking to as 'David'. The name on the lawyer's office is David Sullars. 'But Vonnie, I think you cannot really broke in to this man's room. It is dangerous. The police. You must not do this, please.' I top up our wine.

* * * * *

Just off of Grand Parade, Benito and I stand outside the language school, employment agency and legal chambers. A couple of students come along and sit down on the steps that rise to the front door. They start chatting in what sounds like it might be Spanish. Benito says something to one of them and their faces light up. At my sink comprehensive, you had to be in the top class to study Spanish and unfortunately, I wasn't. They seem to be discovering they come from the same region or town, well something like that anyway. Perhaps he has recognised something in their accents. I stand alone, feeling as much of a spare part as I did at the Hove house party, as they chat and laugh. One of the girls takes a piece of paper from her pocket and writes her phone number on it. She is very tall, wearing the tightest jeans and the tiniest of crop tops. Her spidery eyelashes have an unnatural curl that suggests they're acrylic and her lips are outlined in black. I suppose if I was Benito I might find her vaguely attractive. She looks at me, trying to work out our relationship. I hope she doesn't think I'm his mum. I stare back but clearly not with enough conviction as she goes ahead and hands him the piece of paper.

Benito is excited and animated. There's a light in his eyes. Surely that girl giving him her number isn't responsible? The girls go inside and he turns to me. 'There is a welcome party in the school there tonight. They say we should go along. All are welcome. Music and noise and many people. It will be easy for us to broke the door to the lawman.'

'Easier for me to pick the lock, hopefully,' I say, pulling on my gloves. 'But I'm doing this alone, you understand? You're going to the party.'

'But Vonnie...'

'Go to the party. I don't want to get you in any trouble. I'll come and get you when I'm done.'

We cross the road and wait for the numbers entering the building to increase before stepping inside. The party is, as luck would have it, on the floor below Mr Sullars' chambers. Benito and I saunter into the party. I swerve the free glasses of wine, having realised upon leaving my flat that I'd consumed too much over dinner, while persuading Benito to go along with my plan. We both take a paper plate and help ourselves to the paella and assorted global food offerings. It's a fantastic looking spread, far better than the manky canapés they serve up at arty gatherings. I clearly need to learn English as a foreign language, or maybe train to teach it. Simone, who used to rent the studio next to mine did exactly that. The craze for her collages of beach-found plastic items passed and left her washed up on the strandline herself, so she retrained as a tutor. In her first group of students, she met a Greek business owner and now she's living on Mykonos and posting daily photos of herself lounging on the beach. Her collages are starting to sell again too.

I can't help noticing Benito seems more enthusiastic about this food than he was about the meal I cooked for him. One of the Spanish girls spots him again and beckons him to join her little cluster of equally glamorous friends. With my plate in one gloved hand, wine glass in the other, I tell him I'm going to go look for the toilets. He understands of course what I'm really telling him. 'Good luck, Vonnie!' He winks. I'm about to wink back but he has already crossed the room to join the girl with the spider lashes. I wonder if I would look good in a pair of those. I doubt it somehow.

Benito is too young for me, but then that kind of thing has never stopped Madonna. She looks reasonably good on it too. I've been nearly a year without even a fleeting sexual encounter, not that it's really my thing. I'm definitely a relationship girl. Not the whole church and children deal, at least not yet, but connection and companionship are required. This makes me sound old and feel even older. I'm attracted to Finn, even though, or possibly because he's bad news. He doesn't give much away where his own emotions are concerned, which is a relief. If he did come on to me, I'd honestly find it hard to resist.

The lock-picking gadget from the web didn't come with instructions. In fact, it came in a large, unmarked, brown box, packed tight with the kind of polystyrene squiggly bits that are choking whales in our oceans. Oddly, I feel more guilt about this than actually buying and deploying the wretched burglary device. I wriggle it, I jiggle it and then freeze as a girl with an east European accent comes up the stairs asking for

152

the bathroom. With what I hope is an innocent looking smile, I direct her back down again. It's not on this landing fortunately. A sign beside the door to the legal chambers says, *'no cash is kept on the premises overnight'*. I believe it. I don't imagine many people have paid their solicitor in cash since Dickens' time. I hope the money warning means there is no alarm. There doesn't appear to be a security camera in the corridor, but I have my hood up, scarf ready and keep my face pointed down. No one has ever thought of situating CCTV at skirting board level as far as I know. It might be a good idea for the security conscious. Below I can hear the Ketchup Song playing. Imagining Benito having a boogie with all those young women isn't exactly helping my concentration. It's finished and they're on to the Macarena when the device suddenly and without warning turns in the lock and the latch pulls back. Very slowly I open the door.

After entering the office, I close the door silently behind me, and then risk flicking on the lights. There doesn't appear to be a burglar alarm. I pass the quiet man's reception desk and slip into the office with Mr Sullars' nameplate on the door. Floor-to-ceiling files of the fattest kind imaginable and filing cabinets galore surround a polished teak desk with three padded swivel chairs huddled in close. I try investigating the files first, restricting myself to the section for clients beginning with 'C'. Mr Sullars appears to represent a lot of people called Collins. He seems to be mainly a family and business law specialist. Finally I find a file for Mr James Connell and his various 'trading as' names. It contains what appear to be contracts, deeds and leases of various kinds. If I started reading this lot, I'll still be here when I finally qualify for a pension. That's if I've paid enough voluntary contributions by then that is. Some recent years have been leaner than I like to recall.

After probably ten minutes of rummaging, I decide to abandon the fat files and look for the name 'Connell' in the filing cabinets. Here, in the third drawer down, a thinner folder looks more hopeful. It's again definitely the right James Connell, and seems to be correspondence relating to legal action of various kinds. The first few pages seem to involve an issue with a supplier over payment. After this there is correspondence over on-street parking and contesting a parking fine. This is followed by a number of pages detailing a problem with a shop's landlord over the drains. Connell seems to be involved in a fair number of current or recent legal matters. I want to pinch this entire file. There's far too much in it to digest here. I try scanning a few pages with my phone but the light's too dim for the camera to cope properly. Either that or it's my eyes that aren't focussing properly after too much Spanish wine at my place and whatever I just necked at the party. There's an ornate-looking desk lamp but I can't find how the ruddy thing switches on. The quiet man on reception, when he's in attendance, does however have a photocopier at his personal disposal. It takes another ten minutes to copy the entire file's contents, before carefully returning it to where I found it. Now I realise I should've brought a bag of some sort with me. It's a typically stupid mistake from a burglary virgin. I don't want to be spotted coming down the stairs from a solicitor's with a pile of documents or a file in my hand. In desperation, I stick the A4 sheets inside my jacket and zip it up.

I walk rather stiffly into the party. The room is hot and stuffy now, particularly when you're wearing a hooded jacket liberally stuffed with legal documents. Benito is sitting on a sofa, talking to a young man who appears as enamoured with him as the girls had been before I left. Meringue nests with mouth-watering strawberries in them have materialised on the party table whilst I've been occupied upstairs. I discard my empty glass and refill my paper plate with two of the nests and a slice of a fruitcake. That's tonight's supper and tomorrow's breakfast taken care of. You have to think of these things when you work in the arts. The fresh fruit, in the form of the strawberries, is fairly healthy too. There's egg in those and the fruitcake, but as I said, I do let my veganism lapse a little when absolutely necessary.

Safely back home and alone, I stay up into the early hours looking through the copied documents. If the ransom note is genuine and the motive is money then Gina is probably alive. I cling to that. Connell is the key, I'm sure of it. He's rich, extremely dodgy and his daughter is the only thing that seems to mean a lot to him. Someone knew this is his weakness – someone who wants money or revenge. That's as far as I've got with my profiling. In a detective TV show, Finn would be the obvious suspect, but one who finally turns out to be innocent. He'd be played by some star name and take up most of the investigation, while some sneaky person you wouldn't suspect, probably because they were a middle-aged woman, actually did it. As it happens, there are still no women currently on my list of suspects. That seems a little sexist, but it's just how things have gone. Finn is on the list, but only because I'm failing to add other names. For me he's never really worked as a suspect. If I hadn't been there at the building society raid, I might have believed it, but from what I saw he only hijacked Gina in the heat of the moment. It wasn't premeditated. Yes, he could've then discovered she was Connell's daughter. Perhaps she even said, 'Do you know who my dad is,' and spelt out what that means. What would he then have done? Abandoned her? Held her for ransom? Murdered her? I don't see him being into the kidnap/ransom thing. He must have plenty of cash from the building society raid – and no doubt others – stashed away somewhere. If he was going to kill anyone it would be Connell, not Gina. I don't see him as a cold-blooded murderer. If he was, I think I'd be pushing up daisies by now.

It's nearly two in the morning and my eyelids feel like I could tuck them into my pants. This is the second night running I haven't been to bed. I wish I'd persuaded Benito to come back here with me. That way we could've waded through the paperwork together, not literally of course, though even that might be a pleasant enough experience with Benito involved. Just about anything would be. Time for a black coffee, and then it's mascara-smudged nose back to the grindstone.

Halfway through the pile of photocopied documents, I notice something. The ink, at first so crisp and dark, is beginning to fade. At first a few random consonants and vowels are a little indistinct, and then more and more. So busy had I been making copies while listening out for danger over the strains of the Macarena, that in my wine-numbed state I hadn't realised I was about to be let down by a bloody toner cartridge. I've just reached an interesting letter too. It has the name Margarita Gara on it and the line below says 're: Ms Gara's allegations o…' After that there's hardly a word on the page. All I can make out are 'cons', 'dama', 'acc' and one entire word, 'premises'. The toner cartridge makes one final effort on the next page before finally giving up the ghost, but that appears to be referring to another case, a building work dispute with a Mr Tut- something or other. All I can do, when I've finished using every swear word I know, is try to recreate plausible whole words from the fragments. This is what I come up with: 'considerable damages' (as these two word fragments were next to each other), and 'accident'. The best recreation of what the paragraph should say is: *'Blah, blah blah considerable damages. Blah blah accident, blah blah blah premises.'* Now I need to look into whether a Margarita Gara has had an accident on any of Connell's premises. Unfortunately there is no address for her, so finding her might prove to be a little tricky.

CHAPTER NINE

I presume the letter about Margarita Gara was sent to Connell's solicitor by another legal firm. The words I've had a crack at deciphering sound like lawyer speak, rather than something from a personal letter of complaint. I've searched for the woman online over my language school fruitcake breakfast and think I have a Brighton address for her. At least Margarita Gara is an unusual name. If it was a Susan Smith I was looking for I'd have thousands of Facebook profiles and Twitter feeds still to scan through.

The address for Margarita Gara is unfortunately in Albion Hill and it is very steep. It's all parking meters too, so I decide, probably unwisely, to walk up there. I usually have cereal of one kind or another for breakfast and I often feel a bit queasy afterwards. I'd thought for a while I might be gluten intolerant, but switching to gluten-free cornflakes made no difference. I then surmised the problem might be the oat milk, but switching to almond milk didn't improve matters either. Today I've only had my cake and ate it, but I'm still slightly nauseous. I think I'm just breakfast intolerant, if that isn't simply another way of saying 'not a morning person' or 'hung over'. Whenever I describe my nausea and occasional morning puke, I get a knowing look from friends. They needn't bother. My sex drought means there's absolutely no chance of a little Vonnie junior being the cause of my issues. The only thing kicking indignantly in my tummy right now is my long-suffering liver.

I ring the doorbell chez Margarita and a tall, thin man answers. He might be wearing a striped pastel shirt ready to commute to a job in the city or it might be the top part of his pyjamas. He has the kind of rumpled, static-raised hair that you would probably rub a balloon on first if you felt obliged to stick it to a wall. 'Excuse me, I'm looking for Margarita Gara.'

'Is that a drink or a pizza?' I groan audibly. A joker, and it's not yet nine in the morning. This is too much to take. He goes on to say that he and someone called 'Nat' only moved in nine weeks ago. He doesn't know anything about the previous tenant.

'I don't suppose you still get any post addressed to a Ms Gara?'

'Don't think so. You know most people ask the post office to redirect their mail when they move? It's what we did.' I don't need him to explain this, but I happen to know for a fact that there are other, considerably less well-organised people like myself, who have never bothered, particularly as you have to pay for the privilege of redirection and the only things which tend to come by post are bills.

If I were a proper, professional investigator of missing flatmates, I'd know what to do next. I'd ask stripy shirt/pyjama man a question that would yield substantial results. In fact I'd probably solve the whole mystery right here and now. Trouble is, this guy and Margarita seem to have had

159

no contact whatsoever. Like the woman in a weather house, she had left before he moved in. This never happens to the detectives on the telly. If I was in a Netflix series, I'd have at least found a tantalising clue here after all that uphill walking. Me, I've found diddly-squat and it's all downhill from here.

The only other place I can think of that might yield a clue to Margarita Gara is the chip shop. Benito isn't working today, but there's something about his colleague, Eileen, that makes it seem highly plausible she's been shovelling chips at *The New Atlantis* for centuries. It's her wrist action, I decide, that suggests an elite level of skill, coupled with a world-weariness and a touch of repetitive strain injury. She's there this morning taking in deliveries and stock-taking. It should be Gina's role but it seems that in her absence she's been given a kind of unofficial promotion. I bet she's not being paid anything extra though. If Gina doesn't return then Eileen might conceivably become the next manager, though as like as not Connell will bring in someone else over her. Even if Eileen does find herself bumped up to manager and is given a small pay rise in the process, I don't think she'll be wildly enthusiastic about it. It's not like Gina had this marvellous, covetable role and the only way to ascend to her seat of glory, if you happen to be a wildly ambitious chip-shoveler is to kidnap her. For reasons of equal opportunities, there ought to be some women on the suspect list by now, but I can see suspecting Eileen for what she might stand to gain doesn't really wash.

I ask Eileen about Margarita. 'Margy? Yeah, I remember her. Used to still send a Christmas card for a couple of years.'

'You don't happen to have the address?'

'Well no. I'm lousy at sending cards myself, and I'm not sure I even had her details in the first place. Isn't she on Face Wossit? Or the twitterer?'

'Not that I can see. Did she work here long?'

'Bout a year I suppose.'

'And then she left?'

'Well, she had to, see?'

'Did she?

'She couldn't come back. After the accident. It was that bad.'

'Accident?'

'A fat fire.'

'And where is she now?'

'I don't know. Moved away, I think. I do wish we'd kept in touch actually. She was nice lass, Margy. But you don't always think of it at the time.' Eileen shakes her head every time I hold out my phone to show her a profile photo for Margarita Gara. 'Too young.' 'No, definitely not her.' 'Lord no, she didn't have a chin like that!' I finish my chips. Now I'm back at near sea level my nausea has miraculously gone away. Fruit cake followed by chips might sound like junk food hell, but then you always find the cops breakfasting in a burger joint or munching on a pasty from Greggs. When investigating, do as the investigators do – consume a few extra carbs.

'Is there anyone else who worked here when Margarita did, who might've kept in touch with her?' Eileen considers this.

'No. Not that I'm still in touch with.' She starts to roll a piece of fish in flour. I haven't eaten fish since I was in primary school. I can't remember what it tastes like and the smell of it only reminds me of The Sealife Centre, where I've been to a few after-hours launches for books and albums. The Aquatic Bees played a private gig there once, in the seahorse section. 'There's a woman, Esperanza,' says Eileen, remembering as she batters the cod, 'She worked in the florist's in Western Road. Still does I think. They were friends as far as I can recall. Used to go to the bingo together.' I'm about to ask which bingo hall they attended, but Eileen is called away to answer a customer's query about ethically caught haddock. I've no idea what the woman even thinks she means by 'ethically caught'. If you're going to eat some living thing, it's going to be killed so you can do so. Either you believe in the ethics of that or you don't.

* * * * *

The florist is still closed. I'll have to wait until later to pursue this line of enquiry. I return home and am barely in the door when the landline rings. It's Connell. I can tell immediately by his voice something has happened.

'I've had another letter about the ransom. They've put the price up. Now they want six hundred thousand!'

'And you've told the police?'

'Like I said before, I want to handle this my way.'

162

'But you're telling me?'

'And telling you this goes no further than you. I'm only letting you know at all because I want your opinion.'

'On what?'

'Have you ever heard of a ransom demand going up before?'

'I'm not really an expert on ransom demands, Mr Connell,' I tried to explain. 'Was it posted?'

'Locally probably. Gatwick, it says, which is where anything local ends up. My solicitor says if someone writes to you from nearly anywhere in Sussex you get 'Gatwick' on the postmark.'

'So nothing to do with the airport then?' What I was actually thinking was whether the lawyer had been as observant about the state of his office this morning as he was about a postmark. I have the nasty feeling I may have inadvertently left a wine glass stain and a few paella crumbs on his desk. I also hope I didn't leave the last of the documents I was copying still in the photocopier. I've done that so often in the library, and if I hadn't noticed the cartridge was running out of ink, this too, is a possibility.

'Where's Finn?' Connell asks.

'I've no idea.'

'Can you get in touch with him?'

'I can't,' I lie. 'I don't know where he's staying or even if he's still in the area.'

'Well if you hear from him, tell him to call me.'

'Right, okay… Mr Connell… err are you going to pay the ransom?'

'Ah. You see it's not quite that easy, Yvonne.' It never is. If I had that kind of money knocking about I'd pay up without hesitation, but Connell says he can't lay his hands on that much. He needs to find a way to tell the kidnappers he will need to pay less, and require a few days to get his hands on even that. He needs someone to negotiate with them, which I'm guessing is why he wants to speak to Finn. Perhaps he imagines he'll act as some kind of go-between. I don't see that working. The kidnappers have contacted Gina's dad and that's who they'll want to deal with.

I tell Connell I've no idea how he thinks he is going to contact the kidnappers to discuss financial arrangements, since he only has their letters to go on. Perhaps he needs to put another fuchsia in the window with a message board beside it. He says he's sure they'll be in touch again soon as he hasn't yet been told when or where they want the money delivered. It seems he's convinced the letter writers are genuine now, but when I ask why that is, I don't get a straight answer. I have to ask the question I'd been dreading.

'Mr Connell, have they now sent any actual proof they have Gina?' There is a pause on the end of the phone. I start thinking about severed fingers, I can't help myself.

'They enclosed a Polaroid,' Connell says at last. 'She's holding yesterday's Metro.'

'The newspaper?' I don't know why I said that. What was I thinking the Metro was, a dodgy 1980s motor? She'd hardly be holding that.

'Does she look okay?'

'She looks scared. Scared but alive.'

* * * * *

Today my agency has booked me two cleaning jobs. I know I should probably be devoting myself to the hunt for Gina full-time, but the bills won't pay themselves. That's the problem with temping for an agency, if you don't work, you've nothing coming in and everything going out. Whoever invented zero hours contracts deserves to be shot, in my humble opinion. I have no savings and anything I ever had that was worth anything, like my gran's engagement ring for example, has had to be sold at one time or another to keep food on the table. One year I sell a few pieces, or get a grant or a commission, the next I earn next to nothing from my art. It's fortunate there's always dust falling and dirt accumulating in the world. Without grime and filth I'd starve. Think of that next time you're cursing doing the housework.

On the way to my first job, I do at least have time to pop by the florist again. It seems it doesn't open until after ten in the morning. Esperanza turns out to be the owner of the shop and she's currently busy, working with two colleagues in a cramped back room to make a number of wreaths for a funeral. The colour scheme is blue and white, as the guy was apparently an Albion fan. She's on the phone explaining to someone, presumably the client, that bluebells aren't possible. There are lots of flowers that are dyed blue but the customer wants natural ones. Esperanza wishes she'd known this earlier. She has some scabious and delphiniums, but not nearly enough. There are some blue, potted hydrangeas for sale in the window. One of the assistants will have to behead them so they can use them. She makes a quick beheading gesture as she explains this. I wouldn't like to get in a fight with her. Using the blooms from the plants on sale will considerably reduce the profits on this job, but Esperanza explains, 'it cannot be helped'. The assistant queries whether blue hydrangeas are completely natural. 'Don't they feed them with something?' Esperanza shrugs expansively, 'They grow them in acidic soil. That is natural – or almost natural. Look, they will have do, okay?' She turns to me. 'Sorry to keep you. We are very busy today.' She cuts some lengths of thin wire, then stows her secateurs in her apron pocket.

Esperanza doesn't want to talk to me about Margarita. She says her friend left Brighton after that 'bad business' but doesn't go into details. She seems to suspect I'm in some way connected to Connell, which is true, but not in the way she imagines. If I can find Margarita's whereabouts, I won't go telling him. I just want to talk to her. I say I knew Margarita way back, from the chip shop, having been a regular customer. I'd like to catch up and maybe give her a call. Esperanza says she doesn't have a number or an address. I don't believe her. 'Margarita trusts people far too easily. She doesn't know what they are capable of.'

'You mean Connell?' Her dark lacquered brows angle into a frown beneath her wispy, blue-black up-do.

'Yes. That man.' She all but spits out the words.

166

'What did he do?'

'She couldn't work after the accident. But he stopped her making a claim for damages. The lawyers said she had a strong case. But he warned her off.'

'Who were her lawyers? Can you remember?'

'Me? Why should I?'

'Perhaps they'll have an address for her.'

'And perhaps they won't. Are you with the Home Office?'

'No. I'm a cleaner.' I fish out the card I carry from the company I work for: 'Eaz-E-Klean.' She doesn't look entirely impressed. People seldom do, but at least she is reassured. 'Why do you mention the Home Office? Is Margarita is some kind of trouble with them?'

'We are very busy now. Very busy. I can't chat now. You must ask someone else.'

* * * * *

I'm wiping down rotting bannisters in Rottingdean when my mobile rings. It's Eileen from the chip shop. After talking to me, she called her husband and asked him to flick through an old address book they keep by their phone. Although she was not listed under 'M' or 'G' for some reason, he has, Eileen tells me, found a mobile number and address for Margarita. She must've taken a note of her new details after all. Eileen tells me not to get my hopes of speaking to 'your old friend' up too high. She has already tried to phone Margarita, to tell her of my interest in getting back in touch and discovered the number no longer connects. The address is in Portsmouth.

I tell Mrs Percy I'll need to leave the rest of her wooden surfaces until next time as they require a particular specialised polish my cleaning agency forgot to inform me I'd need today. Use the wrong product and I could stain the grain. She nods, accepting this off-the-top-of-my-head cock and bull story. She wants her children to inherit the sideboard and dresser so she wouldn't want them damaged in any way. Poor Mrs Percy. I suspect there aren't actually many forty-somethings today who would appreciate the bequest of a dark hardwood dresser. They'll probably chop it up and stick the bits in their eco-unfriendly wood-burner. Promising to schedule another visit to finish the job off next week, I back the car out of her drive and head for the petrol station nearest to the coast road to fill up for my journey.

* * * * *

I've never been to Portsmouth, though I've seen adverts for the Gun Wharf Quays shops on the telly so many times it feels like I'm a local. We were supposed to have a school outing to see HMS Victory and the Mary Rose when I was twelve but it got cancelled when the history teacher got shingles.

Since moving to Brighton, I realise I've treated the place like an island surrounded by quicksand, or a shark-infested sea. Until Gina's disappearance I'd hardly travelled beyond its boundaries, save for the occasional train journey up to London to talk to galleries and possible dealers. Now I'm driving along through the West Sussex towns of Worthing, Arundel and Chichester. They're easily reachable from Brighton but for some reason I've never been tempted to explore them. It's a very insular attitude, I tell myself. For all

I know, in one of these places there's a gallery or shop that would be willing to stock and sell my work, and who knows how popular it might be, outside the art-saturated coastal conurbation? When and if Gina is found, I'll start becoming a little more adventurous where exploring the rest of East and West Sussex is concerned. Now I've passed a sign welcoming me to Hampshire. Again it might as well be an exotic foreign clime. This is my first ever foray into this county, I realise again revelling in the ridiculousness of this truth. I've been all over Europe and I've visited the US and India as part of paid-for artist exchange programmes when I was younger. I'm a traveller of the world, but not of my own country. The next time I see a vacancy advertised for an artist in residence at a gallery in Liverpool or Land's End, I'm going to leap at it. Brighton is starting to become too small to contain me. I need to stretch my wings.

I park up near landmark Spinnaker Tower and consult the map on my phone. There's a lot more of Portsmouth than I'd bargained for. Brighton, whilst rather hilly, is reasonably straightforward in terms of geography as it has the sea on one side only. Portsmouth though, sticks out into the water with a harbour on two sides, plus the sea in front, so when you see an expanse of water ahead and assume you're at the southern end, you might well be heading east or west. I should've bought a sat nav for Gina's car. I can use my phone, but have to stop each time I need to consult it. Perhaps the answer is to go completely old-school and pop in a newsagents and buy an A-Z. You can tell I'm a Londoner. My relief when I moved to Brighton on discovering it had its own dedicated A-Z, on sale in the station branch of WH Smith's, was massive. It was my first purchase upon leaving the train in my new home city.

Phyllis Pearsall, creator of the A-Zs, I salute you. If you featured on a poster you'd be up there among my other icons on my bedroom wall. She was an artist as well as a map-maker. The next time a man makes a snide remark about women and map reading, tell him who designed and published the London A-Z. When a woman remarks that this or that person is her personal heroine, remind her they might not have even reached the location where they did whatever it is they are famous for, if Phyllis hadn't mapped it for them first.

I buy a bar of chocolate to eat in the car while consulting Phyllis's Portsmouth edition. I notice the confectionery is a whole ten pence cheaper than in my local convenience store. I realise I might be turning into Sol. Still, it's the kind of information he'll be delighted I'm finally paying attention to, so I'll probably tell him about it. Bridie rings. She's in a London café having a comforting hot chocolate after a 'simply disastrous audition'. It was for a new play by a writer who is known for writing works that are obscene and outrageous. 'Aren't they all these days?' Bridie had learnt a full-blooded monologue from one of the playwright's previous plays, as she'd been instructed by the casting director to 'come along with something you've prepared'. This was, she'd suspected, because the new play she was auditioning for wasn't yet in a finished enough state to read from at the audition. Bridie had turned up, ready to swear, curse and froth at the mouth for England. Unfortunately the director's child-care arrangements had fallen through and he had his three year-old with him in the room. Thinking on her feet, Bridie had switched to something she knew from memory, a gentle section of 'Shirley Valentine'. Bridie had received four-star reviews for her Kent rural tour of this play and felt she had probably salvaged the audition, until she heard the director sigh and mutter as she left the room, 'Third Shirley this morning.' It sounds like another case of a wasted peak-time train fare and now Bridie has to walk back down Regent Street to the tube without getting tempted by a little retail therapy. I offer as much sympathy as I can muster, but I'm a woman focussed on her mission and could've done without the interruption.

I discover to my annoyance the address for Margarita Gara is back towards Fratton. I've overshot my target and am in Southsea. Sherlock Holmes didn't used to get lost I tell myself crossly, but then he could hail a hansom cab and say, 'Driver, so and so street if you please.' Whether the driver pleased or not, he'd be whisked there pronto. I can't wait for driverless cars to be available and affordable.

* * * * *

I'm outside the address Eileen gave me for Margarita Gara. It's a small, pebble-dashed terrace with a small front garden containing a single, nondescript bush of some description. The door and window frames look in need of a lick of paint and the gate has fallen from its hinges. I press the doorbell and wait. There's the sound of footsteps within. To my relief someone is actually in. I don't think I could afford to fork out for the petrol for a second visit. The door is opened on the chain. 'Margarita?' Whoever is there is standing too far back for me to be able to see them. 'Eileen sent me, from the chip shop.' It's almost true. The door closes again, and I think I've said the wrong thing. Then I hear the chain being taken off.

171

Margarita lets me in. She has a livid scar on her chin that looks like a burn and wears a glove on one hand, a hand she seems to find stiff and difficult to use. She is in her fifties, I estimate and speaks with an accent that sounds familiar but which I can't quite place. 'Gina, yes I know Gina.' She ushers me into a small front room that is sparsely and impersonally furnished. I sit in one navy blue, corduroy armchair and she perches on the edge of the other. There is either a nervousness or shyness about her, I'm not sure which it is. I tell her the whole story, which takes some minutes. She nods occasionally but doesn't offer any comment. I don't know if the concern in her eyes is for Gina in particular, or just an expression of sympathy for anyone who might find themselves in that particular predicament. When I finish, I hope she will be the one to break the silence, but when she doesn't, I have to.

'I know you had some trouble with her dad, your former boss...' I hazard. Margarita looks even more on her guard. 'So I thought you might be the person to ask,' I continue. 'Is Connell an honest person? Does he have enemies? Could he even have harmed his own daughter?' She doesn't immediately answer, but slowly and possibly unconsciously, clenches and unclenches the gloved hand.

'At first, everything seem normal,' Margarita offers at last, 'When I get the job, I do not see him. The job is okay. Soon, I hear things.'

'Things?' Margarita says she thinks the shop is what she calls a 'money laundry'. Connell owns another two at least, she thinks, one in St Leonard's, one in Bognor. It was a woman called Helen who visited from the Bognor shop who

172

had told her about there being underhand business practices going on. Helen and Connell had a brief relationship, but it had soured.

'Was he like that? Trying it on with staff?'

'Not with me or Eileen.' Helen it seemed had been wined and dined by Connell, but she had hoped for more than a commitment-free relationship, and that hadn't materialised. She had, in Margarita's words, wanted to be the new Mrs Connell. At some charity ball or similar event for corporate types, Connell had been talking to an attractive man, who was clearly an associate of his. This man had been rather obviously taken with Helen and had flirted with her. Helen had seen the opportunity to make her lover jealous and taken it. Since Connell had given no indication he and Helen were in an exclusive relationship, she arranged an evening out with the new guy and continued to see him for a few weeks. He was more generous, or 'flash with cash' as Margarita put it, than Connell, and keen to boast about his business interests. He'd suggested Helen might like to move on from working in a smelly, old chippy to running one of his tanning salons or nail bars. He said he'd pay her more than she was getting at Connell's shop and explained why he could afford to do so. When he told Helen about the money laundering for local drugs gangs, they were sitting in a pole dancing club, which Helen was already not feeling terribly relaxed about. What the new guy didn't know however is that Helen's niece had nearly died from taking MDMA as a teenager. When she said she didn't approve of becoming involved, however indirectly, in anything connected with drugs or criminals, the new man, whose name Margarita had not discovered, laughed and asked her if she knew Connell was 'in the same game' and that the chip shops were also cleaning up dirty money. Helen had not seen the nail bar owner again after that, but she'd stayed at the Bognor shop and had continued dating Connell for some weeks. She'd told Margarita she had no concrete evidence Connell was in the same line of business as his friend, but her eyes had been opened and the very moment she found any evidence of it, she would leave her job and Connell. A month later, Margarita had to call the Bognor shop over a delivery error. The man who answered the phone said Helen no longer worked there. She had quit unexpectedly and he was now the manager. 'So?' Margarita held up both hands, inviting me to draw my own conclusions.

Margarita had, as I'd been told by Esperanza in the florist, been injured when a fat fryer had gone up in flames. A new thermostat in the fryer had proved to be faulty, allowing the oil to heat above flash point. Margarita had been standing nearest at the time and had sustained serious burns. The shop had also been damaged and forced to close for several weeks. I make a mental note to check this out online in archived local newspaper reports. It's not that I don't believe what Margarita is telling me. I do. If I cross-reference and fact check where I can though I'm more likely to reach an accurate conclusion that'll help Gina, than if I let my imagination run wild with conjecture.

After Margarita had been injured at work, she'd been unable to return to the shop and Connell had refused to pay her sick pay, claiming the accident must have in some way been her fault. I ask if that was legal and she laughs bitterly. 'When you are not a citizen of this country anything is legal.' Margarita had apparently stayed here after her visa expired. This gave her few rights and the risk of being deported at any

174

time. Connell advertises vacancies on the shop door and leaves his staff to interview prospective employees. Eileen had apparently filled a few things down on a form and that was as 'official' as it ever got. Margarita had been told that Connell would be in touch to verify details and provide a signed contract later. When this hadn't happened, Margarita had been initially relieved not to have to provide documentation of proof to work here as she didn't have it. It had proved to be a double-edged sword when she'd been injured at work and left unable to claim benefits.

Margarita says she had wanted to live in England, but now isn't so sure. Unable to pay her rent and facing being made homeless, Margarita had risked consulting a personal injury lawyer. Even if it led to her being asked to leave the UK or deported, at least she might get a compensation payout she had reasoned.

A key in the lock makes her stop speaking. 'Alright, Margy?' A gruff sounding man, probably in his fifties, and wearing paint-spattered overalls, puts his head around the door.

'Yes, yes, everything is okay, Stuart.' The man seems satisfied and heads up the stairs, whistling to himself.

'My landlord. I rent a room here. It is all I can afford. Sometimes I cannot pay rent. But he is a good man, always he wait for his money.'

Margarita explains how the lawyer she had hired had gone into the shop asking questions, and she suspected he'd visited at least one of the other branches too. She had employed a large, London based No-Win-No-Fee firm and hadn't imagined this would happen. Eileen though, had rung and let her know to warn her. Her lawyer then told Margarita that he believed serious health and safety breaches were being committed and that she had a strong case. He urged her to let him pursue it. Connell, in his firm's estimations, was a wealthy man and likely to settle quickly, out of court. It had not however gone down exactly like that. Someone from one of the other shops had tipped Connell off about a man in a suit coming in and asking questions about their safety record. That's when Margarita started getting threatening phone calls. Just talking about this now I can see she is still scared. 'They said my face... they would finish making it a ruin...' She lifted her good hand to it defensively. 'They said I should go home. I said I had no money. A man came round with an envelope, I had to sign for it. It contained a ticket. One way. But I cannot go back without money. There is nothing there for me. How would I live? My husband is dead and I have no home.' Margarita currently works part-time as a translator, translating technical manuals for an American multi-national's Spanish speaking market. It's a job she does mostly online. It doesn't pay well, but her boss pays her wages by PayPal, and that means she can exist under the radar over here, without paying tax or claiming benefits.

I tell Margarita that I'm clutching at straws where searching for Gina is concerned. Any other insights she can give me into Connell and his daughter's lives would be invaluable. Margarita says she thinks Connell's financial arrangements are the key to Gina's disappearance. She wonders if he owes someone money or there is some dispute over the fee he is paid for turning illegal cash legitimate. She says she liked Gina.

176

'She wasn't like a boss. She work alongside us. Gina would never say, 'you must wash up or do overtime because I am your boss, or I will tell my father.' She was one of us.'

It's dark as I drive back to Brighton. I know I said I smoke a bit of weed and have been known to occasionally partake of other substances, but I'm not really part of that druggy demi-monde. I mean my cannabis supplier is fat, forty-something and called Nigel. He turns up in an electric car. Very eco-friendly. I can almost see the advertisement: 'Buy your green from a green dealer.' He must get the stuff from somewhere though. It's worth giving him a call.

Nigel is happy to take my money but less happy to talk. 'If you go in the Co-op yeah, and you buy say a strawberry yoghurt and a tin of apricots, they're not gonna let you know who their supplier is are they? Cos that's how business works, see?'

I do like a patronising, middle-aged mansplainer.

'The yoghurt and the apricots will have who made them on the packaging in big letters,' I tell him patiently. 'I don't think there's too much hush hush about Danone or the man from Del Monte, Nige.'

'But you don't know who the wholesaler is.' I take a very deep breath.

'All I'm asking is this. Is it at all possible that some... I don't know... local drug king pin or erm queen pin has kidnapped my flatmate, because business with her dad might've turned sour?' Nigel shrugs. 'I don't know anything about that. I'm a plumber right?' I hadn't known that, though it's hardly an earth-shattering revelation.

'I just got hooked up with someone who does runs — across to Europe on the ferry.'

'I don't suppose you could…'

'Nah, nah, Vonnie. I've said too much and I ain't saying no more. Look, if I hear anything, anything about a girl going missing like, I'll be straight on that blower okay? But I ain't heard anything like that. And I'm not likely to.' He then expects me to make a purchase, so I do — of a strawberry yoghurt and a can of apricots in the Co-op. If by maintaining my bona fide artist's lifestyle by getting stoned occasionally, I've unintentionally contributed to the coffers of a criminal fraternity that are now holding Gina to ransom, then it's time to kick the habit. Either that or I'll try growing my own.

When I get home, there's a message on my landline's answering machine. It's Connell asking me to call him back. I play the message a couple of times. His tone of voice is even, measured. It doesn't sound as if he has had any worrying news at any rate. I don't call him straight back. I need to get things straight in my head. I've heard stuff I don't like the sound of concerning James Connell today, and I'm not sure getting too involved with him will actually bring me any closer to finding Gina.

I find myself looking up private investigators in my area. Yet I can't help thinking I've got so far into this thing on my own, I ought to continue that way. My mum used to have a saying 'Why keep a dog and bark yourself?' Thinking of dogs though only reminds me of Finn. I could do with his advice, but he did say to only call in an emergency. I think it might be prudent to wait.

I start looking online for tips to find missing persons. I'm fully expecting there to be YouTube 'how to' tutorials. It's how I changed the toilet flush valve and the kitchen light pull. They save you a fortune, those generous DIY demonstrators. If anyone ought to be in the New Year's honours list it's them. It's also where I learned some of my specialist cleaning skills, like the fact you never scour marble. There's a real skill to cleaning windows without leaving streaks, but it's fine if you watch a tutorial on your phone first. It's also where I learnt its bi-carb and vinegar for enamel baths but mild soap and water only for hardwood floors. My cleaning agency never bothered telling me any of this. They supply you with a box of the cheapest products they can lay their hands on and you end up buying most of what you actually need yourself. If you make a mistake and damage a Persian rug or parquet floor you're let go and the company's insurance covers the damage. It seems they'd rather do that than invest in training or quality products. Still, our company is one of the cheapest around, which is why they get contracts from councils and housing associations. Ultimately you get what you pay for, though if you're lucky enough to get me and you don't piss me off, I will do my best. Job satisfaction is a happy client.

I can't however find anything very helpful online regarding finding missing persons or negotiating with kidnappers. I leave our friendly neighbourhood copper a message to ask if there's been any more news her end but don't expect to hear back. You'd have thought, after I go to all the trouble of quoting the crime number every time I chase her up, she might bother once in a blue moon to give some kind of response, even if it's to tell me she's nothing new to report.

The doorbell is being briskly rung, again and again and again. I wish this flat had a door-chain. I should've installed one the moment things took the turn they have. We don't even have an intercom. I debate ignoring the urgent presses of the bell but curiosity gets the better of me. It's Connell. He wants to know way I haven't returned his call.

'Is there some news?' There is, the kidnappers have informed him that tomorrow they will be sending him details of when and where to leave the ransom of £600,000. They have apparently, so their latest letter explains, asked Gina to name a trustworthy person to deliver the money. Gina had obviously been at a loss to think of anyone in her life who fits that description, because she has chosen me.

I stare at Connell, not entirely convinced that he has said what I thought I heard him say. Then I laugh out loud. I can't help myself. I can't imagine Gina seeing me as a responsible person, I really can't. Connell, misunderstanding, pulls an envelope from his pocket, takes out the letter and slaps it down on the table in front of me.

Mr Connell, ask Gina's friend Yvonne to bring us the money tomorrow. Gina says she can be trusted. Send her alone. Later, we will give you the location.'

This is the first actual letter from the kidnappers I've seen. 'Oh, they've got a printer,' I say. Connell looks at me as if I've taken leave of my senses. I suppose I was expecting a letter made of cut up bits of newsprint. I mean if the kidnapper insists on using first class stamps on old style letters then it would be in keeping, as would typing it on a typewriter, or writing with a quill pen. This looks like an arial font, 12 point, and the printer cartridge, unlike the one in Mr Sullar's photocopier, is still thankfully fresh. Gina surely was being held somewhere with electricity like a home or office, unless the person posting the letters is sending them from elsewhere. I tell Connell he should be giving the letters to the police to check for fingerprints. 'Yvonne,' he says wearily, 'If you're sharp enough to kidnap someone, you're sharp enough not to leave fingerprints.'

'Or DNA? Licking the envelope?' Connell shakes his head. Looking at the envelope it's one of those self-stick ones anyway.

'Look, what I've come here to tell you is that as you're the one who will be delivering the ransom, you'll need to come over and be briefed by my people on how we're going to go about this, okay?'

'Your people?' He nods. Then Connell delivers another bombshell. He has only been able to raise just over £400,000 of the money, despite his best efforts. The other nearly £200,000 will be forgeries, only that's not exactly what he calls them. 'Coloured photocopies of notes' is how he puts it. To my mind that's worse, much worse than forgeries. I don't mean legally, I mean in terms of the potential to seriously antagonise Gina's kidnappers. I mean I'm sure we've all had the odd dud note slip through our hands without even clocking it, but colour photocopies? Have you ever made a copy of a banknote in the library copier and tried to pass it off as real? Not after the age of eight I bet you haven't. I know

Connell's a bit of a silver fox who harks from the days when the wad in your pocket was actually made of paper rather than plastic, but this is ridiculous. I tell him so and in not so many words.

'I don't have any other option. It's Gina's only chance.'

If the money drop is tomorrow then that only leaves me the rest of today to come up with a plan. I tell Connell I've work today, so can't come round and discuss ransom drops with 'his people' at present. It all seems a little premature anyway, bearing in mind that we don't yet know how or where it's going to occur. 'Are you free tonight?'

'Look, why don't you wait and see what their next move is first? Give me a call again as soon as you hear something. I'll have my mobile on me. There's no point in trying to make a plan until we hear more from the other side.' He admits I'm right and says he's got himself in a bit of a panic. Connell is one of those men who it's difficult to imagine panicking over anything. To be charitable, he does appear mildly flustered. In his books, maybe it counts as panicking.

Me, however, I am genuinely panicking. The thought of being the one delivering the ransom, as he has just sprung on me, is enough to make anyone hyperventilate. I don't like responsibility at the best of times and this could be a matter of life and death, for Gina or me, possibly even both of us. I've noticed that Connell hasn't even asked me if I'm willing to go through with it or not. He has just assumed I'll do it.

CHAPTER TEN

Traffic grinds by in an endless, slow-moving queue, and dust from the exhausts begrimes the pub's smoked-glass windows. I could leave a message in the thick, grey layer if I was into slow means of communication, like Gina's kidnappers. I'd forgotten this kind of old-fashioned London boozer still exists here and there. They're no longer found in the more up and coming areas of course. There they're certified as an extinct species. This isn't one of those newly aspirational areas. It's too far south of the river at the eastern end of things.

Personally, I'm relieved to walk in and spy a paisley carpet and red-flocked wallpaper. There are real dark-wood sofas, chairs and tables too, which is a definitely a bonus. A couple of months back, I met with a woman who runs an arts collective in Islington. The pub she chose seems to think metal scaffolding with narrow wooden bench tops will suffice as seating. To make matters worse it seems they'd built this furniture, and I'm using the term loosely, with the six-foot tall and doubtlessly male customer in mind. As a female of average height, I spent my meeting trying to avoid my arse overhang destabilising my position, whilst swinging my feet, which hung uncomfortably above the floor like those of a toddler in a high chair. The floor was just boards of course, so rough you could get splinters in your feet just by looking at it. 'Course I never heard back about joining the arts collective. I'm not young, hip or middle-class enough, clearly. Well actually I'm not middle class at all. It's probably why I feel more at home in this old-time pub. I bet they used to have proper knees-ups here back in the time of Queen Anne or whatever. Funny how Spain still has the tango, Austria the waltz, but you can't find a cockney knees-up anywhere in London any more. A bit like trying to buy a 'kiss me quick' hat in Brighton, I suppose. Someone should bring those back. The hipsters would love them.

It's quiet in here. The landlord is polishing glasses. He seems to be working alone, so this obviously isn't a busy time. Either that or it's the least popular establishment hereabouts. The only signs of life are three guys having some kind of meeting in a corner snug. One of them clocks me. His face is an homage to the art of shiftiness. Perhaps places like this are specifically preserved as sanctuaries for veteran villains and other old lags. You can almost imagine it on one of those charity adverts in the middle of the afternoon movie on Talking Pictures. 'Ron and Billy Boy used to run this neighbourhood, but every year increased gentrification has reduced their territory by the size of a half a dozen football pitches. Soon there'll be nowhere for them to talk about the old days and offload knock-off watches and dodgy cigs.'

I can't see the person I'm here to meet. Presuming he's not yet arrived, if indeed he is coming at all, I purchase myself a cranberry juice. Alcohol in a pub tends to make me drowsy, especially if there's an open fire as there is here, and I need to stay sharp, not get comfortable.

I've cancelled today's cleaning jobs, or rather I've passed them on to Sophia without going through our boss Janice. I visited a couple of Sophia's clients unofficially last month, when her son was off school sick. She still needed the money so didn't tell Janice about our job swap. That way Sophia was paid and could still make her rent, on the understanding that when I needed the equivalent amount of hours covered, she'd do it for me, unpaid.

My eyes roam back to the three guys in the corner. The one directly opposite with his back to me catches my eye, as he half-turns to keep an eye on the door. It *is* Finn. The reason I didn't immediately recognise him is because today he is wearing a sharp grey suit and his hair's been cut short. The short back and sides, while making him look slightly less roguish, also reveals just how classically handsome he is, throwing his jawline and cheekbones into sharp relief. I can't help thinking like a sculptor, whatever the circumstances.

I catch Finn's eye and he beckons me over. His friends nod to me and move away. Their hard faces, blunt manners, and the way they're very deferential to Finn, make me slightly anxious. Possibly they're even afraid of him. I remember Connell saying Finn was a loner who didn't work with others. This perhaps isn't as accurate intelligence as Connell believes. I sit down opposite Finn. 'You're looking almost respectable,' I tell him, trying to ease my nerves.

'Not for your benefit,' he grins.

'No?' I tease, but add only semi-jokingly. 'Pity.' With a twinge of jealousy, I wonder whose benefit it is for. Finn leans back, watching my face. He's too sharp to hide much from, and I look away.

'Had to impress the judge. I was in court this morning,' he offers at last. 'Only a minor thing. And they've adjourned it again anyway.' Although he acts nonchalantly about the court appearance, I can see tension in his face. Possibly it's rather less trivial than he's making out.

'Perhaps then I shouldn't be burdening you with my troubles.'

'From what you said on the phone you probably should.' I look at him, unsure what he means. 'Look, tell me the whole thing so far. Everything you know.'

'Would you like another drink first?'

'Why not?'

Bringing the beers, I slip into the seat next to Finn, and lean forward to take him into my confidence. He leans in too. We both make the gesture appear slightly flirtatious for the benefit of anyone watching, through nobody is near enough to overhear us talking quietly. I notice he has positioned himself where he can keep an eye on both doors into the bar. It's probably an old habit. I speak softly, telling him all the details surrounding the ransom demands. He says nothing, though occasionally looks slightly incredulous. Finally I tell him about the instructions for the ransom drop. 'It shouldn't be you. Don't do it,' he says immediately. 'We don't know what their game is.' He sits back in his chair. 'It's not straightforward. There's something more to this than we know.' He sips his beer. 'That's what's worried me all along.

186

I can't see the whole picture.' I nod, me neither. 'There's something phoney about all of this, Vonnie.'

'Phoney?'

'It doesn't smell right. Something doesn't add up. There's a reason no one does ransom kidnappings anymore. They don't work.'

'How do you…'

'You watch the news? How many stories are there involving ransom notes?'

'I don't think I've actually ever seen one. Well not in Britain.'

'My point exactly.'

'Perhaps though, people just pay up and don't involve the police. Or maybe the police keep it quiet…' He's shaking his head and I realise I can't even convince myself with this argument. 'We do at least now know that the kidnapper or kidnappers actually have Gina, as they sent a dated photo.'

'You said on the phone they also upped their ransom demand. Like they suddenly decided they'd set it too low, or they needed more money. I mean – what?' He raises his palms in disbelief. 'What do you make of that?'

'Not very professional.'

'Bit of an understatement, Von. To me, it's off-the-scale weird. Like I say, I don't think there are such things as professional kidnappers out there, and this bunch definitely aren't that. In a way that makes it worse. You might expect a ransom to be negotiated down a bit, but for the kidnapper to suddenly up it – why? Do they need the cash for some particular purpose and then the price of that thing went up? Or more likely they've realised they didn't ask for enough in the first place.' I hadn't really thought about either of these options, but they make sense as Finn says it. 'You know this would be funny if you weren't caught up in the middle of it.' I wonder if he was saying this from my point of view or his own. Does it matter to him that I am caught up in it? 'I can tell you this,' he continues, 'They've almost definitely not done something like this before and it'll make them unpredictable to deal with.'

'Unpredictable is bad?' I ask. Finn nods. 'Dangerous. An organised criminal who leaves little to chance is less likely to panic if things go wrong.' For a moment I feel like asking if he sees himself as an organised criminal, and reminding him that something had gone wrong on his last heist, namely his motorbike failing to start after he robbed the building society. Fortunately I've learnt over the years to think before I speak. It comes from being surrounded by artistic egos and it's a skill that's served me well. When Finn's immediate getaway had been thwarted, he hadn't panicked, I realise. He had changed plans quickly and decisively, by forcing Gina to be his driver. He had remained calm in the emergency. I remember too the second motorbike he had left up on the downs to aid his escape, and throw the police off his trail, if they had happened to be following. Finn had been organised, there is no doubt about that.

'Let's get one thing clear though,' Finn says, 'You've come here to ask for my help on your own behalf? Not because Connell has asked you to?'

'He doesn't know I'm here. He wants me to discuss how we're going to proceed with 'his people' as he calls them. But seeing how successful they've been so far at anything they've done, I'm not too keen.' He smiles at that, then looks at me, eyes serious again.

'So has Connell got the money together? Presumably he's going to pay up?'

'Well…' I say, taking a nervous look around and dropping my voice to a stage whisper that would do Bridie proud. 'He's got some of it.'

'Only some?' I explain about the photocopied notes. He sits bolt upright.

'Fuck! You're joking right?' He's angry, which takes me by surprise. 'That's total shit. That's never gonna work. You didn't say you'd do it Vonn? You didn't did you?'

I try to explain. 'Look you'd have to be incredibly stupid…'

'Yeah. Well perhaps I am stupid, Finn, but she's my friend.'

'Okay' he says more quietly. 'Okay, you're going to make the delivery. But only if he supplies all the cash.'

'Says he can't raise it.'

'Course he can. Sell a bloody chip shop.'

'I'm not sure he still actually owns them. I got the impression he's got serious debts.'

'Well, it's time he added to them. It's his daughter after all.' I nod. I can't say I disagree with him on this point. I'd move heaven and earth if it was my kid. I think most people would.

'Connell will know who he can borrow money from,' Finn says. 'He may not like the terms, but he'll know those people, trust me. You need to tell him to do that. He gets all the money or you're not doing it. You gotta tell him that.'

'Right....'

'He needs to know it's the bottom-line. Not negotiable.'

'Okay.'

'Okay,' he says, giving the room and the doors another quick, casual glance.

I wonder if this is Finn's local area, or if he has chosen to meet me somewhere away from his home patch. Perhaps he grew up around here, maybe even in a council block like me over in Thornton Heath. I wouldn't be surprised if his background is similar to mine. I don't think if art hadn't have come along I'd have ended up as an armed robber though. I expect I'd still have been a cleaner. Maybe these things are pre-destined. 'So why did you leave Sussex?' I ask.

'Well my home being torched for starters.' He asks if I've heard about the building society offering an unspecified reward for evidence leading to his capture. I nod. I tell him there's also been a description of him in the local paper and online. He says he's read it. Possibly it's also a factor in his changing his appearance.

'You weren't tempted by the reward?' he asks. I look at him shocked.

'I'm not that money oriented. Is that why you really left town though? Did you think I'd turn you in for the reward?'

'Someone else could've,' he says, but I sense that's not the whole truth. He definitely doesn't entirely trust me, though there's no reason why he should. 'Look, I don't understand why you don't give my name to the police. Or set me up.' He's finally levelling with me and saying what's on his mind.

'Did you think I was doing that today?' The thought creeps into my head.

'It crossed my mind.' I had thought the keeping-an-eye-on-the-doors thing was simply his usual level of vigilance.

'But you still met me?'

'I took certain precautions.' I don't ask him what they are. At a guess he's had me watched or followed. It's a little unnerving. I hadn't even considered he might believe I was setting him up. If I had known he thought that, I wouldn't have come here. I'd have judged it too dangerous. I suppose I'd naively thought we had some kind of understanding, due to my not telling the police about him earlier.

'Look Finn, I wouldn't set you up because I believe you're telling the truth about leaving Gina unharmed.'

'Or you're worried what I might do if you did?' he asks, but with no threat in the tone. I lower my voice.

'Armed robbery - you know they might shoot you?'

191

'Yeah.' He looks at me levelly. 'I do.'

'Well, I don't want that on my conscience, alright? If you want to go and get yourself gunned down by the cops then that's up to you, but it won't be my doing. I don't want anyone's blood on my hands – even yours!' Infuriatingly, he finds this amusing. 'Oh!' I find myself exclaiming, 'If you understood how guilty I feel about my flatmate. Not treating her as well as I should. Not being the friend she needed me to be. So I don't want anyone else's life or death weighing on my conscience. I don't want that responsibility.'

'Well you've got that now, haven't you, thanks to Connell.' I can't really argue with that. 'You didn't think perhaps you could use the reward for giving the police information about me as part of the ransom for your friend?' Again I hadn't even thought of this but he's clearly been mulling it over.

'No. No, I didn't. It hadn't crossed my mind. We don't even know how much they're offering and I'm sure they don't pay out instantly. It's probably only if or when you are convicted. That could be months or years down the line.' He says nothing, but continues to observe me closely, as if looking for some sign or tell, that I'm in some way trying to play him. I'm annoyed and frustrated. I'm not devious or a schemer, it's not how I am. I came here for one honest reason – I need someone to watch my back when I'm delivering the ransom. If he's not up for doing that, fine, I'll go home. I try one last time to explain. 'Look, Finn, grassing you up for cash is not something I'd feel comfortable doing right? It would be different if there had been violence or a murder involved. Then I'd have volunteered any information I had. And I wouldn't have asked for a reward. It's… it's kind of blood money…' I trail off. I'm still not sure I can really explain my feelings at this point.

'Vonn,' he says 'You need to keep your emotions out of things. You need to think about your situation clearly and coolly.'

'That's so much easier said than done! Especially with you winding me up. And you always seem to do that don't you?'

'Me?' he makes a big-eyed look of innocence, before conceding, 'Yeah, people do say that.'

'I don't want to be responsible for anything bad happening to Gina.' I say 'Or to anyone else for that matter. Even you.'

'Even me? Right.' A knowing smile flickers across his face.

'What?'

Finn drains his glass and rises. 'Come on.' He heads towards a narrow staircase at the back of the room. I'm aware of the barman glancing in our direction and then looking pointedly away, like he knows it's none of his business. He strikes me as a guy who is all too aware what not to see and what not to hear. Following Finn up the stairs, I notice for the first time there are a few flecks of grey in his hair, revealed now it is shorn close on the back his neck. I wonder how old he is and what's brought him to where he is today. I've been able to obtain so few pieces of his story. I wonder too about the silent respect of the guys in pub. What has he done to earn it? I dig my nails into my palms. It's irrelevant. My mission is to save Gina, that and nothing more.

We enter a small box room. There is a brown patch of damp spreading from the edge of the ceiling. The wallpaper has an orange geometric design, which would be ironically retro back in Brighton, but here it is merely old, mould-spotted and peeling. A bed is covered with an old, brown blanket and there's an old-fashioned alarm clock, and a slightly threadbare curtain impaled on nails rather than hanging from a rail. 'You live here?'

'I can tell you're impressed,' Finn says, perpetually evasive. He pats the bed for me to sit down. The mattress is not as uncomfortable as I'd expected. He stoops to take a small wooden box from under the bed. For a moment, for some bizarre reason I think it's one of those urns that contain someone's cremated remains. I can't imagine why he'd want me to look upon a dearly departed friend or relative, but then it has been one of those weeks. He undoes the latch and lifts the lid of box. It doesn't have ashes inside. It contains a handgun.

Seeing my eyes widen, Finn slowly unloads the gun, letting the bullets roll on the chipboard bedside table. I can't help but stare at them. If you discount Phil's leg, this is the closest I've ever been to a bullet. He offers me the gun. I hesitate. 'You take this, you go home and tomorrow you sit tight until I get there. If I do get delayed or can't make it for any reason, at least you've got this as a deterrent.'

'Take it with me when making the ransom drop?' He nods. 'If it was loaded you might have a problem pointing it at someone, I don't know. But like this it's easy.' I take the pistol and point it at him.

'See?' I wonder if he's right. Could I point a loaded gun at someone? Possibly, though I'd need to know what I was doing and that I couldn't shoot them accidentally. How do you know if you could shoot someone? Perhaps you don't until you try. 'Up a couple of inches, both hands, brace yourself.' He takes my hands and guides the gun up a little. 'Legs slightly apart, so you've a solid base.' I don't think I'm totally convinced I could point a loaded gun at someone. As it is, it still feels powerful. I guess this is what Finn wants me to feel. I'll have some way of exiting after leaving the money and hopefully collecting Gina. It'll be something the kidnappers probably won't have bargained for, particularly if they're as disorganised as Finn thinks they are.

Holding the gun though is only acting, I tell myself and I must do it convincingly. I'm definitely not in Bridie's league. She played a spy in a straight-to-video thriller, and I remember her character shooting some baddie while jumping over a car bonnet in a short skirt. She still has a scar on her knee where she caught it on the aerial stub. The only acting I've done was in a few school plays. I was a female shepherd in the Nativity, a shopkeeper in something written by the drama teacher and Juliet's sister Jackie in 'Romeo and Juliet.' Yes, I know Shakespeare didn't write a part for a sibling of Juliet, especially one rather improbably named Jackie, but there aren't enough female roles in the original, and the drama teacher thought she could do rather better. Jackie did at least get to wave a rapier about and do a little fighting, after I badgered the teacher to make her less soppy and give her at a bit of sword action.

Despite my thoughts drifting back to my only previous experience of weapon-wielding, I manage to keep my expression hard, eyes and gun focused on my target – Finn's heart. He nods and says he'd believe that. He opens my shoulder bag and drops the gun inside, then checks the time on his phone. 'Looks like we've both time to grab a quick lunch. Unless there's anything else you fancy.'

It's a moment before I realise what he's meaning. My expression of slow-dawning incredulity makes him laugh out loud. 'Okay, okay, it's definitely the pub's ploughman's.' He moves towards the door. I find myself stepping quickly sideways to prevent him leaving. I can tell from his eyes that he knows how badly I want him. It's infuriating. He holds back, daring me to make a move on him. His mouth twists, hungry, cruel but completely bloody irresistible. I'm buzzing but still shocked at the sharpness of my desire. Too light-headed to remember why or how, I feel his cheek beneath my finger as I stroke its contours. I must make another attempt at sculpting this head. Then I'm stroking the back of his neck and we're kissing hard and hungrily. 'Come on, muss up my hair and get this suit off me.' It's more than lust though, or feels like it is. It's good.

* * * * *

I'm on my way back to the bus stop when I realise I've left my jacket slung over a chair-back, downstairs in the pub. It's only denim, but it's a nice one, even if it did come from the Dogs Trust shop. Retracing my steps, I see Finn leaving the pub. He doesn't see me. He has an elderly lurcher on a lead. Peggy! From this distance I can't be sure it's the same dog. He certainly didn't have a dog with him downstairs or upstairs in the pub. She must've, I'm guessing, been asleep under one of the tables, in the saloon part of the bar, or the beer garden behind. It is a very disconcerting development.

I wait until Finn and his canine companion have disappeared up the street before re-entering the pub. My jacket is not on the chair where we sat. I don't know whether I'm surprised or not. If my trust in human nature were a compass it would currently be veering wildly. The barman sees me and beckons me over. He lifts the jacket from behind the pump and hands it to me. He tells me to take care, rather pointedly. I look back as I go to leave and there is something akin to concern on his face.

'That dog that was in here?' I ask. 'It belongs to Finn?'

'Yeah.'

'Is she called Peggy?'

'Might well be, I don't know.' He walks away and turns his back to pick up a tray upon which he'd been previously cutting up lemons. If I was an actor depicting him in a play, I think this is what Bridie would call 'a bit of business.' Its purpose would be to end an uneasy conversation the character didn't want to be having about someone he isn't meant to talk about. I take the hint and go.

On the train back to Brighton, all I can think about is that wretched dog. Finn had, after all, told me she was dead. He attacked Connell over it. I've seen the dog's grave in the woods where he buried her, after collecting her body from the vet. 'Finn,' I say to myself, 'Congratulations, you have just returned to my list of suspects.' While it feels satisfying to say this, I realise returning someone to the list of suspects when

197

you've just had, albeit very satisfying, sex with them is unfortunate to say the least. I know I've made a hasty and serious error of judgement. The sex also makes the resurrected dog thing feel like a bigger betrayal than it probably is. There's a reason why Miss Marple, Poirot and Sherlock Holmes didn't sleep with anyone involved with their cases. It's because it would impair their judgment. Okay, in Miss Marple's case, perhaps it just wasn't the done thing. Mickey Rourke in 'Angel Heart' doesn't share these scruples, but then he's not really the kind of private detective I should be modelling myself on. I've always needed role models – whether rock musicians, artists or movie stars. I like to start each day with their posters looking down on me because that way I can channel a little of their confidence and banish the self-doubts and impostor syndrome. The ticket inspector makes his way along the carriage and automatically I unzip my bag to rummage for my purse, almost exposing the .45 calibre pistol it contains. I need to be careful, much more careful.

It's raining again as I leave Brighton station and it's starting to get dark. I keep looking behind me to see if I'm being followed. I wish Finn hadn't put that idea in my head. Earlier he'd seemed to hint he'd had me followed on my way to meet him. I know I'd be ultra-careful too in his position, but it does nothing to calm my jitters. If someone is following me, or was earlier as I walked back to the station, then I'm none the wiser. It reminds me of Connell leaving the plant in his window as a message to the kidnappers. His camera didn't pick up an image of them and yet they must've seen it as they responded. I hate things I know are probably happening, but that I can't see. I shiver and it's not just the rain running down

198

my ears. Tonight my own street feels creepy and menacing. I swing around at every footfall. A man putting something in a communal recycling bin makes me jump. I see a woman at her window and feel her eyes watch me walk on alone down the street. In my head, I keep seeing Finn and that brindle lurcher.

The one thing I am sure of is that Finn didn't see me as he left the pub with the dog. His back was to me and he didn't turn. He doesn't seem to feel the need to watch his own back, despite putting this fear into me. Maybe he has enough others watching it for him. There's something I know I need to do. It's something I'm not entirely comfortable about, but given the situation, I've not been left with much choice. If I'm making this ransom drop, I must be thinking clearly. While there's a distracting side-mystery, or unanswered questions to trouble my mind, I won't be able to do that. I wish I hadn't contacted Finn. I should have left him out of all of this.

* * * * *

Grave robbing isn't something I ever thought I'd need to stoop to. There are probably fewer grave robbers left in the UK these days than there are highwaymen, or for that matter kidnappers. Not that I'm really going to be grave robbing in the true sense. I'm heading out into the woods just outside of Steyning, with a shovel on the back seat of Gina's car. If the dog is dead and lying in the earth, then I'll let her be. I simply don't know what I'm going to find until I start digging, but I'm hoping it will be nothing. If that was Peggy I saw in London, there should be nothing there. I don't want to do this, let alone on my own, but I can't get any of my friends involved. It could be dangerous, and it would need a lot of explaining. I can't even tell Bridie, as she's a dog owner herself. If I try to explain to Sol or Jake why I need to know whether or not a dog is buried in the woods, it would involve mentioning Finn and what has happened today, or at least the downstairs part of it. What happens in Deptford stays in Deptford, that's how I feel about that. The thing with the dog though, well that's slightly more complicated.

I set my torch on the ground to give me something to work by. The earth covering Peggy's grave is solid, firm and hard to shift. I've only just broken the topsoil. Every time I push the shovel in it sounds horribly loud. I think of Connell's man Phil getting shot in the woods. Anyone could be lurking about out here. Finn could have followed me back down here, or one of his friends. Connell could be around, or more likely some more of his associates. The sound of digging could summon the landowner, presumably the local farmer. He or she is another person who might well be carrying a shotgun and happy to use it first and ask questions later. The shovel is a new one and cost a pretty penny from the only reasonably late-opening DIY chain in Brighton. It shines silver in the moonlight and when caught in the glare of my torch. A dog barks, nearby. I freeze, and put out the light, crouching in the wet grass. For a moment I wonder if it is a real dog I heard or the ghost of that poor deceased hound, horribly disfigured from the fire. I dig my nails in my palms hard enough to draw blood, which isn't very sensible mid-dig. My hands are getting sore from all the tension lately and I've mouth ulcers from grinding my teeth at night. I've enough problems being caused by the living, I tell myself, so it's hardly the time to start worrying about ghosts.

I hear the bark again and recognise it from my Queen's Park shape-shifting session. It's only a fox. Returning to the excavation I work determinedly. The more I dig the surer I am there's nothing at all buried here. I must be a good metre into the earth now. There's a sudden rustling and snapping of twigs. This time I take cover among the trees, shivering, partly with cold but partly in fear. It's a cliché but my heartbeat sounds so loud to me I'm convinced anyone in the vicinity can also hear it. My fingers are numb in my gloves. I pull my woollen hat down further over my face. If someone is about, I don't want to be recognised. I'm wearing a full-length coat tonight, not the jacket I wore to London. It's emerald green and I wish it was a duller colour like olive or khaki. If I'd thought about it, and had the time, I'd have kittled myself out properly in camouflage gear from the army surplus store. I dislodge a bit of soil from my forehead and in the process somehow manage to rub it into my eyes. They sting and water. I must look like I'm crying and I'm starting to feel I will be in a minute. I'm on the verge of giving up.

Out of the thicket in front of me steps a roe deer. I can just make its silhouette against the sky. I recognise it from drawing one from a wildlife book as a child. It sniffs the air then, no doubt getting a whiff of my Miss Dior perfume, bolts back into the woods. I decide to give the excavation one last go. I dig deep, so to speak, shoving the spade in and stamping it down into the hole with my foot. I feel a jolt as I hit something unyielding. Reaching down, I scrabble with my hands, snagging a fingernail on a plant root. There is something here. It feels smooth and slippery. I recoil. The torch identifies it as a black plastic bin liner with something wrapped up inside it. I feel sick. It can only be the poor dog.

I've just dug up someone's beloved companion. Finn wasn't lying. This must be the remains of old Peggy. There has to be another explanation for what I saw in London. Finn must have another, second dog, who looks remarkably like Peggy. Maybe it's one of her puppies or a sibling. Either that or he's obtained another similar animal straight away. I realise I'm only coming up with these logical explanations because I don't want to lift the sack from the hole and actually look inside to confirm the identification. I'm trying to convince myself that I don't need to take a peek. Yet I know I need to. It will be a tiny look to see a glimpse of brindle fur. That's all I need do. Then I'll replace the poor dog in her grave and bury her again, as respectfully as I can. Tomorrow I'll bring some flowers to put on her grave. The thought of tomorrow makes my stomach lurch. Tomorrow is also the day of the ransom drop, and Connell hasn't even been in touch about the details yet.

I lift out the sack. It is heavy and firm. Laying it carefully on the grass by the grave I fumble to remove the masking tape holding it shut. I make a little hole but there's no way I'm putting my hand inside. Nervously I shine the torch into the bag. I see a small eye looking back up at me. It doesn't belong to a lurcher. It's the Queen looking back at me.

*****

I sit in the Brighton all night café, alongside the cabbies and truckers. They're tucking into fry ups but I'm simply nursing a coffee. I don't feel hungry. I've parked Gina's car outside in a space where I can see it. The dirty shovel is on the back seat. In the boot is a large, black polythene sack bursting with money. It is a great deal of cash by the quick look I took of it

202

upon digging it up. It's bundles of new looking notes. In the newspaper, they said that the raider of the building society must have had some kind of inside knowledge. On that day the branch had, unusually for them, a large quantity of cash bagged up in the small safe behind the counter. It was waiting for a customer to collect. It didn't say exactly how much he got away with. I suppose they don't want things like that getting out. I can't even estimate the figure the bag contains, but I remember seeing the wads of notes being handed over during the raid.

I wish the late night radio station they favour in the café wouldn't play heartbreakers. I could do with an angry song right now. My phone sits in front of me, still waiting for a call from Connell. A group of young clubbers come in for strong coffees and chocolate bars. They were me, a decade ago. They are the kind of people I still like to see myself as: a kind of freewheeling bohemian with no responsibilities. There comes a time when it starts to feel a little false and hollow, and I think that time might just have come. Tonight I wish I was tucked up in bed either alone or with a reliable partner. I think I just got real – or do I mean old? One of the clubbers calls out to me. She wants to know if I know the stop for the night bus back to Mile Oak. Of course I do. I know where to get all the night buses from and at what times they're likely to arrive. I could still tell you where all the best club nights are too on any given evening, and even which ones will still admit people at this late hour. I'm tempted, very tempted, to go and hit the dance floor myself, to work off some stress and frustration. Then I look down at my mud-caked boots and realise that in this state I'm unlikely get past even the friendliest of door staff.

Why did Finn lie to me about burying his dog in the woods when she is alive and well and clearly living with him in London? I wouldn't have expected him to tell me where he'd hidden the proceeds of the robbery in a field. I wouldn't have been offended by that. This lie about the dog though, feels personal and ugly. I sincerely wish I'd taken him up on that cheese ploughman's sandwich rather than the other option. I'm sure I wouldn't feel so deceived and bitter if lunch was all we'd shared. Afterwards, when we lay cuddled up together, I realised it's that relaxed warmth and togetherness I've been missing as much as anything else. Loneliness has made me let my guard down. It's making me doubt I'll have the ability to see clearly, act rationally and do the right thing tomorrow, at the moment when it'll count the most. Finn's played me, presumably because he's intent on protecting his loot. Money clearly comes before anything else for him. The irony is, if he'd trusted me enough to let me know the cash was there, I'd have left it alone.

* * * * *

Back in my too quiet flat, I start preparing things for the next day. I'm going to wear dark clothes for the ransom drop, in the hope they make me slightly less of a target. Not camouflage gear though. I've now decided against the whole army surplus thing. I don't want the kidnappers to think the military or plain-clothes police officers are now involved. It might scare them into doing something rash or stupid. I remember what Finn said about them needing to get rid of a hostage as soon as possible, and that having a prisoner with you would slow you down. If they are spooked into feeling they need to make a fast getaway, Gina might end up paying with her life.

I'll wear my navy puffa coat. If I've time I'll pop into a shop first thing in the morning where I get my aprons and overalls, for both cleaning and sculpting. It's a workwear specialist where they sell everything from chef's whites to hi-viz tabards and hard hats. I'm sure the last time I was in there, to stock up on rubber gloves in the annual sale, I noticed stab vests hanging up on a wall. If they do bulletproof ones too, that would be all the better. I can probably get one or the other reasonably comfortably under my emerald puffa coat. It's probably better to just wear a t-shirt underneath that, despite the chilly weather, as I imagine it could get a bit hot and sticky in a stab vest. Holes to let the wearer breathe would, I imagine defeat the whole object of the thing. I try putting the gun in the pocket of my coat and drawing it from there but it doesn't work. As its not loaded, I suppose I can stick it down the back of the waistband of my jeans. I've seen them do that in cop dramas on the telly. With a long coat like the puffa it doesn't work. I ditch the coat for a short, quilted bomber jacket. Unfortunately it's in a silver metallic colour that will make me a bit more of a target. If I put the gun in the right place though, it is completely covered, but I can draw it reasonably quickly. I'll practise a few times in front of the mirror until I get the hang of it. I was thinking of wearing sunglasses, but since I don't know if I'll be delivering the money during daylight hours, perhaps I won't bother. The BBC weather app is suggesting overcast and rain for the morning anyway. Stepping out of the bath, I look at my face in the mirror and wonder what on earth I've let myself in for. Will today be the day I finally see Gina again, or will it be my last day on Earth?

CHAPTER ELEVEN

My phone alerts me to a new message. It's not from Connell but my boss, Janice at the cleaning agency. She wants to know if I could cover an emergency in Hove. An elderly woman named Maggie has left her bath taps on all night and flooded her bungalow. She's one of Samira's regulars normally, but Sam is currently in Scarborough visiting a new niece. I accept the assignment on the understanding I've a bit of an emergency of my own that could mean I have to leave the job and rush off at any time. Clearly nobody else is readily available, as Janice accepts this without the usually gripes and quibbles. I've been on her books for over three years now, which makes me something of a veteran at the company. I'm not saying Janice's management skills leave something to be desired, but as most people leave before even completing their trial periods, it might be considered a fair assessment. I usually work solo but on the occasions I have been teamed up with another cleaner, he or she has tended to be full of moans and grumbles about the penny-pinching company and how unreasonable they are over allocating the work. These people always say they could get paid more and obtain better hours elsewhere and then they leave. I suppose I ought to keep in touch next time, so I can discover whether there really are benevolent, generous cleaning firms out there, ones that don't expect you to buy your own kit, and don't deny you any hours for a week at least if you don't agree to sanitise a filthy hovel for a difficult client. From what I've seen from the job sites however, it's a case of the grass not being much greener elsewhere.

Maggie, as it turns out, is a lovely woman. She is deeply apologetic about the sopping mess she has made, and despite being barely able to shuffle with a walking frame, wants to help me strip the bedding and armchair covers. It takes all my powers of persuasion to make her sit and drink her Ovaltine, while I take up the rugs and start mopping. 'Clothes airers?'

'Oh yes!' says Maggie, 'In the kitchen cupboard, dear.' Older folk do tend to have a reassuring amount of airers. Gina and I don't possess one between us. I don't even know where you buy them, unless it's from one of those specialist letter-boxed sized catalogues that are always piled up on my clients' doorsteps. Perhaps I should take one home and have a look at it one of these days. I'm sure I'd find lots of useful gadgets I've been struggling to live without. Since Gina and I don't even have a balcony, I don't know how we'd dry our rugs and other non-washables if we were flooded the way Maggie is. I do however have four large chequered laundry bags that I take on these kinds of jobs, plus I know a really good, cheap and efficient laundrette. If you own a washing machine and tumble dryer you may not have noticed this, but laundrettes are becoming rare now. The days when you could find one along with a betting shop, a hairdressers and a bookie in every shop block are long gone. The bookies are still there, but not much good for laundering, unless of course you're talking about money. Mr Connell, I am thinking of you here.

Regarding dirty money, or at least money that was wrapped in a very dirty bin liner, I have at least counted it. There is £220,520 in 50s and 20s. It's sitting at home, in a holdall, as sadly I have plans for it. Unfortunately those plans don't include a holiday somewhere warm where I might meet a handsome Mr Right who doesn't commit robberies for a living or tell lies about the health of his canine companion.

This particular launderette is the best in Brighton. Unlike most, they've invested in the latest machines and dryers. Time is everything today. I'd like to get Maggie's settee cover bedcover, and full-length, lined curtains back to her before Connell calls me with instructions.

* * * * *

At midday, the washing is done, the rugs are drying nicely and there has been no call from Connell. Feeling a little jittery now, I call him. He answers immediately. The post hasn't yet arrived. 'Is that *still* the only way these kidnappers communicate with you?' He says it is and it's usually arrived by lunchtime.

'And what if you don't get post today? Or you do but the instructions aren't clear?' Even over the phone I can hear him pacing.

'I don't know, Yvonne. I don't know.' I ask if he has tried calling the post office, to see if the postal worker serving his street has headed out on his or her round. He says he has indeed tried and received an automated response.

I suggest I come round and collect the ransom money. He expresses surprise, but I tell him it means I'll then be all ready to roll, if we only have short notice when the demand finally arrives. Connell reluctantly agrees. Perhaps he thinks I'm going to do a runner with the money myself. There's precious little trust in my life at present, either from or towards me. That was the thing with Gina. I could trust her and in spite of everything, when it mattered, she knew she could trust me.

* * * * *

At Connell's house, he ushers me into his study. One of the big, burly guys who work for him is sitting in there already. Looking up from his phone, the man-mountain stares at me gimlet-eyed as I walk in. Connell waits for me to sit down before telling me he actually has no intention of handing me the case of money in advance. I start to suspect by asking for him to do that, I have made him again imagine I might be in some way involved with the kidnapping. He says the one thing he isn't is stupid. That's a shame as it happens, as I had been hoping to be able to pull some sleight of hand. My reason for wanting the money in advance isn't the one I've given Connell. What I'd like is time to swap out all of the dud notes for the real ones from Finn's bin liner. If you were going to accept a ransom, you'd check it carefully and count it before you released your captive, wouldn't you? After going to all the trouble of staging a kidnapping, anyone would. I'm sure Finn is right when he said it was incredibly dangerous for Connell to try to short-change Gina's captors. If I leave Connell's photocopied bank notes in the case, that's risking her life, and very possibly mine. This way, as long as Finn doesn't find out I've taken his robbery proceeds, I've at least some chance of no one getting hurt.

I'd also like to return home to collect the empty pistol before making the drop. I haven't brought it over to Connell's house with me as I couldn't have been sure he wouldn't have me searched on entry. Telling him about the gun is another complication I could do without. I need to do this thing my way.

I notice the big, heavy briefcase being used for the money drop has a combination lock. I tell Connell he'll need to let me know the combination, as the kidnappers may want to meet face to face and have me show them the money. They will certainly want to check it before they release Gina. Connell grunts that it won't be locked. Then he sits there in silence, as does his employee. I get up to go, but as I do they both stand too. It's a little unnerving. 'I think we'll all sit here and wait together, Yvonne,' says Connell. He doesn't say it like I've any choice in the matter.

'Do you fancy a game of cards? Either of you? Poker or whatever?' Neither of them answers. I could sit there scrolling my phone now I've run out of small talk. There are some photos I've taken of some of my new pieces I could do with uploading to Instagram and my website, but I don't really feel like doing it. What is the point of advertising your new work if you're not entirely sure you're going to live long enough to sell any of it? I've a few emails to answer, but most are from galleries or dealers saying while they enjoyed looking at the links I sent to my most recent pieces, they don't feel quite strongly or passionately enough to take me on or offer an exhibition. The other most common response is that my sculptures aren't 'quite the right fit for us' whatever that means. There are a few invites to forthcoming private views, from people who are friends of friends. Gina has a Facebook site, but rarely updates it. I check again out of habit, but then I expect Connell has been doing so regularly and would have told me if there had been any recent posts. There's nothing. Idly I try to find a website or socials for the pub where I met Finn. It doesn't seem to have an online presence, or even a review on a travel site. It's as if yesterday afternoon was just a figment of my imagination, either that or I'd stepped through a portal into an alternative reality. I wish either were true. I sigh and fidget. Connell sighs without fidgeting. It's lunchtime. 'I don't feel particularly hungry,' I say, 'but I probably ought to eat something to keep my strength up for the job.'

'We're on the app.'

'Sorry?'

'The chip shop. You can order and have it delivered here.'

'Right. And hopefully you'll pick up the bill.' This doesn't raise even a flicker of amusement. In fact we're all so tense that if like Bridie we'd been to LAMDA, we'd all be audibly cracking our knuckles, or at least the blokes would. I've never seen a woman crack her knuckles in a movie or TV show. I think that's rather sexist, as it is perfectly possible, trust me, though I'm not going to demonstrate right now. I'm a very loud knuckle cracker. I think the blokes would jump out of their skins.

This theory is almost proven as we all jump in unison as the letterbox bangs. Connell's colleague heads out down the hall. If it's just a pizza leaflet and guff about cut price bikini waxes I think I will actually scream.

It's an envelope. A small brown envelope, like the sort HMRC use when demanding my national insurance contribution, only without the address window. The last envelope the kidnappers used was white, but this may or may not be relevant. Connell opens it and lays the letter out on the table for us all to read. The ransom drop is to be tonight.

The letter is in the same font as before and says I'm to drive alone to a lay-by in a country lane on the other side of the South Downs and '*await instructions over the exchange*'. It also gives the exact grid reference as to where I'm supposed to wait. We all consult our separate map apps. Connell has the current iPhone. Even calling my mobile smart is stretching it a bit, but unlike my fellow map readers I go straight to the street view of the location. It's a narrow, winding road, with woods on either side. 'Not in the woods again,' I groan, before I can stop myself. Connell looks at me quizzically, but I'm saying nothing about undead mutts, shot guys named Phil, psychics mentioning trees or puking bank robbers.

'It's to be at ten pm,' says Connell, unnecessarily confirming what we've all just read. 'So they've chosen a location that will be quiet, no doubt.' I say I'm very sorry but being as the ransom drop has now been confirmed as scheduled for the late evening, I'm definitely going to need to go home in the meantime rather than wait about here. For a start I'm going to need my waterproof jacket, torch and probably my wellies, in case the kidnappers expect me to yomp across muddy countryside. It's no good my wearing my current hi-top sneakers and becoming stuck in a mire while Gina's captors are waiting. Connell is not keen to let me go. 'My ex left a number of coats here. I'm sure one of them would fit you.' I wonder whether he means his former girlfriend was a stick insect, but at least one of her coats is a baggy enough style to cope with my curves. I'm not wearing some other woman's abandoned clothes for the ransom drop. It's not that I've a problem with pre-loved outerwear. Almost everything I own comes from a charity shop, jumble sale or skip. If the coat belonged to Helen from the Bognor chippy or some other former woman friend of Connell's, however, I can envisage that might cause me a problem on the night. 'Mr Connell, they did ask for me specifically to deliver the money. Now if I turn up in somebody else's coat, they might very well not realise its me.' Helen had, after all been on a couple of dates with some other dodgy geezer in the money-laundering racket, if what Margarita had told me was accurate. Suppose he was behind Gina's abduction, and then he saw what he thought was Helen approaching having been primed to look out for me? Ending up dead in a ditch sounds like a possible outcome.

'So you're assuming they'll know what you look like?' asks Connell, still keen for me stay. I clearly need to spell it out for him.

'If they have Gina with them. She knows what I look like. Well I hope she'll be there. They do mention it being an exchange. I take that as meaning they'll take the case, and I'll take Gina, rather than them taking the money and her being released later. Is that how you read it, Mr Connell?'

'Possibly.' If he knows more than I do on this score, he's not giving anything away.

'And if they ask, 'is that Vonnie?' and Gina hesitates cos I'm wearing...'

213

'Yes, I get it,' Connell snaps. 'Mitch will accompany you back to your place and wait there with you.' So the big guy is Mitch. I wonder idly if that's his first name or surname.

We all jump again as the doorbell rings. Mitch goes to answer it. Connell looks at me, I look at Connell. Today he looks as though he hasn't slept. He still, to my mind, doesn't look quite as worried as he ought to. I'm still not one hundred percent convinced he doesn't know more about who has Gina or where she is than he's telling. I could be completely wrong about that though.

Gran used to have audio books when her eyesight started to go. She used to like detective stories, particularly hard-boiled, American ones. When I was round there I used to sit and listen with her. One of the first things I noticed was that the police officer or private investigator always had hunches that proved correct. It was either that or a sixth sense that told him or her when someone was lying, or intuition that guided the sleuth in the right direction. The gumshoe or cop themselves tended to be the one telling the story. '*I had the sense something wasn't straight about that dame the moment she walked in off the street*'. You know the kind of thing. I don't know if any of the writers of those books had worked as an investigator, but I assume if you are in the detecting game full-time, you quickly learn how to read people or how to finely tune your bullshit detector. I'm a sculptor who cleans, or a cleaner who sculpts. I don't have an 'A' level in criminology, skills in forensic what-do-you-call-it or a degree in psychological bollocks. If I filled in one of those online recruitment agency forms where an algorithm identifies your skill set, it would probably suggest I stick to the arts and hygiene related fields. I'm not just out of my depth, I'm lying on the bottom of the swimming pool with my lungs full of chlorine and wee.

Mitch returns to the room. He carries three take-away boxes. The person at the door was a courier from Connell's shop bringing pies and chips. I hadn't even realised they sold a vegan pie until I asked the boss. He'd got on the phone and apparently Eileen found a few in the bottom of the freezer. She has cooked up this mushroom and chestnut special for me. It looks so good that on any other day I'd have taken a photo for my Instagram, despite being generally against posting photos of food. Today though, my stomach feels so tight I don't know how I'm going to get my lunch down. Don't get me wrong, I've nothing against the countryside and especially not trees. I mean, we all need to breathe from time to time. Jake used to belong to a group that lived in makeshift tree houses, while trying to stop the building of the Hastings bypass. I admire him for that. I cut down my soya consumption when I realised rainforests were being cut down to grow it. I switched to almond and oat milk, which I hope, have a little less environmental impact. So while I'm not a tree-hugger, and tend to swerve the whole climate change protest scene, I don't take issue with tall things bearing leaves. It's simply, I'd feel a lot happier about this ransom thing if it was happening somewhere in the city. I'm a townie at heart and my natural environment is the urban sprawl. Right now, I'd take a grubby industrial estate or rubbish-strewn back alley over having to enter the woods again alone. I know I'm not really going to be alone. Mitch will be tailing me, like a great, clumsy bear looking for a picnic. That will, I fear, make things worse, and a lot more perilous for both me and for Gina. Over lunch, I try desperately to make Connell see this, but he is insistent he won't let me make the drop without one of his guys tailing me. There must be some way of getting rid of Mitch. When we're back at mine, I'll try to concoct a plan.

* * * * *

Mitch is sitting in my lounge, but he keeps the case containing the money next to him. Connell has stayed at his own place in case the kidnappers should, by some means or other, be in touch again. He muttered something about, 'in case of a second post,' but that hasn't happened since about 1983. Back at mine, I offer Mitch a coffee, and when he accepts, I make it in the biggest mug I can find. Unless I'm the biggest mug myself of course. After yesterday's London trip, I fear I might be. Anyway the plan behind the near gallon of coffee is that Mitch will then need to visit the loo at some point soon. While he's powdering his nose, so to speak, and providing he takes long enough over it, I can switch the fake money for the real notes from Finn's bin bag. Knowing my luck however, Mitch'll take the money case into the bathroom with him.

Finn did tell me to let him know when I had the full details of the ransom drop, and if I'm going to do that, it needs to be now. That's if I still want him on board. I could do with some skilled help, it's true, and I don't trust Mitch or any of Connell's other goons to provide that. Now, of course I feel considerably less warm and fuzzy towards Finn as well. In an emergency however, I've no doubt he's the person I'd feel safest watching my back. At the very least, he's someone who can shoot straight. I don't have the luxury of time to mull over in my mind the pros and cons of contacting him. Hard

216

though it is to trust someone who has told you their dog is dead when it isn't, I'm not in a position to be especially picky.

On impulse, I head for the loo. Once the door is locked, I text Finn to let him know the time of the ransom drop. I'm aware it's a little duplicitous to indirectly ask for his help but not to let him know I've dug up the proceeds of his robbery and intend to give it away, under his nose, without him knowing. Still, if he hadn't carjacked Gina, none of us would be in this mess. There's no way he'll ever know it was me who took the money. At least I presume he won't. They don't have CCTV cameras in the Steyning woods, as far as I know. I suppose that's a positive about tree-filled areas, I hadn't considered.

Mitch has parked his own car outside, so he is ready to follow me later, at a discreet distance, when I leave to make the drop. He wanted to know if I've a spare resident's permit rather than use the meter, but I said I hadn't and he's had to pay to park. I certainly wasn't coughing up the readies for the pleasure of entertaining this unwanted, muscle-bound babysitter. Mitch answers the landline when it rings, but hands it to me with a slightly baffled expression. It turns out to be Bridie asking for a favour. Her living room light fitting has fused for the umpteenth time, possibly due to the squirrel she insists lives in her roof nesting in the wiring. I think 'squirrel' in this case is a euphemism for rat. Bridie's house is reasonably sized and in an upmarket street. She bought it with the proceeds of her TV work, but it's becoming a little scuffed around the edges now she spends so much time 'resting' and can't afford the maintenance. She has invited a couple of mutual friends over this afternoon. They were going have a round-the-table first read-through of a play one of them has written and is hoping to put on in next year's Brighton Fringe. It's not going to be easy to read their copies of the script in the half-dark, 'especially with Mel's cataracts,' Bridie explains. She's hoping I'll invite them round to rehearse here, as I've done in the past. I'm about to say I can't do it today, but then a thought comes to me. I tell her to by all means pack her mini theatre company into her car and come on over. 'I might even pay your parking.'

The play is an all-female four-hander about eco-activism. They should really have asked Jake about it for research after his stint at the bypass protest and brief flirtation with Extinction Rebellion, but haven't of course. Bridie is going to be performing in the piece with friends Jazzy, Mel and Emmeline, her usual troupe for home-grown endeavours. It's the presence of Emmeline I was relying on and she doesn't disappoint. Emmeline's ex-husband, with whom she is still on amicable terms, owns a French vineyard. I've never known her not bring a couple of bottles of Chateau Whatever to one of Bridie's drama sessions. It's no doubt the reason she is so regularly cast. I fetch glasses in anticipation and open a jumbo-size packet of salted popcorn I'd been keeping for the next movie or box-set night I have with Gina. Emmeline uncorks the wine and the actors all insist they'll only have the tiniest one as they're working. I know from experience this means they'll all be bladdered before they've even got through the first act.

Of course, I have to firmly refuse to imbibe even the smallest glass, but the hapless Mitch is prevailed upon. It's only a modest drop of wine, certainly not enough to put him over the driving limit, but Emmeline has a habit of discreetly topping up drinks before you've even got halfway down the glass. Sitting there among the rehearsing women, Mitch doesn't appear to notice as I flit in and out the room, slipping from something more comfortable into my stab-proof vest and carefully getting the rest of my things together. It's rather a long, shouty and sweary play, with a passionate romance between the eco-warriors thrown in. 'I'm a creature of this planet too!' Jazzy's character appeals as she and Mel choreograph something that isn't quite an embrace and isn't quite a tussle. Perhaps, they'll leave deciding on which it is when they 'get it on its feet and start blocking', as Bridie is keen to do, if they get far enough along with their reading, discussing and drinking.

'With every breath of carbon dioxide you expel from your lungs, you wound both me and the Earth!' Mel declares, pushing Jazzy away then pulling her back.

'Did that look a bit eggy, Vonnie? I think the intention is right, but it feels a little awkward.' I'm sure with a bit more work it'll be fine. It's very similar to all Jazzy's other pieces I've seen or heard read, and they aren't at all bad. She really does deserve to be paid for one of them soon, rather than having to stage everything herself in sweaty, forty-seater spaces over pubs or under office hubs. The new play's development process certainly gives Mitch something to watch. He's not remotely drunk, but finally he does feel the urge to empty his bladder. I let him close the bathroom door behind him and then judge this to be my own dramatic cue to exit stage right. Snatching up the case of money and his car keys off the table, I make a dash for the door. Everything I need for tonight is now in grabbing distance in the hallway. The women are moving chairs back to try and work out how to choreograph a proper fight scene between a protester and the spy who has infiltrated their group. The spy has inevitably turned out to be one of the lovers, I could see that signposted from a mile off, but I don't have time to give constructive feedback. Anyway, as a plot it seems pretty realistic. I think I've recently established that it tends to be the person you've chosen to place your trust in who turns out to be harbouring a dark secret. Silently, I let myself out. I know it's rude to leave a show halfway through, but I've a hopefully not too final act of my own to prepare for, and must do so alone.

* * * * *

I take Gina's car. I only pocketed Mitch's keys to delay him from coming after me. I do seem to be making a habit of stealing men's keys. My aim is to go somewhere where I can swap the fake money for the real stuff. While I'm driving, my phone starts ringing. I pull over. I hope it's Finn, but inevitably it's Connell and I don't answer. Mitch hasn't wasted much time in telling him I've done a runner. I'm not going to speak to Connell, but I do send him a text, '*Still doing the drop tonight. But want to wait somewhere alone.*' Then I switch my phone off.

I'm not being entirely truthful about waiting alone. I head to Sol's, who is thankfully in, rearranging his store cupboards in date order as he does from time to time. Once he embarks upon a task like this he likes to stick with it come what may, so I make myself a coffee, and settle down to the serious business of swapping out the fake banknotes. Although it's all neatly rubber-banded together in wads with the phoney money hidden among the real ones, giving each pile a quick flick gives the game away. It makes me wonder how Connell expected to get away with it. He's a complete cheapskate. It's his daughter's life at stake after all. When I check my phone he's called several more times. Finn hasn't called though. I wonder whether to phone him again, but end up deciding it sounds a bit needy. He'll have received my message, and if he chooses not to respond, I can do this thing on my own.

* * * * *

Sol has finished his cupboards and wants to play me his latest composition. I'm not a great appreciator of modern, classical music, if that's even the term for his work. The piece to my mind goes on a bit and is a tad repetitive. I tell him it's very nice, which doesn't seem to be the response he's hoping for. Right now I'm in no mood to concentrate on a violin concerto or whatever it bloody well is. Checking my phone again, I discover Bridie has recently sent me some photos from her rehearsal at mine. She's going to post them on her socials to remind people she's still available for castings. The session went well apparently, and they're all now in the pub on the corner, the one below the crack den, if I feel like joining them. I suppose I should be amazed my friends' lives are continuing exactly as normal. Clearly Bridie and her thespian cohorts didn't even notice anything awry when I slipped out of their session while they were still arguing over the blocking of the first scene. There's no mention in her message of Mitch, who presumably left in rather a hurry shortly after I did. In fact I know he did because I can see my empty sofa in the background in the first of the photos, which shows Bridie pointing a meaningful finger at a chastened Mel, all in character of course. This surely confirms Mitch left as soon as he discovered I'd vanished, as well as giving the impression the play contains one of Jazzy's slightly preachy, long speeches. People in Jazzy's plays do a lot of soul searching, virtue signalling, shaming and blaming, usually very loudly. In real life she wouldn't say boo to a goose and lives with her decidedly scary mother in a Peacehaven chalet bungalow.

Jake, also shamelessly still sending me his self-promotional materials despite my current circumstances, has emailed me a flyer for his latest gig. I mention it to Sol who makes an excuse about it not being a night when he's free, unfortunately, despite not having been told what evening it's actually on. Sol and Jake aren't great fans of each other's work, I get that. They work in different musical genres, but I do think my friends should show each other at least a little generosity from time to time. I turn out to most of their events, to show solidarity, and if I think the play is too long, the music exactly not my thing, the workshop or class too peculiar for words, I never say so. I buy them a drink, albeit just the cheapest one I can get away with, and tell them it was great. I don't go in for 'Amazing! Incredible! You smashed it, darling!' type language, as it's not the world I grew up in. My mum would tell me a drawing was 'not bad' and I'd be chuffed enough with that. Although I'm not effusive with praise I do try to accentuate the positive and never offer criticism unless it's requested and helpful. Whenever I have a gallery exhibition, I make sure all my friends have flyers, virtual and paper. I plaster the details all over my socials and make sure everyone knows there'll be free wine and nibbles on offer. Then I wait at the gallery and because my work is starting to get known, people do turn up to peruse it. Occasionally a small piece or two even sells. My friends, however, are inevitably a no-show. I've read a few biographies of famous sculptors – well, Rodin, Henry Moore and Barbara Hepworth to be precise. Nowhere does it say they ever had this problem. It never says, '*none of their mates could be arsed to show up,*' but then I suppose it wouldn't. It's not something you'd want to publicise.

Sol is preparing for an evening's busking outside Waitrose in Western Road. It's the first time he's ventured back there since an altercation with some Peruvian panpipers over the pitch beside the main door, he tells me. Things had become heated and it had led to him needing stitches in his right eyebrow. Who knew pan pipes could be so sharp, well apart from musically I mean. I've never bought into the thing that listening to them is relaxing. It's too breathy sounding, like an asthmatic drunk blowing across a beer bottle. At least this explains why he's recently moved to a new pitch outside M&S.

I'm sure I could stop at Sol's while I wait to exchange the cash for Gina, but the thought of lingering too long in one place is making me nervous. I put the money in the boot of the car and drive Sol to his old busking pitch. He appreciates the lift. That way he can keep an eye out for any territorial South American woodwind combos before he's committed to setting up there. Everywhere I go there seems to be a South American connection. Maybe I've just not noticed them all before. I'm certainly not adding panpipers to the list of suspects.

Sol asks if he can have a couple of the fake notes. Screwed up in his hat, it might encourage shoppers to donate more generously than usual. I let him have them but I'm sceptical about it increasing his earnings. I mean no one gives a busker anything more than a quid, even outside Waitrose.

Checking my phone again, I see there's now a voicemail from Benito. He wonders if I've heard any more news about Gina. I don't really know how much to tell him, but I call him back because I like talking to him. He says he'd dropped by my studio earlier looking for me, but had been surprised to see a man standing in the entrance, asking another artist for directions to it. 'Maybe he want to buy one of your little naked men but I'm not so sure.' By his description of the bloke who was looking for me it sounds like it could be Mitch or another of Connell's interchangeable loyal staffers. My studio is one of a number in an old print-works, but I don't have its address on my website, as I don't want people dropping in unannounced. If they did, my models would have no privacy and I'd be constantly distracted. Visitors are by appointment only and no one has recently requested one. I hadn't told Connell where the studio is, but it sounds like he's found out. There are a number of large buildings that have been separated into individual studios in the city, but not so many that it would be very difficult to find me. I ask Benito why he was there looking for me, hoping it was just because he enjoys the delights of my company. He says it is just because he and Eileen want to know if there was any more news about Gina and he happened to be passing. I don't tell him I'm making the ransom drop. I wouldn't want to get Benito involved in something risky like that, and he's another person who would probably insist on trying to help, but only end up hampering me. I say I'll meet him for a catch-up tomorrow. 'That will be so good, Vonnie,' he says. I finish the call with a stupid smile on my face, fool that I am.

For me, the danger of my current situation is curiously starting to add a certain frisson to everyday life. I think even

Sol might have been the subject of a little frisky flirting, had the date-ordering of the cupboards not made me suspect his lovemaking might also involve certain off-putting quirks. Where my sex life is concerned, I still accept my afternoon sojourn with Finn was ill-advised. I think it's safe to say, after his dead dog deception, that delightful though it was, it is an event never likely to be repeated.

When I listened to those detective audio books with Gran, I loved that you always knew the murder would be solved right at the end. I wish real life was like that, and I don't mean full of murders committed with blunt instruments in downtown New York. I just wish there were tidy and fair endings. If I were Perry Mason or Sam Spade, I'd definitely get Gina back safe and sound.

I drive on my way as Sol lifts his violin to play the first note to the passing shoppers. I sensed he'd have liked me to take a cruise around the block to ensure the panpipers are definitely not going to bring violent discord to today's musical proceedings, but I don't have the time. I'm heading out of Brighton, across the Downs towards Ditchling. Gina's car finds the steepness of this road a bit of a challenge in every gear, but it's both a direct and scenic way to reach my destination. I want, before the daylight fades, to take a first look at where I'll be heading later to hopefully exchange a case of money for my flatmate. On the sea-facing side of the South Downs it's all gently rolling slopes dotted with walkers, sheep and cattle, but the north sides of each adjoining hill are as steep and rugged as any mountain. Up here, I can look across Ditchling Beacon and see the Jack and Jill windmills at Clayton before turning off towards Pyecombe and heading west through the little village. It has occurred to me that

Connell's people might also be out and about doing a reconnaissance trip. Either that or they could be in the area looking for me and the cash. It stops me calling in at a delightful looking village pub that would ordinarily be a great place to wait. As it stands, it's the nearest hostelry to the site of the ransom drop, so it's possible someone from Connell's mob might either make an appearance, or already be there lying in wait for me, or possibly the kidnappers.

Further into West Sussex is the narrow country lane, snuggled between a wooded area and the Downs, where the lay-by picked for the exchange is located. As I drive up, I spy tree tunnels again. I can almost hear the sinister movie music start in my head. I think I'm gaining a lifelong aversion to narrow roads where the branches of the trees meet above. The only advantage I can see is that it stops you being spied on by, say, a police helicopter, or drones. I can imagine Connell might have a drone operator sitting up on the Downs, controlling a remote flying device equipped with a camera. It's the kind of thing he'd do, employing a 'Phil' or 'Mitch' type character who'll completely fail to get it off the ground. It makes me understand why Connell lets his shop managers hire their own staff. I couldn't see him making it big in the world of recruitment. In a way I suppose, he has hired me to make the ransom drop, albeit on his daughter and the kidnapper's recommendation. His inability to choose his stooges wisely may explain why he has not opposed leaving the ransom delivery to me. It's not something that boosts my ego and self-confidence, at a time when they both could sorely do with it.

I am only a few kilometres east of Steyning and the farm where Finn was living in his caravan. This is a coincidence, I tell myself. I mean, if you're looking for a quiet, rural spot near Brighton, you need to travel north of the Downs. Go west or east and it's all built up for miles around and head south and there's the English Channel, which, unless you're a nautical type, is pretty off-putting. I stop briefly in the lay-by, noting a water-filled rut on the driver's side of the car, and that there are two gaps in the fence and tall hedgerow beyond. The lay-by has no streetlamp, so tonight I will need the torch, which is stashed with the rest of my stuff on the back seat in readiness. I get out and look through the hedge. There is thick woodland beyond and no discernible path between the trees. The kidnappers might arrive by car or they could walk in through here, after parking up elsewhere. There is little undergrowth as the trees shut out most of the light. I risk a quick walk into the leafy gloom. It's just starting to get dark, but somewhere above me a blackbird is singing what is probably his last song of the day. I hear the sound of an engine in the distance, and realise nearby on the other side of this patch of woodland is another road. Ducking through the trees, I can see a car pass down what appears to be another lane, as small and quiet as the one I've parked on.

I retrace my steps and get back in the car. Driving on to the north, I put a little distance between myself and the lay-by I must return to in three hours' time. Further along the road, standing completely on its own, is another country pub. It's a chocolate-box perfect one with timber-framed, white walls and a thatched roof. I pull into the roomy car park and enter warily. There are a couple of middle-aged men enjoying a quiet pint in a corner. They're wearing those checked shirts and padded, green gilets that still appear to be all the rage in the farming community, and among those who buy their clothes at a garden centre. I glance at the menu, chalked in neat calligraphy above the bar and the prices are eye watering, never mind they include such horrors as roast wood pigeon, pig's-trotter jelly and a tripe pie. Whether this is designed for well-heeled foodies down from Islington who imagine this is what people eat out here in the wilds of Sussex, or whether the chef has escaped from 'The Texas Chain Saw Massacre' I can't decide. This place would never survive in Brighton. Fellow vegans would rase it to the ground before you could say 'pheasant parfait'. A coffee and a packet of ready salted are what I order. I don't get much change from a fiver. One of the farmers joins me at the bar to order his 'same again'. 'Eat here much?' I ask. He laughs, knowingly.

'I used to. Not so much these days.'

'Tripe pie not your thing?'

'They used to do lovely fish-fingers and chips. Affordable it was too. But you know what happens if you stand in the way of progress eh?'

'No, what happens?'

'It runs you down.'

'Like a runaway tractor.' I throw that in to sound a little less like an ignorant townie, but in doing so of course sound exactly that.

'Ha.' he says and returns to his friend. I keep glancing out the window at the car. The ransom is safely locked in the boot, but safely only applies as long as the car isn't stolen.

I check my phone again. Connell has texted me. I almost don't bother to read it, but seeing the word 'urgent' compels me. The kidnappers have been in touch again. He doesn't say by what means, but I think it's safe to say it isn't the mythical second post. They are bringing the ransom drop forward. It's now happening at seven pm.

The rendezvous is now in less than an hour's time. It will barely be dark. The kidnappers apparently now have my phone number too. Again he doesn't say how. I'm doubting somehow it was a Zoom call, but it must've been some kind of two-way exchange for him to have given it to them. Either that or he's scrawled it on a board and displayed it in his window. If so, I'm glad he lives in a quiet street, far from the red-light district, or I'd be fielding calls from middle-aged men all night. If there are further changes of plan, the kidnappers will, Connell says, contact me directly. This sounds a little ominous. I'm not a person who likes a change of plan at the best of times.

I text Connell back to let him know I'm ready. As I press 'send', a man and a woman enter the pub. They are wearing smart, city-style clothes – she expensively blonde and wearing a thin, optimistically showerproof coat, rather than those actually waterproof green anoraks that people who live out of town wear. Her patterned wellies must be Boden or Kath Kidston. He has slicked back hair and a cagoule with a North Face logo, like all the TV reporters wear when reporting in bad weather. It's not outside the realms of possibility that they are a news crew or journalists. I don't know how they'd have got wind of what's going to be happening nearby later. I know Connell wouldn't have tipped them off, but then maybe the kidnappers themselves have alerted them. I can't fathom a motive for them doing so, but then Finn did say they're disorganised and unpredictable.

I wonder if there is also a chance that the newcomers are undercover officers. The police could theoretically have had us under surveillance, tapped Connell's phone, and intercepted his texts or whatever. Possibly, it's not even the kidnappers they're after. Maybe Finn is the one they're closing in on. I'm starting to feel claustrophobic in here. The couple are looking around as if searching for someone. They're not being discreet about it and their body language is tense and is making mine tense too. With my back to them at the bar, I watch them in the mirror behind. They walk to the other side of the room. He murmurs something and she nods and takes out her phone. She's looking up now, directly at me. It might mean nothing, but it might mean trouble. I risk another mirror glance. She is saying something to him and now he's looking my way. I think I can safely assume the conversation didn't go along the lines of, 'Wow, darling, isn't that the famous sculptor Vonnie Sharpe? What an absolute privilege to be in such esteemed company.' I pick up my drink and wander as casually as I can towards the door offering a 'beer garden'. It turns out to be a couple of picnic tables with ashtrays on them, surrounded by a low post-and-chain fence. Once outside, I leave the half-empty coffee cup on one of the picnic tables and step over the fence into the car park. Hopefully by leaving this way rather than the front door, I'll have bought myself enough time to make a getaway, if indeed that is what I need to do.

There's a new car in the car park, which I presume belongs to the couple. It's a shiny, black Peugeot. There is no mud spatter, and it doesn't appear to be four-wheeled drive, so again, I'm thinking it has come from the city. I don't know if the couple are in any way connected with either the kidnappers or Connell of course. I might simply be getting paranoid, though as a vegan, killing time in pig-trotter central certainly didn't help. I start the engine and drive back out onto the road. It's far better to be safe than mess this thing up before it's even begun.

As I turn into a narrower lane, a black, high-performance car roars past in the opposite direction, almost forcing me off the road. It's a common enough occurrence, but today I keep checking the mirror, half expecting to see it reappear behind me. There's the possibility it's an armed-but-undercover police unit. It could of course also be to do with the people who are holding Gina. Being lured out here to an isolated country road leaves me open to being carjacked myself if someone wants the money, but doesn't want to or can't release my flatmate. Alternatively, one of Connell's team might decide to go rogue and muscle in on the action himself. I keep an eye on my mirrors. I don't want any other cars getting too close, either in front or behind. Whenever I see brake lights come on ahead, I slow up, having first checked I'm not being trapped in some kind of vehicle sandwich.

Spotting a board advertising a farm shop offering various items of produce, I pull into their yard. A flint outbuilding conveniently shields the casual parker in search of hearty, country fayre from the road. I take out my phone and text Finn the new, brought-forward drop time. He'll have to be already on his way down here to be any help to me now and he hasn't replied to my previous message, but I figure it's worth a try.

When I leave the car this time, I take the case of money with me. The woman working in the rather draughty barn, which serves as a farm shop, starts when she sees me. 'I thought you were from the Ministry for a minute there,' she comments when I pick up a reasonably priced sourdough loaf. Even the word 'ministry' makes me jump in turn, thinking some official organisation is also somehow now involved in solving the kidnap. In hindsight, sitting in my car swigging pure apple juice made from the farm's own Cox's, I realise she was most likely talking about someone from the Ministry of Agriculture inspecting their dairy, chicken sheds or whatever else they inspect. I've purchased the bread and a jar of damson jam, along with the apple juice. It gives me provisions for later on, which I hope to share with Gina.

My mobile rings. I don't recognise the number. 'Yvonne? Have you got the money?'

I don't recognise the voice either. It's a man, slightly northern, very nervous.

'Have you got Gina?'

'You'll see her at seven.'

'How do I know that?' There's a pause so long I think he's rung off.

'You don't,' he says at last, as if it's taken him some time to think of this answer.

'Then why the hell would I turn up with a caseload of cash?' I'm angry now. I've had enough of being jerked around by these idiots. Talking to the kidnapper, he doesn't sound scary. He sounds boring and average. I still don't even know if he has Gina, or that she's even alive. Sitting here, parked in a farmyard, watching a border collie licking its balls, makes negotiating with a kidnapper seem completely unreal. It makes me take a big risk. 'You want that money, I want to hear from Gina. Put her on the phone. Put her on the phone now.'

'Not gonna happen.' I mutter a well-known phrase ending in 'off' and hang up on him. A cold feeling of dread starts in my toes and works its way up to my chest. That was probably the wrong thing to do. I needed to have kept him talking, got some clues as to his mindset and what he has planned. I don't even know for sure he is a kidnapper. There's still the chance he's an opportunist who has seen a story about a missing young woman and is using it to make a dishonest buck. He might simply be one of greedy lowlifes who bought up all the hand sanitizer and toilet rolls during the Covid crisis and stuck them on eBay. One of those people who does a similar thing every Christmas to ensure harassed parents have to buy the latest must-have toy from them, at three times the shop price. If I'd kept him on the phone, rather than made an unrealistic demand, then I might now be in a position to know if he has Gina. Instead, it looks like I've blown out the whole money-for-hostage exchange.

I feel like taking my list of suspects from my bag and ripping it up. The man who called is no one I've spoken to since Gina disappeared. I'm pretty certain of that. No, actually on thinking about it, I'm not even sure of that. I think I *have* heard that voice before, but I can't place where or put a name to it. I'm trying desperately to remember but in my panicky state I'm drawing a complete blank.

My phone rings again. 'Vonnie!' This is a voice I do instantly recognise.

'Gina! Oh my God, Gina.'

'You're coming, Vonnie aren't you?' I hear her gasp as the phone is snatched from her hand. It's the man with the slight northern accent again.

'Seven o'clock. You know where. With the money.' The line goes dead.

CHAPTER TWELVE

Now I know Gina is alive, I'm ready to see this through. Reinvigorated and fired up, I head back out onto the road with a new determination. I need a calm, clear head, but I've never had one of those at the best of times. I'm also not usually the first to turn up to a party, but I think in this case I might as well head for the rendezvous point again, despite being half an hour early. The plans may well alter, and if the exchange is brought forward, the last thing I want to do is risk Gina's life by being late.

I sit in the lay-by and fish out the plastic, disposable cutlery Gina and I have a habit of stashing in the glove compartment. On buying a lunch out, we always pick up a knife, fork and spoon each if they're available free of charge, and then end up eating with our fingers anyway. I know plastic cutlery is bad for the environment, but at least ours is stashed away in the car rather than binned. Now it means I don't need to get my penknife dirty as I slice my sour dough and make a thickly spread damson jam sandwich. I checked the jam very carefully when I bought it and it doesn't contain gelatine, in case you're wondering. Even so, I'm not very hungry to be honest. It's just something to do. I might make two sandwiches and eat them with Gina after the exchange. I don't suppose the kidnappers have fed her very well. She didn't sound weak or ill or the phone, merely a bit scared and that's of course, only natural. I don't know how well I'd hold up in her position. Not too well at all probably.

Five to seven and the sandwiches are made and I've left half the bottle of apple juice to share too, even though my mouth is now so dry with nerves my tongue is sticking to the top of it. I look at the clock on my phone as I wait for something to happen. Two minutes past seven and nothing. Three minutes past and still nothing. The phone rings. A Geordie woman says she's calling about my recent motor accident. I cut her off as she burbles on with the standard script. I'm sorry Gina, I need a swig of your half of the apple juice after that. It's five past seven. A text arrives. It's from an unknown number, and contains a link to a map and a map reference. I enlarge the map on my phone. Unfortunately the kidnappers are expecting me to leave the car where I'm parked and walk through the woods to leave the money at a spot near that road that runs in parallel with this one. I suppose there's nothing for it but to get out of the car and obediently follow instructions.

As I move silently through the trees, I'm more alert than I've ever been in my life. The whole fox visualisation thing was, I realise, utter bollocks. My own fight or flight chemicals are coursing through my veins, making me hyperaware of my surroundings. No fox, badger or other forest critter could currently creep up on me even if it felt inclined to. I don't need to pretend to be a wild animal to tap into these instincts. They were a part of me all along and automatically unleash themselves now they're needed. I've my hand on the unloaded pistol in my pocket and I'm ready for any potential ambush. I'm not letting anyone take the money until I know Gina is free.

My phone receives a text, making me start at the sound. 'WE ARE BEING WATCHED.' It's all in capitals. I don't know who the 'we' is they're referring to. Do the kidnappers only mean themselves or are they including me? I can't see or hear anyone about. Undoubtedly someone has spooked Gina's captors and I don't know what'll happen next. I wait. Minutes pass. There is silence apart from a slight rustling of leaves in the breeze. My bad knee is starting to fix. I sit down on a fallen tree trunk. It feels damp and threatens to leave a green powder on my jeans, I hope will wash out. Trees really seem to have it in for me, despite my eco-friendliness. I don't know what I'm supposed to do now.

Ten minutes pass. Slowly and quietly I retrace my steps to the car. I sit inside and lock the doors. Perhaps the kidnappers will come to me if I remain here. I put the radio on. The DJ is chatting away, inviting us to phone in about how our dogs have embarrassed us in public. It's the kind of pointless chatter I'd normally switch off, but currently I'm glad to have this link to another, far more normal world. Not that I really want to be reminded of dogs, though it's not like anyone's going to call the station and say they saw a dog which had come back from the dead. Tammy phones in from Carshalton while she's waiting for her dinner to cook. She isn't sitting in a lay-by waiting for kidnappers to release her flatmate. Her world is cosy, cheery and normal. Somehow I've made the wrong choices in life, that much is clear.

A wood pigeon hurtles towards the car, nearly colliding with the windscreen. I didn't think many birds apart from owls flew about in the dark, and it is dark now. Then I realise, the bird has been flushed from its roost because something or someone is out there. Maybe it's the person who makes them into a parfait, whatever that is, or maybe this is finally the moment. A shadow is moving among the trees. It's feeling a bit like 'The Blair Witch Project' or any one of those low budget slasher films they screen on the Horror Channel with 'woods' in the title. I won't be watching another of those for a long while.

Two men emerge from the gap in the tree hedge. One of them is Mitch. I grind my teeth in exasperation. They walk towards me. I wind my window down but only a crack, so they can speak to me.

'You're here,' growls Mitch, stating the bloody obvious. 'With the money?' Staying in the car, I flip open the case and show him. There's no point in Connell's people thinking I was doing a runner with the cash.

'I was about to make the swap, but something scared them off.'

'You're not supposed to be here until ten pm.' My mind's whirring. These guys are severely behind the curve. Surely Connell should be keeping them regularly briefed.

'Connell texted me, said it has moved forward to seven.' The look on Mitch's face as he turns to the other guy suggests this is indeed news to them both. Mitch takes out his mobile and punches in a number. He strides off to take the call. The other guy watches me suspiciously. I leave the radio on. They've paused the canine gossip temporarily and are playing 'It Feels Like I'm In Love'. It doesn't, believe me, although my knees may well be shaking as the song suggests. Mitch returns. 'Connell knows nothing about any change of plan.'

'He texted me.'

'No.'

'Well someone did.' I realise something 'It must've been the kidnappers then!'

'Nah, it can't have been, love. They only deal with Connell.' I'm riled by Mitch calling me 'love' and suggesting I'm the one who's not the sharpest chisel in the sculpting kit. You'd think by now he'd realise that it's not me, it's him.

'Err that's not actually the case, *Sweetie*. One of the kidnappers rang me just now. He even let me speak to Gina.' This shocks him. He's completely gobsmacked and immediately takes his phone out again. 'Vonnie says Gina is alive, and she's spoken to her.' I beckon him up to the window while he still has Connell on the blower. I raise my voice so Connell can hear me too. 'And for you and your boss's information they've just called off the exchange because they saw someone hanging about, presumably you two. You need to leave and let them see I'm alone here. Back off and leave. Now are you going to tell Connell that or shall I?'

'Why should we believe you?' I shake my head.

'Because, Mitch, what other reason would I still be sitting here in this lay-by with a case full of money? Now as I said, you can either tell Connell and explain this to him or I can.' I suspect Connell has actually already heard me, but he might as well get the message reinforced by his own employees.

239

Mitchell strides away again to consult with his boss again. While he's gone, I have an idea. I call to the other guy, who is standing around like a film extra who is surplus to requirements in this particular scene. I have a partial view of the South Downs from through the trees behind me. I point. 'I can see the hill there. Could the kidnappers be watching us from up there? Is there a track, or a car park or something? I was wondering if you guys might take a look, when Mitch gets off the phone. I mean they can obviously see you, wherever it is you're parked.'

As Mitch starts to return, the extra goes up and speaks to him. Mitch comes back over to me.

'Connell says you're to stay put. And as soon as you hear from the kidnappers again, call him.'

'Of course.' They walk away and vanish into the gloom of the trees. They must be parked up somewhere on the other road. Presumably they were here doing what they'd assumed was an early location reconnaissance too, without knowing the time of the ransom drop had been changed.

I check my phone messages. The one that signs off 'Connell' has come from a mobile number I'd naturally assumed was his. When I check it against the recent numbers in my missed calls log, I find the numbers of several different mobiles. The text message changing the time of the drop, which wasn't actually from Connell at all, is from the same number the kidnapper let Gina call me back on. It is not the same phone number the man with the northern accent used to call me from though. I suppose this means there are two kidnappers both using separate phones. I try calling the number the text and Gina's call came from but it's now switched off. It's the same story when I try the number for the northern-sounding kidnapper. It sounded to me like a genuine accent too, not something being put on by someone I know, to put me off the scent. I'm sure it's not Connell, Finn or even René pretending to be somebody else. I suppose there is the possibility that René is in fact British and was putting on the whole Belgian thing. He only dances rather than speaks in his Tik Tok videos after all. His whole internet persona could be fake. I don't really buy it. It's none of Connell's staffers who've spoken to me either. The 'extra' sounded like he might be Welsh, but it's not Mitch or Phil. I still think I've heard the kidnapper's voice before though. I'm rummaging in what passes as my brain for someone either I or Gina know, or knew. I do know a lot of people but I still can't put a face to that voice. It's really bugging me.

The radio is now playing 'I'm Not In Love' and promising an upcoming anecdote about an over-sexed French Bulldog. I switch it off. Sorry Gina, I'm going to need to eat my own sour dough sandwich and drink more of your portion of the apple juice. I've saved you your sandwich. It's on the back seat waiting and I'm clinging to the hope you'll be enjoying it later tonight.

Connell rings. I knew he would, but this time I do take his call, while stressing he needs to keep it short as I'm waiting to hopefully hear back from the kidnappers again. He wants to know if I'm really sure it was Gina I spoke to and if so, how she sounded. He doesn't mention my previously giving Mitch the slip or his presumed worries I'd made off with the money. Hearing Gina has spoken to me seems to have made all of that forgotten and maybe forgiven, for the present at least. I tell him I'm doing my best to get Gina back, adding that she would probably be with me now if he hadn't sent his people out here. 'Can you please leave me to do this alone as I was asked to?' I don't catch his answer, as I end the call, but I hope it was a 'yes'.

* * * * *

I hear a car engine. While I was talking to Connell, a police car has pulled into the lay-by behind me. This is a disaster, or more accurately, worse than a disaster. Two cops emerge and walk towards me. Again I wind the window down a crack. 'Evening officers.'

'Is everything alright here?' says the younger one.

'Yes, err I stopped to make a call.'

'Okay, but you should be aware this isn't a good place to linger in the evening.' I look at the cop, wondering what she's warning me about. It could be anything from werewolves to doggers I suppose. 'It's a dimly lit lane and this is one of the few places where vehicles can pass. There have been accidents at this spot as recent as a fortnight ago.' I start my engine and thank her for the advice. If the kidnappers are still watching they now undoubtedly think I'm in league with the law. There's nothing I can do about it but drive off. The police follow behind me until I reach a main road, then pass and head on their way.

I return to the gastro pub with tripe and wood pigeons on the menu but stay in my car in the car park. It looks like it's bustling with locals now. Perhaps there are people residing in Sussex who are partial to overpriced offal. It's an unsettling thought. Then I notice a blackboard outside, declaring it is quiz night and that there are big prizes. I decide to go and sit in the warm. There is after all a certain amount of safety in a crowd.

It's a music round as I sit down at one of the few empty tables. People are playing as individuals rather than teams. A member of the bar staff expectantly slaps a piece of paper down in front of me. A bald man with a microphone is booming out the questions. I realise he has a different northern accent than the guy on the phone. My description of it was woefully inadequate, but I think the kidnapper's sound might've been more Nottingham or Sheffield, whereas this guy is Mancunian. 'Who sang 'I Don't Like Mondays', 'Ruby Tuesday', 'Wednesday Week' and 'Friday I'm In Love'. That's four separate bands, folks. You need all four to get one point.' This seems hardly generous. I suspect they don't give away many of those big prizes. 'I'll repeat the question...' It's music from before my time, but mum used to always like a radio on when she was doing people's hair, usually a local station or Heart FM. I grew up drawing to the classic sounds of the 60s, 70s and 80s. I scrawl down 'Boomtown Rats, Rolling Stones' then leave a gap for Wednesday, and add 'The Cure'. A voice behind me whispers, 'The Undertones.' I gasp and spin round. It's Finn, in his motorcycle leathers, leaning over my shoulder and grinning. 'The third answer.'

'Ta.'

'So you're waiting here?'

'Yes, err no... look there've been developments.' He suggests we go and talk somewhere more private.

243

We sit in my car in the car park. He notices the sandwich meant for Gina, so I let him have it. She probably won't need it now tonight. I'm not sure I'll hear from the kidnappers again now. 'What is it?'

'Damson jam.'

'Damn what?'

'Like a plum.' He makes a face but devours it anyway. 'You don't want to go back and finish the quiz?' I tease him to lighten the mood.

'If it's all on music it might be worth it. My dad ran a second hand record shop.' I smile. I think that's the first thing he's told me about himself. It might not be true of course, I remind myself, as the image of the lurcher comes back to mind. I stop grinning like an idiot.

'How did you know I'd be here?'

Finn says he found me by spotting my car in the pub car park. As I haven't updated him since the exchange was scheduled for seven pm, he'd assumed upon seeing my car that either it hadn't happened, or it had, and I was sitting in the pub waiting to hear if Gina had been released yet and ready to pick her up if she had. It's now just before nine. While he eats, I bring him up to date on everything that's happened.

'Good,' Finn mutters when I mention having spoken, albeit briefly, to Gina. He seems much less surprised about it than Connell was. The thing that interests him most though is the arrival of the police car. 'Did they have the blues and twos on?'

'No siren.'

'Lights?' I can't remember if they did or didn't as they pulled in behind me. Finn isn't satisfied with this answer. 'Think. It's important, Vonn.' I try to recall my image of the patrol car pulling in. I remember I noticed it was the police because when I saw their headlamps reflecting back on their reflective chequered stripes.

'If they were flashing the blues then everyone in the vicinity, or from any vantage point will know about it. In that case we're probably done for the night. If not, then it's possible the kidnappers weren't close enough to spot them.'

'That could mean it might still be on?'

Finn's motorbike is parked up next to my car. I ask if he's ridden down from London. He says he'd have been here earlier but the traffic was bad.

'You didn't call me.'

'I wanted to get a look at spot where the drop was meant to happen first.' It seems we've all had the same idea.

'You didn't happen to see any of Connell's guys hanging around.'

'Nah. Luckily for them.' I thank Finn for coming. He shrugs. 'I want this thing cleared up. I don't want the blame for it. Especially...' He stops.

'Go on.' His jaw tightens. He looks out of the window.

'Vonnie, this whole things seems completely out of control. Out of ours, out of theirs...'

'Yeah, tell me something I don't know, honey.' A spark of amusement darts across his face as he looks back at me.

'I mean I've asked around. To see if anyone can get a handle on it. Even internationally, people who are ransomed tend to be worth millions if not billions, and the ransom would be much, much higher. I mean what are they going to do with £600,000? Buy a little flat in Hove? There are other, commoner and uglier reasons young women are abducted, but as soon as the ransom notes started coming, that was a positive sign for your friend. Now you've spoken to her, even more so. But it's highly unusual. Unheard of in fact. That's what I thought originally, and that's what other people have told me since.'

'So you remain certain they're amateurs, not professionals?' Even as I say it I can hear Bridie saying, 'It's professional theatre, darling. Not Am Dram. Even if it isn't paid.' I'm not sure I believe there's strong distinction between amateur and professional theatre. Am I an amateur sculptor because I need a job to support myself? How can you be an amateur kidnapper? 'Maybe they've not done this before, that's what you're saying?'

'It would've been all over the media if they had. When they got caught.'

'So bungling and pretty clueless? Only here we are, and they've still got Gina and we're no nearer knowing where or who they are. They're giving us the run around and that makes us look more like the amateurs don't you think?'

Finn says he is definitely of the opinion that if the kidnappers didn't see the police approach me, they'll make another attempt to get in contact soon, possibly tonight. The way he sees it, keeping a live hostage is a lot of effort, so now they know Connell has taken the bait and is following their instructions by sending me out with the money, they'll want to get the exchange made as soon as possible. 'With money you can move fast, stay one step ahead. Less easy, with a human captive in tow.' Why then, did they delay for so long before setting up the drop? Again Finn thinks it's because they don't know what they're doing. 'Blundering around in the woods, asking for cash, rather than a fast money transfer via encrypted communications. Definitely not technically able.' I point out that I'm not very 'technically able' and come to that, couldn't he have robbed the building society electronically. 'I wouldn't know where to start,' he says. 'And besides it wouldn't be as much fun.' The man who put my flatmate's future in peril committed the robbery for fun. I hope that means he won't mind too much when he eventually goes to dig up his loot and finds someone has beaten him to it. Of course Finn has no idea that his ill-gotten gains now make up a large amount of the ransom sitting in the car between us. That subject and the resurrected dog are not topics for conversation. 'My other theory as to why they didn't get on with it is that either they couldn't decide or agree how to go about it.'

'Or they were waiting for someone or something.'

'True. We still don't know how many people are involved. But if they're planning on dividing up the cash, it definitely won't be worth their while if there's more than two of them.'

'So…' I say. 'Now what?'

'We sit tight. And wait.' I nod but hope that we won't be hanging about here too much longer. I'm not particularly enjoying sitting in a car in a moonlight car park with someone I don't trust and very definitely shouldn't have slept with. Annoyingly, I still fancy him madly too, and I'm sure he knows it. I wish you could switch things like lust off at times when you don't need them, like the extra functions on your phone when you need to save the battery. I definitely need to save my battery. Who knows how much yomping through the woods may lie ahead?

My phone alerts me to a text. 'St. Leonard's Forest.' I show Finn. 'We're on.'

'Where's that? I'm not from these parts,' he asks.

'Neither am I, babe, and I didn't know there's a forest at St. Leonard's.' Presumably it's somewhere near the outskirts of Hastings. The internet though, says otherwise. It's nothing to do with the town of St. Leonard's, which is on the coast between Hastings and Bexhill. The forest is in fact just north of us, near Horsham. I text back to the number. 'Where in St. Leonard's Forest and what time?' Finn gets out of the car.

'I'll follow.' He climbs onto his motorbike. I try to commit the route to memory and put my phone down on the passenger seat. I've never understood the phrase 'a wild goose chase' as I think hunters stand below flocks of geese and shoot up at them, rather than go running about after them. Perhaps the expression arose because to chase wild geese is futile, as you're on foot and they have wings. Anyway, what I'm saying is this is starting to feel a bit like a wild goose chase. The mention of a forest again doesn't exactly fill me with optimism either. Despite getting pleasantly sloshed at a beach barbecue in aid of Greenpeace and Surfers Against Sewage last year, I'm definitely still not warming to the natural world.

I drive off, glancing in the rear view mirror. Finn is hanging back; all I can see is his headlamp. There are plenty of signs to Horsham but not many to the forest. I hear another text drop in but frustratingly there's nowhere to stop to read it. A lorry passes in the opposite direction. 'Aggregates' it says on the side. That's what I need right now – lots of grit, albeit mixed with a fair amount of determination. Up ahead is the wide gateway to a house set back from the road. I flash my tail lights to alert Finn to my plans and pull in. He gets off the motorbike and comes over. It's another map reference, to a spot near somewhere called Pease Pottage. 'Time?' I text the kidnappers again. 'Where are U?' is the reply. Good question. On the wrong bloody road as it happens. 'Ten minutes away?' I suggest. We seem to be at somewhere called Mannings Heath and by doing a U turn, and then heading up the A23 to turn off at Pease Pottage, reaching the spot the kidnappers have indicated, looks doable in that time. Finn though has his own phone out and is looking at it.

'It's roughly two sides of a square. If I keep on north and go straight through Horsham I should reach the same place at the same time you do, Vonn, but from the opposite direction. That way I'll get there without them knowing you've someone riding shotgun.'

'How did they even know I'd still be waiting around?' I ask. 'If I'd gone back to Brighton there's no way I'd be able to make it to this rendezvous.'

'They can't know. They're just hoping. It sounds like they're getting a bit desperate to get this thing over with. The question is, why the sudden hurry now? Why risk another attempt tonight?'

'I hope it's not anything bad about Gina. Like she's injured or needing medical treatment. She does have some nasty allergies that can flare up suddenly. I mean if she eats oranges her lips swell like Mick Jagger's. She's supposed to carry one of those pens in case she has a worse reaction, but she never remembers to.'

'No time to dwell on that now,' Finn says firmly. 'We need to move.'

As I make the Pease Pottage turn off, all the signage is to the next big town here in West Sussex, which is Crawley. There are also signs pointing to Gatwick Airport. It's possible the kidnappers are planning a getaway abroad. Driving through the woods, I'm again looking for a lay-by, but this time the map reference only takes me to a spot at the side of the road. I pull in as far as I can, up onto the deeply rutted grass verge, then switch off my engine, but not the headlights. All is still. I check the clock on my phone. Thankfully, I'm on time, but again there is no sign of anyone else being out here. I wait. A rabbit hops out from the hedgerow ahead of me and starts scratching the inside of one of its ears before eating the contents. Although that sounds a bit disgusting, I hope it sticks around. I had a rabbit when I was kid. They have fantastic hearing. If the rabbit decides to hop it, then I'll know someone is about.

My phone starts to ring. It sounds ridiculously loud. It's Connell.

'Any news?' I see a movement among the trees in front of me.

'I think it might be going down. I'll call you back.' I cut the call. This indeed looks like it. The rabbit is gone. There is a man approaching, walking slowly along the side of the road towards my car. I can't make out much detail. He appears to be dressed in black or something dark at any rate, with his hood up. As he comes nearer I can see he is wearing a balaclava. I go cold. His eyes look wide and scared. He stops a little way from the car. I receive a text message, but only dare give it a quick glance. '*Open your door. Put the case down. Close the car door.*' There are clearly two or more people involved. The one who is texting and the man standing in front of me. I hesitate.

'Where is Gina?' I text back. There's another movement among the trees. A torch shines a light, illuminating a face. It's Gina, or at least I think it is. Certainly it's a second person. The torch snaps off and I can no longer see her. Another text comes in.

'*Put the case outside the car. Shut the door. She goes free.*' I do as I'm bidden, wishing now I hadn't involved Finn in this. If the kidnappers hear the roar of an approaching motorcycle it will all be over without Gina being freed. The man walks over and takes the case of money by the handle. He walks backwards away from the car. Then he opens the case, to glance at the contents in the light from my headlights. As he bends his head to examine the wads of notes I hear a scream from the trees.

'Gina!'

Gina emerges from the trees ahead of me. Finn is beside her. He must've crept up on and silently dealt with the second kidnapper who was holding her there. Gina is free. As Finn approaches he levels a pistol at the second kidnapper who stands frozen, money case in hand, staring at Gina.

'Don't move!' As Finn and Gina approach I can see she still looks terrified.

'It's alright, Gina.' I call. 'It's alright.' I can see now though that Finn has hold of her arm and he is dragging her roughly with him as he comes over to us. This isn't right. Something is in fact very wrong.

'Drop that case,' Finn commands. The kidnapper does as asked. He is now staring wide-eyed at Finn.

'Vonnie, get out the car and search him,' Finn orders, adding, 'And don't you move a muscle, mate,' to the kidnapper as he keeps his gun trained on him. I leave the car to search the kidnapper. He is definitely male, and very slight and slim. I would guess he's a youngish person, in his twenties perhaps, though with his balaclava I can't be sure. I suppose I'd expected some thick-set, thirty or forty something, hard-man type like Mitch. This kidnapper appears not to even be armed. This is getting strange again.

'Where's the second one?' I ask Finn as I step back.

'Second what?'

'Kidnapper. The one who was holding Gina.' He looks at me, almost mockingly.

'Still haven't caught on, Vonnie?'

'What?' He releases Gina and steps back. To my amazement she runs straight to the kidnapper, who hugs her protectively

'What the...' I trail off. 'Gina? Then I realise. Even with his hood up and balaclava on I know who the guy hugging her is. 'Benito! Oh my God!' Finn leans on the bonnet of the car. He lowers his gun slightly, but keeps his hand on it.

'Oh and you know him, Vonn. That's perfect,' he says snarkily, 'Just perfect.' Gina and Benito both look at me.

'Vonnie, you've got to help us!' she pleads.

'Gina, I've been trying to help you. I've been trying to help from the moment you were...' I correct myself, 'From the moment I thought you'd been abducted.'

'I *was* abducted.' She glares at Finn. 'That bastard abducted me. He's the robber, Vonnie! He's the one from the building society!'

'I know that...' I don't know why I should be the one trying to explain or justify my actions. It seems to me it should be Gina and Benito.

Benito puts his hood down and removes the balaclava. Finn strolls over to them. Benito stands protectively in front of Gina. Finn isn't impressed.

'I left you safe and sound in your car. So then what did you do?' Gina looks at me but says nothing. 'You tried to call someone for help?' Finn asks her. 'But I stopped you, took your phone. Okay fine. Then what? What did you do?'

'There was a phone box. I had no coins. I had to reverse the charges. To call the chip shop…' She stopped.

'You rang to order chips?' Finn is incredulous.

'This is Benito. He works there.' I explain.

'Right. So you call your boyfriend to come and collect you.' I wonder when Finn calls him that, how I hadn't realised. I suppose I thought Gina would've been punching well above her weight to be involved with Benito. I don't think she's even had a boyfriend before, but I don't even know that for a fact. It seems I don't know half of what I thought I did before all of this began. 'So,' Finn continues, 'Then what?' Benito looks at Gina and shakes his head. She clams up.

'But who… who else is involved in this, Gina? Apart from Benito?' I look at her, still barely comprehending the situation. She says nothing.

'It was my idea,' says Benito.

'No, we came up with it together.'

'Extorting money from your Dad? Why on earth would you do that? He's been so worried Gina, and I thought you two were close.'

'We are. We were.'

'And I've been worried sick. I mean I thought you could've been murdered.'

'You don't understand…'

'Too right I don't.'

'We had to.' Benito nods in agreement. 'You see, Vonnie, we had to help his mum.'

'Benito's mother?'

'Yes, my dad owed her money. He sacked her when she had an accident and…'

'Margarita Gara is Benito's mum?' I ask, as the penny drops for me. I think I'm beginning to get an idea of what's happening now. Gina looks at me mouth open. I think she's beginning to realise how much effort I've put in to try to save her from this non-existent kidnapping.

'I've met Margarita' I tell Gina. 'I know she was badly injured in the shop.'

'He sacked her. And he warned her off claiming compensation. Threatened her.'

'I saw part of a lawyer's letter,' I say.

'He was using his law man to threaten her,' says Benito.

'But it wasn't just Dad's solicitor.' Gina says. 'It was Dad. She left town because he said if she took any further action against him, she might have another accident. He said that! By then she had taken the case to a no-win no-fee lawyer. And she knew he was about to contact my dad. I didn't believe he would threaten her like that. I didn't believe Benito when he told me. I couldn't. But Margarita had recorded all Dad's calls. She played them to me. I was so shocked.' Benito squeezes her hand. 'So look, we were working on a plan, okay? Secretly,' she continues, 'We were going to try to blackmail my dad. Without him knowing it was us of course. But it was difficult. And Margarita – Benito's mum – didn't know at that point.'

'So when was this?'

'Just a few weeks ago. We kept meeting up. Working out how to do it. The blackmail. Because Benito's mum needs the money. Urgently. For medical care. She needs an operation to be able to use her hand again, but here she's just stuck on a long waiting list. Back home she could have it done privately. We were going to ask for enough money to cover it, and for our air tickets. She's waiting for us to bring the money. At the airport. Our flights are booked.'

'Gina – you, you're going to Spain?'

'Spain? No. Venezuela.'

'Right… so is he… Benito, you're Venezuelan?' He nods. I wonder why he lied and told me he was Spanish, then realise he's done no such thing. I'd simply assumed by his accent that he was. He'd probably have told me if I'd asked, but again I didn't. I jumped to conclusions without knowing the facts. I've been a pretty crap detective, all things told.

'We're getting married,' Gina tells me. Benito smiles as she gives him a loved-up look.

'So,' says Finn, looking unimpressed, 'Let me get this clear. You staged a bogus kidnap with your fella here, to get some money from your dad for his mum.'

'Yes,' Gina says simply. Another thought has occurred to me though.

'So, who else is involved in this… this… well, fraudulent extortion, if that's even the right term?'

'No one, Vonnie. Just us. It took us ages to persuade Margarita it was the right thing to do. She's such a good person.'

'What about the man?'

'What man?'

'A man phoned me about leaving the ransom. And I know it wasn't you, Benito. He had an English accent.'

'I asked Margarita's landlord, Greg to call you.' Gina continues, 'He's the only other person who knows what we're doing. He heard how my dad treated her and he was angry about it. He said if there was ever anything he could do. So I got him to make that call from Fratton. Then I called you back, pretending I was being held prisoner.' I can only stare at Gina. She suddenly seems so much older, more in control and I suppose downright devious than I could ever have imagined. I'm starting to see her in a whole new light. This is a new scheming, clever and cunning Gina, though I suspect it is Benito turning her head that has brought about this metamorphosis. The things we do for love.

257

Finn, who has been getting fidgety and fiddling with his gun, takes out his phone.

'Shall I do the honours?'

'Are... are you calling the police?' Gina asks, her voice small, barely a squeak. Finn laughs, harshly. Gina looks at me, realising almost immediately that of course he isn't. He's someone who robs building societies. 'I'm calling the chip shop, once I've found the number. Maybe I fancy some battered cod, or maybe I need your old man's number.' I wonder why he doesn't ask me for Connell's number.

'No, please! No don't!' Gina gasps. Now I start to suspect Finn isn't particularly interested in calling Connell at all. He's trying to rattle Gina and Benito. I'm not calling Connell myself either right away. Whatever Benito and Gina might've done on his mother's behalf, I'm not sure I want him being the one to deal with it, particularly for Benito's sake.

'Okay then, fine.' Finn puts away his phone. Gina looks relieved. Benito smiles at him.

'Thank you,' Finn shrugs.

'Don't mention it, mate.' He picks up the case of money. The smile is wiped from Benito's face. Finn steps back with it, covering himself with the gun. I get that sinking feeling.

'No, no, no,' Benito moans.

'Wait...' Gina says. 'We need that.' She advances on Finn, her need for the cash making her reckless.

'Like I need people thinking I've kidnapped and probably murdered you,' Finn says coolly. 'Give me your phone.' She stands her ground and says nothing.

'I can turn you upside down and shake it out of your pocket if I have to.' I suspect he means it. Benito takes a step forward protectively.

'And you'll what?' says Finn, levelling the gun at him. Gina takes out her phone.

'Here. Look I have it.' She holds out the phone at arm's length to Finn. I don't say anything. I just let it play out. I don't know whose side I'm on or what I'm supposed to be doing.

'Call your Dad yourself,' Finn tells her.

'No!' Gina is horrified by the idea. Accepting this as her answer, Finn takes a wad of notes from the case. He throws it as far as he can into the darkness. Gina wails in horror and tries to run at him but Benito wisely grabs hold of her arm to stop her.

'Throw me your phone,' says Finn. Gina looks like she is about to refuse, then suddenly takes it out and flings it violently at his head. Finn flinches aside, then backs up to pick it up. He crouches, rests the money case on his knees, lays the gun on top, and scrolls through Gina's phone.

'Tell him Vonnie. Don't let him call Dad,' Gina pleads.

'Gina,' I say, 'Why didn't you trust me and talk to me? Why didn't you include me in your plans?'

'You'd have tried to talk me out of it. You wouldn't have understood. You'd probably have thought Benito and his mum were taking advantage of me, or something like that. You wouldn't have understood I can make my own decisions. Everyone always thinks they know what's best for me. But they don't. I do.'

'And this mess, Gina, this is what's best, is it?' I reply. Finn puts the case and gun down and stands up again, holding up the phone. He has Skyped or Zoomed Gina's dad who is on the screen.

'Here you go Connell, look, here's your daughter safe and sound, and here's… well probably your future son-in-law.' Finn pans around the action with the phone like a cameraman. 'Oh and here's your case of money they were about to run away with.' Finn tosses the phone back to Gina, more carefully than she threw it at him. She catches it and faces her father on the screen.

'Dad…' Gina breaks down sobbing. 'Dad, I'm sorry. I'm so, so sorry.' She cuts the call. I walk over to Benito.

'What time's your flight?'

'We check in, in half an hour.'

Finn picks up the case of money again and the pistol too. Unfortunately the person I've called in to help is now the one making this situation more complicated and fraught than it need be. It's not just Gina where I've been a bad judge of character.

'We should let them go,' I tell him.

260

'Nobody's stopping them. I'm certainly not staying put babysitting them till Connell's goons get here.'

'And we should let them have the money.' Finn immediately looks at me like I've taken leave of my senses, as I'd feared he might. He turns and walks away with the case.

'Hey! No!' Gina yells. She tries to go after him but Benito again holds her back. Instead I rush after him.

'Finn. Wait.' He ignores me. I follow him through the trees to the spot near a rough muddy track where he has left his motorbike. He opens the box on the back and the briefcase of money. 'You are not taking that cash!'

'Seriously? After the hassle those two have caused me? I think they owe me. And they're getting off pretty lightly all things considered.'

'Margarita needs that money, and Gina and Benito too, I mean it needs to be a fresh start for them all out of the country.'

'Yeah, well I think we could all do one of those now, don't you?' As he goes to empty the case into the bike box I grab his arm. 'Get off!' I hang on grimly, grabbing at the case handle with my other hand. As we wrestle over the case, he manages to shut it again. It becomes a frantic and frankly undignified tug of war. He reaches for his gun.

'Oh, what and you'll shoot me will you?' I am pretty certain he won't, although after everything that's unfolded, I'm not sure I know anything about anyone after all. We are both stubbornly holding on to the case, pulling and trying to wrench it from each other's grasp. He tries to prise my fingers off. I try unsuccessfully to headbutt him.

A scream of a siren approaches and flashing blue lights illuminate the surrounding trees. Gina or maybe Connell must've called the police. Suddenly the case is in my hands, and I topple backwards with it onto the ground. A shadow flits into the trees, a motorbike roars away.

I sit up, clutching the prize. An ambulance hurtles past in the same direction that Finn's motorbike took. Of course the police wouldn't have got here this fast, even if one of us or someone watching on had called them. I doubt very much that either Gina or Connell will even have summoned them now. If he's sending Mitch and his cronies anywhere, which he probably is, since he hasn't been given our new location, it's likely it'll be to the previous location for the ransom drop. No one knows we're out here in St. Leonard's Forest. I dash back to Gina and Benito with the case. By now the ambulance will be upon or overtaking Finn and he'll realise his mistake and come speeding back for the cash. Gina and Benito have remained huddled by the car.

'Gina, take it. Take the case. Both of you, and take this car now. Before he returns.' They must've got here somehow, by cab or by a hired car they've parked somewhere nearby, but there's no time for them to retrace their steps and use their previous means of transport. Finn will roar back along that road at any second.

'Vonnie, I… I just want to say…'

'No time. Save it. Get in the car. You need to get to the airport. Go!' Benito has already climbed in the passenger side.

Gina scrambles into the driver's seat. The key is still in the ignition where I left it.

'Thank you, Vonnie,' Benito says in that to-die-for accent. 'You are our hero.'

'What about you?' asks Gina, 'We can't just leave you here.'

'I'm fine. Just go! GO!!!' I breathe a sigh of relief as Gina finally lifts the handbrake and puts the car in gear. I watch them pull away and stay put until the car's rear lights vanish around the bend in the road.

The moon disappears behind the clouds as I trudge along the largely unlit road leading back to Pease Pottage. I keep listening out for a motorbike. If I hear one I'll have to scramble over the wooden fence and hide among the trees until it's passed. When I fell back with the case I must've landed in a large muddy puddle. Now my adrenalin level is dropping, as I walk, I can feel that the whole of my bum and most of the backs of my legs are cold and wet. My jeans are clinging to my numb thighs and calves. I hope I'm not going to have to go very far like this.

At Pease Pottage nothing is still open, but at least there's a streetlight to stand under while I call and wait for a mini-cab. 'Yes, we can take you all the way to Brighton but it'll be a largish fare.' Fortunately for me, I found the single wad of notes Finn had thrown from the case, as I retraced my steps back to Gina and Benito. They are slightly short of their £600,000 now, but in the circumstances they should be bloody grateful for what they have. I tell the mini-cab controller that the fare won't be a problem. I hope the driver won't turn me down and drive off when he sees the muddy state I'm in. After all that's happened tonight, I wouldn't rule out anything else going wrong.

* * * * *

Bridie expects me to tell her everything that happened whilst simultaneously consuming the large and very hot pancake she has made me for breakfast. I've not slept a wink. I'm still coming to terms with the fact that it's all over. Across the kitchen, my jeans are reaching the end of their wash cycle. My arms feel stiff and my shoulders ache from wrestling with Finn over the money case. It's funny, when my friend Fern split with her partner over their joint finances, I thought to myself that the last thing I'd ever be likely to get in a fight with a man over was money. My relief Gina is alive and well is tempered with an anger at all she has put me through. In spite of this, it does feel like a weight has been lifted. This morning is the first since her disappearance that I've not felt a gnawing sense of dread.

Benito, Margarita and Gina will no doubt be heading out of Caracas airport sometime today. When I got home last night, I received a final text from Gina in which she said her flight was boarding. She also promised to stay in touch. I hope she will. Nevertheless, I do feel there is one person who still deserves a full explanation of the situation. That is Connell. I had after all, given him my word to do my best to get his daughter back safe and sound. I have certainly found her unharmed, but she certainly won't be returning any time soon. I need to put his mind at rest and let him know that she is loved-up, safe and happy as she embarks on her new life.

Bridie shakes her head when I confess where I intend heading this morning.

'I really don't think it's a good idea,' she tells me. 'I don't know what good you think you'll do. I thought all the stress and worry was over, and yet you're now wanting to jump out of the frying pan into the fire.'

'He's her dad. I owe him an explanation. I need to try to put his mind at rest.' Eventually, as I won't be dissuaded, she insists on coming to Connell's with me.

* * * * *

'Nice place. Very nice,' Bridie mutters as we wait on the doorstep. 'Not currently married, I think you said?' It's funny how knowing they own a prime piece of real estate can so swiftly restore someone's reputation. Connell ushers us through to his study. Today, I'm relieved to say there are none of his associates hanging around like jackals at a kill. He pours us both decaf coffees from a cafetière. It turns out he and some of his colleagues had set out to look for Gina last night, as soon as Finn contacted them, but as I'd surmised, they had gone to the wrong location. One forest looks very much like another on Skype. I'd expected him to be angry with me, demanding to know exactly what had happened and why I hadn't returned with Gina. Instead he seems very calm, perhaps dangerously so.

'I want to know everything,' he says, eyes unblinking. 'Tell me exactly how it went down.' So I tell my tale again, from the point where the second attempt at the exchange was set up. The only part I leave out is the fact that Margarita's landlord had been slightly involved in things, by making that call pretending to be a kidnapper. If any of this sets Connell out for revenge, I don't want someone who is still in the country punished, particularly as, like myself, he has only tried to do the right thing and help a friend. I'm guessing that over in South America, Gina's new fiancé and future mother-in-law will be safe from Connell's ire. Connell might be a big fish in the Sussex chip shop money-laundering racket, but nothing I've seen has given me any indication he has anything like a global reach.

'I have heard from my daughter, actually,' Connell reveals. I note he doesn't refer to her by name. 'She sent me a text to say she'll let me know when her plane has landed.' He looks at me, almost accusingly. 'Venezuela!' he spits, 'What the hell is she going to do out there?' I can't exactly tell him that what she's going to do is live the life she's been longing for, hopefully out of Daddy Dearest's reach.

'I can hardly believe this. I wouldn't have thought she had the nerve... I bought her a flight in a biplane from Shoreham one year for her birthday. She was too scared to take it.' I nod, we've all misjudged Gina, there's no doubting that. 'That Gara woman from the shop. You say you met her?' he asks, pointedly.

'She seems very nice.'

'For someone who's conspired with her son to take Gina away?'

'I'm not sure that's quite how it was,' I say carefully. 'I got the impression Gina was making all her own decisions.'

'Having fallen under the spell of that Gara lad. Didn't give that name on his application form, or he wouldn't have got a job with us.'

'Benito's lovely,' I insist, further risking Connell's ire. He tenses his fingers on the desk, but says nothing. I sense he both does and doesn't want to learn this. 'And from what I could see, they make each other happy. He loves her very much. I mean they're kind of alike in some ways. Quite sweet. Maybe a little bit unworldly.'

'Yet they've led us all on a merry dance.' This is certainly true, I can't argue on this score. 'Do you imagine… do you really think she'll be happy out there?'

'Yes,' I say, emphatically. 'I know this might not be want you want to hear, Mr Connell, but having seen Gina and Benito together, I think she will be. Very happy.' He gives me a sharp look, but then his face starts to relax a little.

'Okay,' he says, holding out his hands in a gesture of surrender. 'Clearly this isn't the way I expected things to end. And I was hoping to actually get my daughter back… but, she's safe, she's well…' Bridie and I both nod. 'And she's shown a little of her old man's initiative. I mean, when I met my wife, Gina's mum, her father didn't approve so we eloped.' He sips his coffee, ruminatively, 'So I can hardly judge Gina for doing something similar, even if she has, in the process, left a very large hole in my finances.' Not just your finances, I think to myself. There's a certain bank robber who may soon find he's considerably less well off than when he buried his money.

'You know,' says Bridie as we head off, me towards a cleaning job, her an Alexander Technique session, 'do you think this whole saga might make a little play? I could ask Jazzy to write it and maybe I could play you. I can see it doing rather well at next year's fringe.'

'Well I hope you'll consider paying me for my story?'

'Of course. Though it'll only be profit-share. You might get enough out of it for a coffee and a croissant at the Inner Sanctum.'

'Well,' I tell her, 'That's something I suppose.'

EPILOGUE

I unlock the door and enter my flat. Even without switching on the light, somehow I know he's there. I can sense it, like those hard-boiled gumshoes in my Gran's audio books. I swallow, heart pounding. I've been both dreading and expecting this day since I left Brighton. Even though I didn't leave a forwarding address, I knew he'd eventually find me.

'220,000 pounds, Vonnie,' he says flatly. I can barely make out his shape, sitting on the sofa. Oddly, I felt more frightened when he was just a shadow waiting to return into my life.

I walk into the room and stand opposite the window. From this angle I can see his face in the light from the street-lamp outside. It makes the angles appear sharper, harsher, his eyes not visible in the shadow.

'How did you find me?'

'Your latest exhibition. You tweeted about it.'

'And you came all the way up here to Edinburgh to find me?'

'To find what you've done with my money.'

'Your money?' I try to make my voice sound completely innocent. I should've got Bridie to give me some acting lessons.

'Yeah, Vonnie. My money.'

'I don't know what you're talking about.' This is, after all, what he'd said to me in the Primrose Café, when he'd denied having anything to do with Gina's abduction.

'Only you knew where I buried it.'

'What? I don't recall you burying any money.'

'You're a bad liar.'

'I don't think so.'

'You were seen. The guy who owns the land saw someone fitting your description in the area, the night before the ransom drop. And there aren't many people in Steyning that look like you, Vonnie.' He says this in a way that is almost flirtatious, but I now know better than to let my guard down.

'The only thing I saw in that clearing was a cross with a dog's name on it. Well unless somehow it wasn't a dog's grave at all, and you were lying to me about her dying.' He says nothing. 'Yeah, unless…' I continue, 'Unless she was actually making a good recovery – so good in fact that I saw you taking her for a walk, very shortly after we'd been getting all cosy in a room above a south London pub.'

'Mmmm,' is all he says to that. I'm not sure what it means, or if it refers to being rumbled over the deception, or reminded of the sex.

'That didn't exactly make me feel all warm inside, you know. Seeing you with the dog. Why did you lie to me?' He sighs.

'At the time I was leaving Brighton, I didn't imagine we'd ever meet again. And if you did happen to return to where I'd been living, and found a spot I'd marked where I'd obviously buried something… well with your inquisitive nature, I needed to give you a reason not to dig it up. Though obviously you still did.'

'Only when I was pretty sure it wasn't a dead dog,' I counter. 'So you thought I'd try to steal your money if I knew it was there?'

'Clearly I was right.' That is, I suppose, factually correct.

'And anyway, where is she now – Peggy?'

'You passed a camper van just down the street on your way home just now. She's in there on the sofa having a snooze.'

'I didn't go looking for the money, Finn. I dug up the bag because I knew you'd lied to me,' I say, more emotion in my voice than I'd intended to betray. 'I just wanted to find out the truth. Because I'd started to trust you and…' He reaches over and switches the table lamp on, presumably so he can see me more clearly. His hair is a little longer again now and his face appears thinner and paler behind his glasses. '…And that was clearly a mistake.'

'As was burying the money,' he comments dryly. I say that if he wants it back, he'll have to go to Venezuela, explaining about swapping it in for the counterfeit notes.

'What? So that was my money in that case!' He sits up straight and stares at me.

'So if you've come here today expecting me to hand it back, clearly you've had a wasted journey. Plus you had, in fairness, told me that taking fake notes to a ransom drop was dangerous and stupid, so in that respect I'd been following your advice.' He continues to stare at me. It's a little unnerving but I'm almost tempted to laugh. 'And I'm not sorry I did it either,' I continue defiantly. 'Not if it's helping Benito's mum get the medical treatment she urgently needs and gives her the chance to rebuild her life. Gina sent me a postcard. She and Benito are getting married next month.' He's smiling slightly now, in that mocking way he has.

'Ah, that's cute. A happy ending. For them.'

Finn puts his boots up on my rented coffee table. I glower. 'So you can't pay me back, eh? Despite the fact you're now living in an arty part of Edinburgh? That must cost a fair bit I should've thought. And your exhibition seemed to be going well.'

'You've been to it?'

'Well since I'm on the poster, so to speak.'

'Yeah, it's going okay. I've sold four pieces – that's four grand, for probably three years' work. It would be six if you'd like to buy your head, it's priced very reasonably at two thousand pounds. You may as well have it,' I add, emboldened, 'As you always did fancy yourself. Tell you what, if you like, you can knock it off what I owe you from giving Gina the case.'

'It's not for sale,' according to the woman in the gallery.'

'So you actually tried to buy it?'

'Nah. But I enquired out of curiosity.'

'It's not for sale, because I thought I should keep it to remind me not to be so gullible in future.' I tell him.

'I did wonder about the title of the piece – *Out Of The Frying Pan.*'

'Gina's not the only one who's done some growing up recently.' I end up confessing I've been expecting a visit from him for the past six months – jumping at every shadow. He sits up again, removes his feet from the table and regards me intently.

'You really didn't move up here, to make it harder for me to find you?' I bite my lip.

'Only in part. I couldn't afford the rent on my old place without Gina sharing with me, and then my friend Connor who owns this place decided to go travelling for a year, and needed someone to flat-sit so I thought…'

'New start?'

'Yes. Plus I've a group of friends wanting to take a new play to Edinburgh this year for the Festival. It could be a big break for them, and it'll be a lot cheaper to do now they've somewhere to stay.' Finn doesn't seem interested. He gets up and strolls over to the window, and in his constantly vigilant way, looks out, up and down the road. Being him must be exhausting. I was glad to escape from being under that kind of pressure.

'You didn't answer my texts,' he says, without turning round to look at me. There's a surprising bitterness in his voice, more pain than anger.

'Texts? What texts?' He doesn't move or reply.

'Look, I lost my phone. That night. Just outside Pease Pottage. When you, Gina and Benito had gone. After I'd called a cab home. It must've fallen out of my pocket. When I bought a new one, I kept the new number, rather than transferred the old one. New start.'

'Mmmm,' is again all he says. The room grows cold between us.

'So you'd sent me texts to ask me to give back your money?' I say at last, simply for a way to relieve the tension. He knows I don't have the money so there's not really anything else to say on that account. The crucial thing is to find out what he intends to do about it. I don't imagine he's going to offer that I pay him back in easy to afford instalments at a reasonable rate of interest, or even take out a debt consolidation loan. He has not, however, turned up mob-handed or threatened to break my legs as yet, so that is a positive.

'I wanted to check you were okay,' Finn says. 'That Mr Chip Shop hadn't taken it out on you when he didn't get his daughter back.' I tell him that Connell has dealt with his daughter running off with his money to Venezuela remarkably well considering. Finn says he's glad of that and adds that he hadn't liked having to abandon me in the middle of the woods at night. I say that's not quite how I remember it, when we fought over the case and I ended up toppling

274

back in the mud. He'd been about to make a get away with the money if a passing ambulance hadn't spooked him into fleeing.

'You see I've no illusions about you, Finn my friend. It was only ever about the money for you. You had no interest in saving Gina or helping me.'

'That's not entirely fair, Vonn,' he says softly. 'I came back that night because you asked for my help. And I'd intended returning to Brighton again the next day, to check you were alright.'

'But you didn't!' I find myself raising my voice. 'Okay, so I didn't get your texts, but you could've come back, the next day, the next week. I didn't move up here straight away. You could've come and found me if you wanted to.' I look down, digging my nails in my palms again. It's been a while since I've made those bloody little half-moon imprints in my hands. I don't know what I'm feeling, even whether I'm scared or angry that he's finally found me. In fact in some strange way I feel almost glad he's here.

'I couldn't come back to you,' Finn says quietly. 'When I got back to where I was living, the police were waiting.'

'Over the building society robbery?'

'Not that. Thankfully. Something else. From weeks before.'

'Something else like what?'

'An exploding cashpoint. Not my job. I just acted as a courier. Shouldn't have got involved.' He shrugs, as if he's talking about a bad day at the office. In a way I suppose that's what it was to him.

'So you got caught?'

'Yep. I've been inside,' he says, slightly less matter-of-factly. 'Six months, did four. You didn't know? I suppose you didn't, if you didn't get my texts.'

'When did you get out?'

'Monday.' I mull it over. All this time I'd been worried about him finding me, he'd actually been in prison. In fact it seems like he's only recently, upon being released, discovered his money was gone. The texts he'd sent from prison hadn't been about the money all. Then suddenly I understand. It hits me like a jolt. I've got him all wrong. I walk over to him. He tenses up, ever on his guard.

'You once told me you don't play games,' I say, both angry with him and sad at once. 'But you do. It's all one big game to you. I don't think you even know how to stop.' He looks away. I put my hand up to his face, and he flinches away, as if expecting to be struck. No trust at all, or no expectations. I gently take his face and turn it back to look at me. 'You need to stop playing, Finn, because you're not winning anymore.' I let my finger stroke his cheek. I need to stop playing too, I realise. This isn't kind, it isn't fair. I can only imagine how hard prison has been for him, the free spirit that he is.

I move away, leaving Finn to his thoughts. I suspect now he'd actually texted to ask me to write, or even visit him in prison. If so, for someone like Finn, that had no doubt been a hard thing to do. He doesn't like admitting he needs anyone

276

or anything, and neither do I. I know now he's not here for the money. He's here for me.

On the top of the bookshelf is an unopened bottle of Champagne the art dealer I've recently signed with brought along to the private view. I take it down and go to the drawer to fetch my absent landlord's corkscrew and a couple of glasses. 'Let's have a drink, eh?' I don't look at him, still giving him a moment. 'I'm not really sure Champagne is entirely appropriate, all things considered, but it's better than me sitting here necking it all by myself.' Without a word, he joins me on the sofa. I uncork the bottle. 'To new starts?' We sit side by side and sip the Champagne in a companionable silence.